THE BOOK OF IONA

The Book of Iona

An Anthology

Edited by
ROBERT CRAWFORD

for Blyth Iona,

for Lewis,

and for Alice

with love

First published in Great Britain in 2016
by Polygon, an imprint of Birlinn Ltd

Birlinn Ltd
West Newington House
10 Newington Road
Edinburgh EH9 1QS

www.polygonbooks.co.uk

ISBN 978 1 84697 351 2

The editor and publisher gratefully acknowledge the permission granted to reproduce the copyright material in this book. Every effort has been made to trace copyright holders an[illegible]rial. If there are any errors [illegible] any corrections that shou[illegible]ook.

B[illegible]
A [illegible]

Contents

Introduction ix
CANDIA McWILLIAM *The Loopholes of Retreat* 1
ADOMNÁN *Planks* 13
Communion 15
The Gift 16
The Drowned Books 17
ANON *Fil Súil nGlais / A Blue Eye Glancing Back* 19
THOMAS PENNANT from *A Tour in Scotland* 20
ADOMNÁN *War* 26
Sithean 27
EDWIN MORGAN *Columba's Song* 29
VICTORIA MACKENZIE *Crex Crex* 30
ST COLUMBA *Altus Prosator / The Maker on High* 42/43
Adiutor Laborantium / All Labourers' Helper 52/53
GEORGE BUCHANAN from *The History of Scotland* 54
WILLIAM SHAKESPEARE from *Macbeth* 56
ROBERT CRAWFORD *Icolmkill* 57
ADOMNÁN *The Coof* 59
The Copyist 60
The Light House 61
I 63
MICK IMLAH *The Prophecies* 65
DAVID KINLOCH *Between the Lines* 68
MEG BATEMAN *Peploe and Cadell in Iona* 70
ROBERT LOUIS STEVENSON *Dining at the Argyll Hotel* 71
ROBERT LOUIS STEVENSON *The Islet* 72
ANON *Meallach Liom Bheith i n-Ucht Oiléan /* 80
Delightful to Be on the Breast of an Island 81
ADOMNÁN *A Gaelic Quatrain* 84
ANON *La Chaluim-Chille / The Day of St Columba* 85
Achlasan Chaluim-Chille / Saint John's Wort 88
SEAMUS HEANEY *Gravities* 91
FIONA MACLEOD *The Sin-Eater* 92
FIONA MACLEOD *The Sun-Chant of Cathal* 116
ADOMNÁN *Acts* 117
Among the Picts 119

ADOMNÁN *Broichan* 121
SAMUEL JOHNSON *In the Morning Our Boat Was Ready* 122
ADOMNÁN *Dùn I* 129
Forecast 131
Iona Fragments 132
Blessing 133
Pilgrim 135
LOUISE IMOGEN GUINEY *Columba and the Stork* 137
ALICE THOMPSON *Hologram* 138
ALAN DEARLE *The Iona Machine* 150
QUEEN VICTORIA *On Visiting Staffa* 157
ANON *A Traditional Gaelic Prophecy* 158
KENNETH STEVEN *Iona Poems* 159
ROBERT CRAWFORD *The Marble Quarry* 160
AMY CLAMPITT *Westward* 161
SARA LODGE *The Grin Without the Cat* 167
NORMAN MacCAIG *Celtic Cross* 183
ADOMNÁN *Columba's Deeds* 185
Cronan the Poet 186
Neman 187
Day 188
Raiders 189
JAMES BOSWELL *Tuesday 19 October 1773* 190
ROBERT CRAWFORD *Iona* 202
ST COLUMBA *An I Mo Chridhe* 203
BECCÁN MAC LUIGDECH *Tiugraind Beccáin do Cholum Cille /* 204
The Last Verses of Beccan to Colum Cille 205
ADOMNÁN *The Excommunicant* 210
The Loch Ness Monster 211
The Whale Blessing 213
The Trudge 214
JENNIE ERDAL *Listening in the Loose Grass* 215
CHRISTABEL SCOTT from *Iona: A Romance of the West* 228
ADOMNÁN *Bed* 230
The Cry 231
Mother 232
The Foster-Mother 234
Erc 235

JOHN MacGILVRAY from *Elegy on Donald McLean, Esq. of Coll (1787)* 236
WILLIAM WORDSWORTH *Iona* 237
RUTH THOMAS *All the Treasures We Can Have* 238
MICK IMLAH *I* 252
ROBERT CRAWFORD *MC* 253
HERMAN MELVILLE *Clarel, XXXV* 254
ST COLUMBA *Noli Pater* 258
ADOMNÁN *Calm* 260
Fifty Yards 261
LIONEL JOHNSON *Saint Columba* 262
ADOMNÁN *Lightning* 264
Old 266
Retreat 268
WALTER SCOTT from *The Lord of the Isles, Canto IV* 270
JOHN KEATS *Letter to his Brother, while travelling with Charles Brown, 23 and 26 July 1818* 271
MEAGHAN DELAHUNT *To Pick Up a Stone* 276
ADOMNÁN *Machair* 287
Script 288
Diarmait 289
Columba's Death 290
Drought 292
The Work 294

Notes on Contributors 295
Acknowledgements 305

Introduction

Iona is an island of lives and afterlives. Some families have lived there for generations; the lie of the land is enriched by genealogies. For the many visitors – pilgrims, tourists, walkers, painters, photographers, birders, bathers or paddlers – who travel by ferry from Oban on the western mainland of Scotland to the large island of Mull, then by car, bus or arduous bike ride across to the hamlet of Fionnphort on Mull's south-west coast before proceeding on a further small ferry over the Sound of Iona to the jetty at St Ronan's Bay, the experience of arriving on Iona in a present-day crowd often turns into a haunting encounter with long-gone individuals. Almost no one can catch sight of, let alone set foot on, the island without a stirring of the imagination. Eyeing the abbey from the approaching ferry, modern tourists come thinking of the sixth-century Saint Columba and his monks, or of later, determined visitors including Samuel Johnson, James Boswell, and John Keats. Iona's many elaborately crafted medieval sculpted stones, and the heroic tale of the modern rebuilding of its abbey by unemployed Glaswegians marshalled by George MacLeod, Kirk minister and founder of the Iona Community, mean that afterlives on this island are insistent presences. Iona is a site where spirit, imagination, and physical exertion mingle.

Under snow or summer heatwave, it's a vivid place. Emerald, turquoise and viridian tides passing over sunlit sand towards the north end are as striking as the lash of Atlantic rain when storm clouds scud across the sky above the machair. Iona's light – brilliant, windswept, strong yet often fleeting – has attracted generations of painters, best known among whom are those early twentieth-century Scottish colourists S. J. Peploe and F. C. B. Cadell, conjured up in this book by Meg Bateman and David Kinloch. The sensory intensity of being on Iona involves not just that light which heightens a sense of inhabiting what George MacLeod called 'a thin place' where this world and a world beyond seem to intersect; it also involves Iona's distinctive simplifying smallness. However great its reputation, this island is only about three miles by one and a half in size; its fame derives from focus, not from vastness; it is, in several senses, a place of concentration.

To most folk today, Iona can seem remote; but for many centuries it has been richly connected. For Columba, sailing from Ireland to Iona in the year 563 AD, and for his medieval monastic successors the island was at the heart of a navigable archipelago extending as far as Ireland to the west, Mull to the east, and with the rest of the Hebrides on all sides. Through the language of Latin, the earliest, Gaelic-speaking writers associated with Iona were linked not just to the surrounding islands and the mainland but also to Europe and international Christendom. When Adomnán, the seventh-century abbot of Iona (whose Gaelic name is pronounced 'A-gov-nan') authored his prose account of Columba's life, he wrote in the international *lingua franca* of the day, confident that his Latin prose could and would be read in many countries. Adomnán tells of Columba's founding of the monastery on Iona, of his development of a religious community throughout the surrounding islands (a community whose influence went on to extend far across Europe), and of Columba's mission to convert the Picts in mainland Scotland. Even today, Adomnán's *Life of Saint Columba* remains arguably the most important Iona text, but its extended assembly of hagiographical anecdotes and narratives can strain the patience of modern readers. Since worshipful medieval audiences may have given Adomnán's string of stories the sort of attention that today is associated more with poetry than with prose, in *The Book of Iona* passages from Adomnán's Latin are recast throughout as English verse. Often this recasting results in a free translation which nonetheless stays close to the original trajectory. My aim is to preserve something of the direct, visionary clarity of the original, but also to present the content as patterned matter for poetic contemplation.

Though it includes memoir material, *The Book of Iona* is an anthology given over to literary imagination, not to historiography, ecclesiastical chronicling or journalism. Just as several of the Adomnán passages in this book fuse together kinds of remoteness and connectedness, so many of the contemporary pieces included operate in related imaginative territory. The new, specially commissioned stories and some of the recent poetry were produced as part of Loch Computer, a project which (thanks to generous support from the Scottish Government and the Royal Society of Edinburgh) assembled in St Andrews and Edinburgh between 2014 and 2016 a rum crew of fiction writers, poets, computer scientists, digital humanities specialists, and visual artists to ponder the meaning of remoteness and connectedness in the digital era. Most but not all of the participants have visited Iona.

In this book several of them take small imaginative liberties with its topography. After Loch Computer's discussions between computer scientists and creative practitioners, the writers were asked to produce an imaginative piece centred on Iona and involving both remoteness and connectedness. A few pieces in this book, such as Alice Thompson's story 'Hologram' and Al Dearle's scientifically inventive account of 'The Iona Machine', explicitly engage with digital technology; most of the contributors deal with remoteness and connectedness more tangentially, yet frequently in ways true to earlier Iona texts: so, present-day writers ponder spirituality, interpersonal distance and closeness, as well as aspects of what it means to experience on an island an intense sense of concentration.

Often modern visitors' awareness of Iona as a place of concentration and contemplation has been heightened by a realisation that getting there involves giving up technology. Only local people can bring their cars on to the island; tourists have to leave their vehicles on Mull. For most folk, Iona is a place to walk or to cycle, not to drive. On arrival, strangers are unsettled to realise that few mobile phone networks provide coverage, and internet access is at best patchy. A physical slowing down and a deliberate or enforced exile from some of the most insistent distractions of technological modernity accompanies many people's sense of Iona, though for year-round residents getting or losing a phone signal can have a different, sometimes biting, importance. To city dwellers, Iona looks depopulated: few houses, surprising amounts of space. If you head in the right direction, then, even if you arrive as part of a group, it is easy on the island to achieve both solitariness and communion with nature and with God. Pilgrims come seeking this, making their own *peregrinatio*, their testing voyage of contemplation; others, however, come from far places to experience human communion, working and praying for a sense of common purpose. Whatever their journeys' purpose, large numbers of people ponder on Iona the relation between remoteness and connectedness. That seems one of the things Iona is for.

Clustered throughout this book, the verse versions of sections from Adomnán's biography of Iona's most famous saint give readers a sense of Columba's life. They show, too, how this revered figure, who was among other things a writer, became an icon for the meditations of later generations. Other medieval texts associated with Columba –

some in Latin, others in Gaelic – enhance this sense, helping to explain why Iona was so important to medieval imaginations. Though, as both George Buchanan and Shakespeare attest, the island was not forgotten by the time of the Renaissance, its buildings were ruined, its treasures dissipated. By the Enlightenment era, travellers including Thomas Pennant, James Boswell and Samuel Johnson knew of Iona's allure and evoked it with eloquence. Grandly, Johnson wrote of how 'That man is little to be envied, whose patriotism would not gain force upon the plain of *Marathon*, or whose piety would not grow warmer among the ruins of *Iona*!' Yet he was aware, too, of the island's antiquities being 'incumbered with mud and rubbish'. The ruinous state of Iona's ecclesiastical heritage, however, heightened the appeal of the place to the Romantic imagination. Visitors as different and distinguished as Walter Scott, William Wordsworth, John Keats and Felix Mendelssohn made the journey to view the ruined abbey, sanctifying Iona as a site of imagination as well as religious pilgrimage. By the time Romanticism metamorphosed into the late nineteenth-century dreams of the Celtic Twilight, Iona had become for some a sleepy haven, and for others a locus of troubled imaginings. William Sharp, better known by his pen-name 'Fiona Macleod', made the island central to his finest story, 'The Sin-Eater', while Robert Louis Stevenson, unimpressed by local cuisine, presented the lights of sacred Iona as longed for but unattainable when glimpsed from a more threatening shore in his 1886 novel *Kidnapped*.

Just as modern visitors see a very different abbey, so contemporary writers view Iona differently from their Romantic and Victorian predecessors. The poet Mick Imlah's treatment of Adomnán and Columba is inflected with present-day irony as well as with fascination; for short-story writers Sara Lodge and Alice Thompson, Iona is a location where the politics of gender are to the fore in a way that might have startled the island's earlier inhabitants. The Iona of several contributors to this book is very much a place of twenty-first-century people; yet it is haunted, too, by afterlives, memories and longing.

Sometimes that longing has a markedly spiritual quality. However, the point of this anthology is not to hoard religious texts. Rather, *The Book of Iona* offers in a kaleidoscopic yet coherent design imaginative works that resonate together and may prompt reflection on secular as well as spiritual ideas. The focus on an island that is a site both of concentration and contemplation makes pondering the shifting relationship between remoteness and connectedness unavoidable. It takes a long time to get to know Iona in thorough detail, and Iona is a place where detail always counts. I have been visiting the island for over forty years, and have come to associate it with all the people I have loved – both living and dead. This book is an attempt to share in literary form several aspects of Iona's beauty, and to provide some refreshing perspectives on places and prospects that may have come to seem over-familiar.

A note on form: in *The Book of Iona* works originally written in Latin or Gaelic verse are presented in parallel text, in order to give the poetry the dignity of its original shape, and to allow readers to experience just a little of the 'otherness' of the untranslated text in addition to the translated version. Where texts were originally written in prose in a language other than English, only an English translation is given. Unless otherwise specified, versions of Latin and Gaelic texts in this book are by the editor; readers seeking the original Latin prose of Adomnán's *Vita Sancti Columbae* can find it in several editions, including that of A. O. and M. O. Anderson (Edinburgh, 1961; second edition, Oxford, 1991); readers who wish to read a prose translation of the whole of Adomnán's *Life of Saint Columba* can find several versions on the internet, including one that is part of the site called the Internet Archive (where a digital copy of William Reeves's 1874 translation, originally published in Edinburgh by Edmonston and Douglas, is available free of charge); there are also a number of translations available as printed books, the most recent and most authoritative being the 1995 Penguin Classics edition translated by Richard Sharpe. The present anthology's editor and several of the other contributors have found these earlier works of great help, not least as starting points for the imagination. Bringing together for the first time such a wealth of imaginative writing associated with Iona from the early Middle Ages until the twenty-first century, *The Book of Iona* returns repeatedly to notions of remoteness and connectedness. I hope it will appeal to lovers of a very special island, to lovers of imaginative writing, and to those who have a passion for both.

Robert Crawford,
St Andrews, 2016

CANDIA McWILLIAM

The Loopholes of Retreat

We knew the veil was thinning for Nana Effie after the drookit handbag in the Post Office.

Peggy, who took a shift at the busy times, called me down from the old house where I was spreading seaweed on the lazy-beds we'd made Nana agree to. I was over from my place of work to bide awhile with my mother's mother who had mostly raised me, as far as ever I did grow.

It was odd having the dulse in slippy limpet-buttoned armfuls not in leaves like dried-out summer salty handkerchiefs off the washing line. I've grown used to those where I live now.

It turned out Nana'd put her milk-thermos for the morning cup she had now to take alone into the depths of her good handbag. She only found out the thermos-top was loose when she'd had to pull forth in the Post Office, some days later, from out the soor dook in her bag, the sticky banknotes, with that thin line of metal through them, a vein now of cheesy green. She took them out from the soggy pastry of her wallet.

Coin was unaffected.

There's the swollen-up clam of compact. She thought of that powder puff as a teacher might of the board-duster. This was clear to any who had chummed Nana forth the island. By the time she was at any destination but the first her face would be sifted with powder white as a morning roll.

She was postcarding me, Peggy insisted, though there I was, staying with her in the house where she'd lived with all us children and our mother and sometimes our father, till he wasn't, and Granda Niall till he went.

She was looking for the money to pay for the stamp to reach the place where I was not, for I was with her, in that house that had held the clutch of us, but that now felt right tight for just two, even though it was distance I'd filled up on in my life, not space; my next island being crammed as a sack of roe. She was looking for the money to exchange for the stamp that would ensure the flight of words so they might reach me, all those miles away, where I was not. The unposted picture postcard, showing a blushing sky and the old cross against, it read on the reverse, under the instruction 'Correspondence', 'I wish you were here.'

It had clearly been written some time before. Most likely the words were those she thought most suited for the open craft of a postcard. I had received several such cards from her over the years and thought of it as not much more than one half of the antiphonal affection we held for one another.

I looked at the address. All was as it should have been, the effective exact numbers, too big to grasp, and the concrete nouns, Sago, Marina Fort, all pre-written-out by me on my last visit to spare her trouble. Where my name was, though, she had overwritten, 'to GOD'.

Leather-infused cheese, somewhat set, holding the shy essentials of the days of this woman who had once known that everything had its pigeonhole within her own mind, was what tipped us children, in our thirties and forties, the wink that she was maybe readying herself for flight.

I did keep the postcard's addressee to myself.

The texture of the curd, when she showed it to me, was gelatinous, a bit shiny; to do with the chemicals for tanning the handbag, reacting with proteins in milk. You'd think I'd know the science; but, though I've cooked many things, I'd not at any point tried slow-seething small sums of money in milk.

The substance in the handbag was blueish whiteish, something like the frost-glow of a zinc bucket or, then again, of sashimi cut from the head of the squid. A squid's tentacles retain a flirty pinkness. Little bunched rosy-tinted fingers, those tentacles are most prized when the head of the squid itself is the size of a strawberry.

To eat these sea-strawberries feels like a purr; the sort you might offer before announcing warmly anticipated news. The modest sound of justifiable satisfaction. Announcing a good exam result, say, in a subject once discouraged on account of its perceived difficulty; remembering the name of your father's reputedly drowned first love without sounding dismissive or even at all angry; revealing that although you are not tall you are well able to use the hands.

In my work, texture is important. Among my customers, texture is considered and debated. Cool-slippery, sticky, ointment-tacky, unctuous, warm-dense, half-resistant, gelatinous, glutinous, bubble-quivering, rubbery, cornflour-custardy, eggy-decided, fungus-cloudy, woody-granular, soft-shred curdling, hot-melting, glass-silken, satin-sweet, tongue-answering, dusty-spicy, all these are terms with which I have become familiar as I placate the circling appetites of the Hungry Ghosts, those dead who cannot rest on account of their disorderly or violent passing, in their season of going forth, at its height on the fifteenth day of the seventh month of the Chinese calendar, and to fulfil also the appetites of those not yet departed who would assuage them; and beyond that season, for all the other exaltations, celebrations and observances of my new home, the island republic of Singapore.

It was Nana Effie who taught me to cook; most importantly, for the formation of my sixth and seventh senses, timing and knowing when to finish things off, on the girdle, a utensil that asks a precise calibration of what heat may achieve. Cooking with her I learned what I did not know I knew until I had took it across the seas to another set of islands. That I could steer and control heat; which is everything in cooking; cooking itself, or the offering of a prepared repast, with its suggestion of leisure and a life beyond fight and flight, being all that removes the raw from its primitive state. Where there is cooking there is gratitude and may be grace.

Sashimi is raw you're thinking?

Think again; of the application required to shape the uncooked fish such that it is not only palatable but beautiful. That thought, that attention, that filleting, that sectioning, that feathering, that eliciting from the texture of the lately-living fish how it may fan its petals of muscle or fat so as to flower best on the human tongue, that investment of time – they are all forms of heat, being work.

Work is heat, heat work, we were told it at the secondary school on the mainland as we clamped our retorts over the clean blue Bunsen flame that roared thin so you could see clear through it as it rushed up to its licking limit, shivering the air around itself with a motion not felt as warmth.

'Watch for the rise and the bubbles that tell you the other side of the round is making ready to be uplifted', said Nana, showing me how, by letting me do. The weight in the air around the range changed from the babyish puff of flour to the swell of breathable fat, hot iron. Reliable magic took its course. Flipping the drop-scones without leaving batter-trail on the girdle was like skimming stones on the blue water's thin top, loch or sea-lip; something I just could do. It was in my wrist-bone, Nana said. It was like taking but the one crack to snap the jouncing mackerel still.

I knew at what angle to cleave wood; I used less energy than others to achieve set tasks by knowing the point of entry. I cracked nuts with my hands and could tell where the hen had laid when she made off to a new place to attempt her flustered notion of raising chicks beyond the shell. I could crack an egg and separate it with one hand. I was eye level with the range-top when Nana took me on in the kitchen.

I was bringing what I could to family life; day by day, she seemed assured, and thereby to assure us, things could not break if the daily steps were taken; pancakes or porridge twice a day, harsh reddish tea morn and eve, potatoes boiled in the skin left to divulge themselves under a bunched-up cloth held down by the pot lid, a stone to hold it firm. You could read words through the slim, summer skin that you rolled off the tatties, silken to the fingers over the nude yellow inside. The skin over the white burst baked spud in winter was dry like an unwaxed boot and full with the taste of the ground: peat, iron, bog-myrtle, the spongy heart of the rush.

Not stone; our water tasted of stone; fresh cut stone, cool stone that was to time as ice to water.

I ate skin as a boy. Birled alphabets of apple skin from the cookers that came over on the boat; no trees would fruit for us though they had once for the monks, in an orchard that seemed like a book of another country; you could see the cupped pink and white petals inside your head, stamens furry with gold pollen fallen from the tip of the monk's brush, bees with belted belly hovering fat against the taut margin of gold that was braced against the enclosed garden of letters it fanked.

I ate the rolled or cobbled potato skin. The burned skin of crust fruitcake left in the baking tin. The rusk of loaves. The shiny outer body of a boiled dumpling, glistening with suet that had lately cradled animal innards, and held in the shape of the binding-cloth's folds hard now like a nail to the teeth.

I ate the salt skin of the water when I swam the bays. Through it all, as I did not grow, I read, a kind of skin-eating in some manner. I could not but know that until very recently – mere hundreds of years – reading had to be a transaction with the skin of a creature, imparting to you the words you hunted and wished to eat with a wide open hunger of the head.

We ate our potatoes with salt. Butter was an infrequent cold ingot, troubled into becoming in the worked churn; the girls had the feel for it, could spot the moment before the surrender of the cream to splitting. When first I met shop butter, away at the college, I gorged on its mutable luxury, the stirred richness it gave porridge, the cool dose of it under black treacle after a late night, even the salt on salt of roll, butter, bacon with bootlace of rind. I put myself right off butter in my plashings and sookings, just as I put myself off being a man of law by the gorging indigestible way I read then.

I learned my own way was not to be smooth.

I cannot now touch butter without breaking into salty, uneasy sweat, having lived half my life among people who mostly prefer edible softness not to change its nature halfway through the intimate process of eating.

Yes, bean curd is soft, but it keeps its shape until you have decided what to make of it. Cutting bean curd is like alterations were when I was small; the girls' frocks, our breeks, were made of cut-down clothes refettled by Nana and our mother. Once you had cut into the stuff, that was the size of it. You couldn't uncut. Once you had set out to make the one frock into the two frocks or the one shirt into rags for the cherry-red hearth polish or the dubbin, that was it.

We are asked to believe you can bring the cut edges of things together, kiss it better and have things as before, a healing that tells you the cut never was, like a cut made in water with a knife, forgotten, not even a scar under the water, not inside its surface at the depth of the tides, not within the fat swell of the shifting waters under their keel-sliced skin.

I'm not so sure. I'm not sure that doesn't mean that people think hurt can be withdrawn, on second thoughts, because it wasn't what was meant. It's at the wrong weight, damage, just now; we've seen the copy of it too often to know its first imprinting. Damage will not be seen away by second thoughts. Damage will out. It is, for good. There's no unmaking the deeper partings.

With the potatoes? Salt, as I say, from the earthenware salt-pig, and not yet then monitored for the health of the heart. For sweetness we had rusty sugar in clumps, crystals aggregated yet distinct, resembling one another strictly at different sizes, replicating without limit the principal allotted form, grown onto strings close as mussels or the stacked hexagonal stone pipes out at Staffa, rock sugar sent in chests nailed shut, writing on them that was made in bits like broken biscuits, not flowing like the lettering taught in the school; you'd the sense the letters on the tea-chests that arrived on the boat had been put there flat with a swipe through a grid, not written but declared at the behest of some function that drove what was not still. What was the propulsive force we felt, Agnes and I and the other children? What the stillness?

We thought it to be music, but I have since thought it may have been God in one of the guises He can take on when you live where every stone and star had been looked upon, counted, beseeched and thanked in prayerful words for longer than our own lifetimes many times over and again.

You can learn things about a place from what it discourages. I am not talking about chewing gum or jaywalking. Those are the things everyone knows about the Lion City, Singapore; they touch only the film of skin the tourists see. On the MRT train, smooth and neat in its function, disturbingly reliable to one accustomed to the isles of the west, are graphics that forbid, in the accepted way, encircling what is forbidden in a scarlet ring, drawing a line of veto across it, the carriage anywhere on the Mass Rapid Transport system the fruit of the durian. The durian has a skin it is impossible to eat. Bitter gourd, preserved melon, kumquat, salted plum, resourceful Singaporeans have found ways to enjoy, but the sachets of flesh in the durian are defended by a skin of armorial defensiveness; the fruit is guarded too by its stench, of sweat, of the pit, the latrine. There are no fresh words for it.

The fruit appeals maybe to those without an innate tragic sense, which means knowing the disgust within delight and the impossibility of much simplicity but pain. It drives home a point some are born knowing; mercy can be brutal, it does not exaggerate, and the times event spares us are what we know of peace; ambiguity is rich and kind.

There was a rumour the Mull ferry was to carry a sign with a squeezebox in that red circle with the red line through, signifying the discouraging of accordion-playing aboard. The place for a squeezebox to go unheard might be high weather, on the emptied swilling deck, the waters fraying above and over it, the land bouncing out of sight / into sight so you'd leave your guts in the air for the gulls to catch.

A gull will eat till it is sick then eat that.

Nana thought I was a musician. I'd to practise hard at last to show her I was not. This was good for Agnes, who was, it turned out, the musician among us all; seven of us eight play the fiddle, and Euan Malcolm played the silver whistle; all the boys but me the pipes; I'd not the length of breath though I'd the fingering. Agnes could get on unobserved with her secret work of talent. No one took out their own hopes on her. Her voice ripened, taking the shade my nature afforded, growing as a melon might under sheltering leaves in a hot-frame once well dug with dove-dung in an old garden long neglected, giving accidental shelter to the exotic. She took up the little harp, the clarsach, as you might take up talking to yourself; it answered the sounds she threaded with her own voice into its strings, holding the instrument cooried into her.

Music had for us the glamour. We laughed to learn music was a tongue not much admired by a visitor from England who accounted it a method of employing the mind without the labour of thinking and with some applause too from a person's self. We did applaud ourselves, for, being so numerous, this was near to applauding one another.

I was first to scoot the coop. After that, they clattered and flounced and fell and tumbled free, the brothers and sisters and my pigeon-pair twin Agnes. Now, when I think of the fine rebellion I had undertaken, I see that it was the flight my grandmother commenced to make possible for me when I was eye to eye with the winking drop scones on the high-handled girdle and didn't threaten to take that much more of a stretch. She'd thought books might wing me ready for my fledge, failing to understand that it was in her own gift that my flight feathers hardened and set fair a warmer piety for my life than that to which I had thought myself born.

I confused one thing for the other. It's easy done. I had the one great shame, so I believed, and it could be elided or relieved by escape or distance. These were other days than now. Though you may be certain the old mistakes are there ready to be made again, sheep paths under the snow.

A man in the town ran a firm, agency was the word, supplied waiters for occasions when a Scotsman was wanted. You are not, in this case, right if you have leapt to the obvious, kilted, conclusion. It wasn't the legs, but the voice. In some parts of the world, to this day, a Scotsman's voice speaks louder than words. I will not insult you by reminding you of all we Scots have invented, from probity in banking to the, so they say, psychological novel.

I settled in Singapore after a few years when they shipped me in just for what they call the Caledonian season through from the Yacht Club Balls to the staggered Burns Nights that fill January full as a pluck through to the end of February.

I married Eithne Tang from front of house at her family's crab place, just past the end of the bus route. In the tank that forms the back wall of the restaurant, which is popular with families, are clams called geoduck, more prized even than what is left after the angel's share has gone from the maturing malt. The clams resemble a harvest of heaping grey dildos sighing at shocking length from a set of castanets that has been slammed about their bases and fixed in place with a band of thick grey rubber that could strap a breakdown to a flatbed.

That wall of homed geoduck seemed inauspicious to my courtship of a daughter of the house. They represented sullen but portable wealth in seafood form. They resembled the reprisals of shameful coarse battle. They were gloomy and lewd. Panic, or embarrassment, was their effect. I am quiet and of sanguine nature, which is one of the reasons I have survived the fact I never grew past where I stopped short.

I said sanguine.

I decided that the geoduck were only the clown in the serious play, there to draw off the ugly natural nature of man, leaving behind our better selves, free to act as well as we may; they gave me no trouble after that. To my wife, or so it seemed, they had never resembled what they resembled to me. Or perhaps it was that she had no place for shame and disgust.

I fell for her, in the first degree, when I saw her clipping the paper kerchiefs around the necks of a large family who were attacking several steaming black-pepper-sauced crabs, clacking legs long and thick as deer-femur, not only jointed and chopped into leaking sub-joints but equipped with fastidious pincers like billhook-heads; she was attentive and kind as she clipped the paper bibs with the little metal toggle and pincer, like a librarian whose books are nestlings to her, needing settled in their place, needing their feathery pages stroking, needing to know the information sufficient unto the day, assured they may always fly to a settled place, a good home.

I grew to love her in the ways I suspected I might over my first summer of my new job, planning and catering for funerals of many faiths, occasions that, in want of space or gardens, things few have here in the Lion City, take place mainly in the neutral communal space at the foot of public housing apartments here, known to Singaporeans as the void deck, the space where you might host a ping-pong night, a school reunion, a musical evening, a public meeting, or a funeral, non-denominational, Taoist Buddhist, Buddhist, Roman Catholic, Protestant or several other options offered in our firm's prospectus; including freethinking.

My preference shifts between the options. Perhaps I should not confide that to you lest it give you the impression that for me faith is skin deep; not so; it is as far in me as the weather and the horizon. But I have not yet hauled my coracle up the chosen beach or turned my back upon any other islands or views out to sea; it is not that I am wandering from hawker to hawker in matters of the spirit so much as that I am looking for the niche in which I may most accurately and well prepare myself for dying and for its only end.

I am a not-luxurious man born of an isle steeped with God; one who would provide for those he has loved; and atone for his misdeeds.

I slip sometimes to Little India in pursuit of ecumenism in the city of the Merlion, a beast doodled in the margin of an apocryphal text if ever there was one. Maybe the pragmatic heterodoxy of Singapore has met the certainties I grew among in the packed doocot that was my family's life on the far island and set the lion among some of the pigeons.

I believe that all the feral pigeons, all the utility pigeons, all the bosomy squabs and tatty bands and flocks of the world were once inhabitants of its dovecotes and tended columbaria, and, yes, its doocots, or are descendants of the inhabitants thereof, and that all the fancy birds, the trumpeters whose calls come like low laughter, the collared doves, the imperially coloured birds like Venice glass and Indian sweeties for brightness and sugar-seethed voice, all the trained carriers of love-letters to lyric poets, all the decorated wing-weary hero pigeons of war, the very dove that brought the branch of grey olive to Noah, signifying landfall, each of these has its place in what we could with patience and close work make around us, a place for each. Starting with the end, and concluding with the beginning, shifting our thoughts around their locations within the chambered shelter, we may come to know that simply to be silted into place where you have been put is to lose compassion for the one who is not, apparently, you yourself, alone.

There are those who will try to hard-boil this hope of faith to sterility, or cast it in cold clay, and place it chill and full of deceit beneath the brooding mind to discourage further thought, or specifically to discourage the thought that there must be more than fighting for your place and sticking to it in the cold comfort of your own waste, a bird in lime. But it is not enough; can it be?

Eithne's name came in two parts. Her western name, Eithne, had been selected by her at the age of eighteen, at baptism, as one form of the many-limbedness, the mermaid, or if you'd prefer hydra-headed, or even crablike, quality of the city in which she was born. Why not have, should you be, as she was and I was, an islander from birth, that amphibiousness, with a sail of fin stowed as well as the scales and the strong capacity to swim – and for that matter feet on the ground? It is maybe a matter of evolution after all.

The name Tang was but a Romanisation of the original form of her name, as close as might be made with the components of another way to set down language, bent into new shapes, ovals and pot-hooks, where there might more happily have been not letters but marks made deriving from the form of a sheltering tree or a sipping deer, or a chambered house for pigeons bred to carry secret scrolls in sealing-wax-stoppered sections of bamboo, tied to the pink bird-foot with a red thread.

I watched the dim-sum makers at their work between my shifts when I was first resident here without my full residency paperwork.

The expertise consists in a kind of waking sleep akin to some kinds of prayer, that allows no break in the rhythm, the pinching of the dumpling dough, the contrary rolling with the palms of the elastic pale plum, the flour-dusting of the hands quiet and frequent as wing-dips, the rolling with the white-wood pin to make the dough light and transparent as petal of poppy, fingers never smirching it till the maker's hand thumbprints the filling into that light disc, pleats up the juncture, making of plum plump creamy-jade fig, twisting it sealed, raises and sets it, the first of a clutch, into the woven steaming-basket nest. Each dumpling of as much or of as little interest as it was in those moments when, like an egg, it was most perfectly made.

I like before I sleep to fold my hands into the dove-shadow-making position understood the world over as the sign of concession, intercession, prayer.

New graves here in Singapore lie undisturbed – at the moment – for fifteen years. A limited duration of peace in earth, quite unlike matters back at home in the corridor of the kings or where the monks lie under turf embroidered by toadflax and germander speedwell that stitch themselves across the green under the treadling needles of rain.

At the end of those fifteen years, the graves are exhumed. For those whose religion permits cremation, the exhumed remains will be cremated and stored within the columbarium; within whose niches rest not doves but the ashes of the dead.

Eithne and I make a respectable living catering the funeral services held below the tall apartment blocks. It was a relief to me to discover that the knacks I had had in the kitchen of my grandmother could be of the same weight here. I turned my eye for the measure of bubble in a pancake to the making of black sesame cakes; I offered them with longan fruit, screwpine-leaf juice and rock sugar, a translation of the crystal sugar that had come to us on the island down sea-lanes taken by the Vikings; I cooked winter melon and white sesame durian puffs; I presented them with the same dailiness as I had the pancakes off the island girdle. This assisted in the forbearance from tears and the saving of face. Occasionally it led to mistakes, such as the time when a widow wished me to weep for good fortune, a sort of private rain for her dead man, and I could not, but usually my impassivity was understood to be a form of exotic good manners.

We Scots are known to be inscrutable.

Eithne prefers to pray alone. She likes to go, in the wet especially, to the broken and remade stones and crosses of Iona, whose history has resulted in their being broken and repaired so often that there is a thickness to their story.

I like to pray in her own birth-island after the Taoist funerals; there will be joss sticks and joss papers burning, in the for-once cool concrete bareness of a void deck, with to come the light moment when paper versions of the empty sweets of life are set afire so that the departed may be sent out upon that last voyage, that cannot surely be as jointed and contingent as the journey even from mainland Scotland to the island, with its stages and changes.

Neither may this passage to the afterlife be as apparently direct as the journey from our mainland to Singapore, with the one change only.

This last journey commences with the setting alight of two clothing chests made of bright paper, one paper mountain of silver, one of gold, a paper house of air and, last, two thin paper servants. The sky pulls up the facsimiles into its hungering mouth and scatters their remains, the flame having eaten all shape, all colour, even the air they once held, that filled them with a bulk of nothing.

I am returned to the thin place where it began, from where it is best to fly up as the sparks fly up.

Would you hear my confession now?

You have?

ADOMNÁN

Planks

Pine
And oak planks
Are being hauled
From riverbanks
Along the cold
Sea road
To Mull,
And to Iona,
Towed
By small boats
That stay afloat
Because we place
The saint's books
And arrange his fine
Vestments
To face
The altar
In the shrine,
Intoning a psalm
To ensure
The wind will
Soon falter
Then peter out,
The sea stay calm
So those stout,
Sawmilled
Pine
And oak planks
Can come over
Under cover

Of the name
Of Columba
As proof
There's enough
Faith here still
To build a roof.

ADOMNÁN

Communion

One Iona winter's day Columba wept.
Diarmait asked, 'Why are you crying?'

'I see the monks worn out with work
Building the monastery at Durrow.'

Just at that moment, far away
At Durrow, Columba's friend, Prior Lasren,

Anxiously turned to his monks,
'Ease up. Eat. Wait for good weather.'

And Columba, distant and communing,
Blessed Lasren, for letting them rest.

ADOMNÁN

The Gift

Heaven
Has given
Only a few
This right,
This gift
To gaze
On everything at once
In the clear,
Sheer blaze
Of day,
As if a shaft
Of bright light lit
Each detail,
So the heft
Of the earth might fit
Into a glance,
And all
The whole
Mile-high
Sky
Be taken in
By the human eye
As easily
As angels dance
On a pin.

ADOMNÁN

The Drowned Books

After the message boy
Fell from his horse
And lay
Twenty days
In the Boyne,
A man, passing by
On a nag
On his way
To a fair,
Saw the boy's leather bag
There
Underwater
Still with the body,
And the man yelled
Till he was hoarse,
So that same day,
While dark clouds roiled
Overhead,
Folk fished the boy out
Like a coin,
And when he lay
On his back
On the bank
They undid his bag
Full of books –
Ruined, spoiled
By the water,
Except for one page
Royal
Among the rest,
Dry

As dry land,
Unspoiled.
Why?
It was written
In the hand
Of Columba.

ANON (Eleventh Century)

Fil Súil nGlais (A Blue Eye Glancing Back)

(Columba sets sail for Iona)

Fil súil nglais
Fégbas Érinn dar a hais;
  Noco n-aceba íarmo-thá
  Firu Érenn nách a mná.

A blue eye glancing back
Sees Ireland fading in the wake,
  Destined not to see again
  Ireland's women, Ireland's men.

THOMAS PENNANT

from *A Tour in Scotland and a Voyage to the Hebrides*

9–11 July 1772

Towards evening arrive within sight of *Jona*, and a tremendous chain of rocks, lying to the south of it, rendered more horrible by the perpetual noise of breakers. Defer our entrance into the *Sound* till day-light.

About eight of the clock in the morning very narrowly escape striking on the rock *Bonirevor*, apparent at this time by the breaking of a wave: our master was at some distance in his boat, in search of sea fowl, but alarmed with the danger of his vessel, was hastening to its relief; but the tide conveyed us out of reach of the rock, and saved him the trouble of landing us; for the weather was so calm as to free us from any apprehensions about our lives. After tiding for three hours, anchor in the sound of *Jona*, in three fathoms water, on a white sandy bottom; but the safest anchorage is on the East side, between a little isle and that of *Mull*: this sound is three miles long and one broad, shallow, and in some parts dry at the ebb of spring-tides: is bounded on the East by the island of *Mull*; on the West, by that of *Jona*, the most celebrated of the *Hebrides*.

Multitudes of gannets were now fishing here: they precipitated themselves from a vast height, plunged on their prey at least two fathoms deep, and took to the air again as soon as they emerged. Their sense of seeing must be exquisite; but they are often deceived, for Mr. *Thompson* informed me, that he had frequently taken them by placing a herring on a hook, and sinking it a fathom deep, which the gannet plunges for and is taken.

The view of the *Jona* was very picturesque: the East side, or that which bounds the sound, exhibited a beautiful variety; an extent of plain, a little elevated above the water, and almost covered with the ruins of the sacred buildings, and with the remains of the old town, still inhabited. Beyond these the island rises into little rocky hills, with narrow verdant hollows between (for they merit not the name of vallies), and numerous enough for every recluse to take his solitary walk, undisturbed by society.

The island belongs to the parish of *Ross*, in *Mull*; is three miles long, and one broad; the East side mostly flat; the middle rises into small hills; the West side very rude and rocky: the whole is a singular mixture of rock and fertility.

The soil is a compound of sand and comminuted sea shells, mixed with black loam; is very favorable to the growth of bear, natural clover, crowsfoot and daisies. It is in perpetual tillage, and is ploughed thrice before the sowing: the crops at this time made a promising appearance, but the seed was committed to the ground at very different times; some, I think, about the beginning of *May*, and some not three weeks ago. Oats do not succeed here; but flax and potatoes come on very well. I am informed that the soil in *Col*, *Tir-I*, and North and South *Uist*, is similar to that in *Jona*.

The tenants here *run-rig*, and have the pasturage in common. It supports about a hundred and eight head of cattle, and about five hundred sheep. There is no heath in this island: cattle unused to that plant give bloody milk; which is the case with the cattle of *Jona* transported to *Mull*, where that vegetable abounds; but the cure is soon effected by giving them plenty of water.

Servants are paid here commonly with a fourth of the crop, grass for three or four cows, and a few sheep.

The number of inhabitants is about a hundred and fifty: the most stupid and the most lazy of all the islanders; yet many of them boast of their descent from the companions of St. *Columba*.

A few of the more common birds frequent this island: wild geese breed here, and the young are often reared and tamed by the natives.

The beautiful *Sea-Bugloss* makes the shores gay with its glaucous leaves and purple flowers. The *Eryngo*, or sea-holly, is frequent; and the fatal *Belladonna* is found here.

The *Granites durus rubescens*, the same with the *Egyptian*, is found in *Nuns-isle*, and on the coast of *Mull*: a *Breccia quartzosa*, of a beautiful kind, is common; and the rocks to the South of the *Bay of Martyrs* is formed of the *Swedish Trapp*; useful to glass-makers.

Jona derives its name from a *Hebrew* word, signifying a dove, in allusion to the name of the great saint, *Columba*, the founder of its fame. This holy man, instigated by his zeal, left his native country, *Ireland*, in the year 565, with the pious design of preaching the gospel to the *Picts*. It appears that he left his native soil with warm resentment, vowing never to make a settlement within sight of that hated island. He made his first trial at *Oransay*, and on finding that place too near to *Ireland*, succeeded to his wish at *Hy*, for that was the name of *Jona* at the time of his arrival. He repeated here the experiment on several hills, erecting on each a heap of stones; and that which he last ascended is to this day called *Carnan-chul-reh*-EIRINN, or, the eminence of the back turned to *Ireland*.

Columba was soon distinguished by the sanctity of his manners: a miracle that he wrought so operated on the *Pictish* king, *Bradeus*, that he immediately made a present of the little isle to the saint. It seems that his majesty had refused *Columba* an audience; and even proceeded so far as to order the palace gates to be shut against him; but the saint, by the power of his word, instantly caused them to fly open.

As soon as he was in possession of *Jona* he founded a cell of monks, borrowing his institutions from a certain oriental monastic order. It is said that the first religious were canons regular; of which the founder was the first abbot: and that his monks, till the year 716, differed from those of the church of *Rome*, both in the observation of *Easter*, and in the clerical tonsure. *Columba* led here an exemplary life, and was highly respected for the sanctity of his manners for a considerable number of years. He is the first on record who had the faculty of *second-sight*, for he told the victory of *Aidan* over the *Picts* and *Saxons* on the very instant it happened. He had the honour of burying in his island, *Convallus* and *Kinnatil*, two kings of *Scotland*, and of crowning a third. At length, worn out with age, he died, in *Jona*, in the arms of his disciples; was interred there, but (as the *Irish* pretend) in after-times translated to *Down*; where, according to the epitaph, his remains were deposited with those of St. *Bridget* and St. *Patrick*.

Hi tres in *Duno* tumulo tumulantur in uno;
Brigida, *Patricius*, atque *Columba* pius.

But this is totally denied by the *Scots*; who affirm, that the contrary is shewn in a life of the saint, extracted out of the pope's library, and translated out of the *Latin* into *Erse*, by father *Cail o horan*; which decides, in favor of *Jona*, the momentous dispute.

After the death of St. *Columba*, the island received the name of *Y-columb-cill*, or, the isle of the cell of *Columba*. In process of time the island itself was personified, and by a common blunder in early times converted into a saint, and worshipped under the title of St. *Columb-killa*.

The religious continued unmolested during two centuries: but in the year 807 were attacked by the *Danes*, who with their usual barbarity, put part of the monks to the sword, and obliged the remainder, with their abbot *Cellach*, to seek safety by flying from their rage. The monastery remained depopulated for seven years, but on the retreat of the *Danes* received a new order, being then peopled by the *Cluniacs*, who continued there till the dissolution, when the revenues were united to the see of *Argyle*.

Took boat and landed on the spot called the *Bay of Martyrs*: the place where the bodies of those who were to be interred in this holy ground, were received, during the period of superstition.

Walked about a quarter of a mile to the South, in order to fix on a convenient spot for pitching a rude tent, formed of oars and sails, as our day residence, during our stay in the island.

Observe a little beyond, an oblong inclosure, bounded by a stone dike, called *Clachnan Druidach*, and supposed to have been the burial place of the *Druids*, for bones of various sizes are found there. I have no doubt but that *Druidism* was the original religion of this place; yet I suppose this to have been rather the common cemetery of the people of the town, which lies almost close to the *Bay of Martyrs*.

Having settled the business of our tent, return through the town, consisting at present of about fifty houses, mostly very mean, thatched with straw of bear pulled up by the roots, and bound tight on the roof with ropes made of heath. Some of the houses that lie a little beyond the rest seemed to have been better constructed than the others, and to have been the mansions of the inhabitants when the place was in a flourishing state, but at present are in a very ruinous condition.

Visit every place in the order that they lay from the village. The first was the ruin of the nunnery, filled with canonesses of St. *Augustine*, and consecrated to St. *Oran*. They were permitted to live in community for a considerable time after the reformation, and wore a white gown; and above it a rotchet of fine linnen.

The church was fifty-eight feet by twenty: the roof of the east end is entire, is a pretty vault made of very thin stones, bound together by four ribs meeting in the centre. The floor is covered some feet thick with cow-dung; this place being at present the common shelter for the cattle; and the islanders are too lazy to remove this fine manure, the collection of a century, to enrich their grounds.

With much difficulty, by virtue of fair words, and a bribe, prevale on one of these listless fellows to remove a great quantity of this dung-hill; and by that means once more expose to light the tomb of the last prioress. Her figure is cut on the face of the stone; an angel on each side supports her head; and above them is a little plate and a comb. The prioress occupies only one half of the surface: the other is filled with the form of the virgin MARY, with head crowned and mitred; the child in her arms; and, to denote her *Queen of Heaven*, a sun and moon appear above. At her feet is this address, from the prioress: *Sancta* MARIA *ora pro me.* And round the lady is inscribed, *Hic jacet Domina* Anna Donaldi Terleti + *filia quondam Priorissa de* JONA . . .

* * *

The chapel of St. *Oran* stands in this space, which legend reports to have been the first building attempted by St. *Columba*: by the working of some evil spirit, the walls fell down as fast as they were built up.

After some consultation it was pronounced, that they never would be permanent till a human victim was buried alive: *Oran*, a companion of the saint, generously offered himself, and was interred accordingly: at the end of three days St. *Columba* had the curiosity to take a farewel look at his old friend, and caused the earth to be removed: to the surprize of all beholders, *Oran* started up, and began to reveal the secrets of his prison-house; and particularly declared, that all that had been said of hell was a mere joke. This dangerous impiety so shocked *Columba*, that, with great policy, he instantly ordered the earth to be flung in again: poor *Oran* was overwhelmed, and an end for ever put to his prating. His grave is near the door, distinguished only by a plain red stone.

* * *

Cross the island over a most fertile elevated tract to the S. West side, to visit the landing place of St. *Columba*; a small bay, with a pebbly beach, mixed with a variety of pretty stones, such as violet-coloured *Quartz*,

Nephritic stones, and fragments of porphyry, granite and *Zoeblitx* marble: a vast tract near this place was covered with heaps of stones of unequal sizes: these, as is said, were the penances of monks who were to raise heaps of dimensions equal to their crimes: and to judge by some, it is no breach of charity to think there were among them enormous sinners.

On one side is shewn an oblong heap of earth, the supposed size of the vessel that transported St. *Columba* and his twelve disciples from *Ireland* to this island.

On my return saw, on the right hand, on a small hill, a small circle of stones, and a little *cairn* in the middle, evidently *druidical*, but called the *hill of the angels*, *Cnoc-nar-aimgeal*; from a tradition that the holy man had there a conference with those celestial beings soon after his arrival. Bishop *Pocock* informed me, that the natives were accustomed to bring their horses to this circle at the feast of St. *Michael*, and to course round it. I conjecture that this usage originated from the custom of blessing the horses in the days of superstition, when the priest and the holy water-pot were called in: but in latter times the horses were all assembled, but the reason forgotten.

The traveller must not neglect to ascend the hill of *Dun-ii*; from whose summit is a most picturesque view of the long chain of little islands, neighbors to this; of the long low isles of *Col* and *Tir-I* to the West; and the vast height of *Rum* and *Skie* to the North.

At eight of the clock in the morning with the first fair wind we yet had, set sail for the sound: the view of *Jona*, its clustered towns, the great ruins, and the fertility of the ground, were fine contrasts, in our passage to the red granite rocks of the barren *Mull*.

ADOMNÁN

War

On Iona he said to Diarmait, 'Strike the bell.'
The bell summoned the brethren to the church.
The church was filled with prayers for King Aidan.
'King Aidan now is fighting his far war.
His far war is a victory, but grim.
Grim to see corpses strewn beneath the clouds.'
The clouds were peaceful that day on Iona.

ADOMNÁN

Sithean

When he said,
'I want to go alone
To the machair;
No one
Should follow,'
A sly scout
Set out
By a different route,
Then hid
In a hollow
On a hill
Until
He saw the saint
Spread his arms
Wide
On another knoll
Among the farms
Where all
Round him
And above him
Skimmed bright,
Shimmering white
Angels;
But when Columba returned
He warned
That scout,
'Keep your mouth shut:
Let this sacred
Secret
Stay secret.' –
Though all
Still
Call

That small
Round
Pasture mound
'Sithean' –
The Hill
Of the Angels.

EDWIN MORGAN

Columba's Song

Where's Brude? Where's Brude?
So many souls to be saved!
The bracken is thick, the wildcat is quick,
the foxes dance in the moonlight,
the salmon dance in the waters,
the adders dance in the thick brown bracken.
Where's Brude? Where's man?
There's too much nature here,
eagles and deer,
but where's the mind and where's the soul?
Show me your kings, your women, the man of the plough.
And cry me to your cradles.
It wasn't for a fox or an eagle I set sail!

VICTORIA MacKENZIE

Crex Crex

A strong westerly wind, chilled by the Atlantic, blows a smirr of rain straight at the windows and shivers the foxgloves in the hotel garden. So much for June. But there are small consolations: a coal fire blazes in the hearth and I'm sinking into a velvet-covered chair. I feel calmer than I have for weeks. A young waiter with a Highland accent takes my order. He's bearded and his fingers are long and sensitive; he reminds me of my first boyfriend, who played guitar and thought he was going to make the world a better place, until he discovered how difficult that would be.

The waiter is polite and efficient and brings me a china teapot of Lady Grey and a scone the size of a saucer, the sugar glittering on top like broken glass. I sip my tea and savour the heat from the glowing embers. Bliss. Then my husband appears and my good mood evaporates.

When we were first married I took such pride in saying those words: 'my husband'. Now it's more like a term of abuse. Here he comes, lumbering in wearing multi-pocketed trousers and a tatty anorak the colour of boiled spinach. And yes, he has his camera round his neck and a bag of lenses, weighing at least a stone, slung over his shoulder. Perhaps he thinks he'll spot a rare bird in the dining room. David is obsessed with what he calls his List: a catalogue of all known resident and visitor birds in Britain. Every spare second is devoted to looking for birds, the rarer the better, but it's just a game to him, he's not remotely interested in the birds themselves. He even assigns them points – fifty for a great northern diver, sixty for a red-breasted merganser, that sort of thing. A hundred points is the highest score and it goes to the corncrake. But don't get me started on those sodding birds. *Crex crex. Crex crex.* Everywhere we go we hear them calling, or I should say rasping. The sound is harsh and repetitive: less like birdsong, more like the cranking of a rusty car jack.

David sits down opposite me. 'That looks nice,' he says, gesturing at my scone.

'It is.'

'Then I'll get one too.' His tone is jovial but I push my plate towards him.

'Here, finish this. I've had enough.'

I get up and leave. I know I'm behaving badly but I can't stop myself.

§

It's our first time on Iona. We arrived three days ago, after a four-hour drive from Edinburgh, a ferry to Mull, another hour's drive, and finally a ten-minute ferry crossing. It would be quicker to get to Africa. Iona is tiny: four miles long and a mile wide, with one village, *Baile Mòr*, or 'Big Village', where our hotel is. Apart from the village, there's a smattering of other buildings, including the abbey with its sturdy square tower, and the ruins of a nunnery. A patchwork of green fields, rocks pushing through the thin soil, are dotted with sheep, and a few sandy beaches scallop the edge of the island. No cars are allowed, although the locals have them and it's remarkable how often I have to jump off the single-track road to get out of the way of a speeding Land Rover.

I walk out of the hotel and decide to head for the abbey to escape the rain. Outside its main door is a huge stone cross, three metres tall and beautifully carved. I think about all the hands that have touched it, all the changes it has witnessed. David read up about Iona's history before we left; he hates going anywhere he hasn't meticulously researched first, so I know that this cross is over a thousand years old. Whatever storms raged in the hearts of the people who built it mean nothing to us now. Just as the storm raging in mine is without significance for anyone but me.

I go inside the abbey. I'd forgotten that feeling you get inside old churches. This one feels *really* old – the stones are grey and worn, and it smells of earth and dust. At secondary school my best friend was Catholic and sometimes I went to church with her; I even took communion because I didn't know any better. It made me feel important to think God was watching me and listening to my private thoughts. Empty-headed little girl that I was. I'm just as empty-headed now, when I'm forty-nine and should know better.

I go through a side door to the cloisters where an elderly man in tweed is making agonisingly slow progress. He's tall but stooped, with a kind face and the shaggiest eyebrows I've ever seen. His whole body is trembling, his feet almost beyond his control, each step requiring concentration and effort. Every time he reaches a pillar he clings to it as if it's his long lost brother, and when he holds on he stops trembling. He sits down on a low ledge between the pillars.

He sees me and smiles. 'Here on holiday?'

'You could say that. My husband's a twitcher.'

'Ah! He must be thrilled by the corncrakes.'

'He hasn't seen one yet.'

'They're very shy, but they're wonderful birds. I usually manage a glimpse. But they'll be off to the Congo in a couple of months.'

'The Congo? Why come to Iona when you spend the rest of the year basking in central Africa?'

'Birds are full of mysteries, but I expect it makes sense to them. And we're here, aren't we? When we could be somewhere warm!'

'Perhaps the male corncrakes like it and insist their wives come too.'

'Maybe,' he chuckles. 'But my wife was just as keen on Iona as I am. She's long dead now, God rest her soul, but I still come every year.'

'Like the corncrakes.'

'Exactly so!' He seems delighted with the comparison. 'They're really quite astounding in many ways, but they're not terribly good at getting off the ground. Rumour has it that on the night they leave, they all clamber to the top of the abbey tower and launch themselves from the roof. Once they're airborne they're away! Brave little creatures.'

I'm not sure I believe him, but I like the thought of the birds finding the miracle of flight from the abbey roof.

'When I was young,' he continues, 'this country was crawling with life. Millions of sparrows, lapwings, butterflies, hares – I still remember how it sounded, all that life. You used to hear corncrakes all over Britain, but they've been decimated by nothing more than the pattern a combine harvester makes in a field.'

'What do you mean?' I ask politely, sensing I've got him onto a favourite topic.

'It's very simple. The farmer starts at the edge of the field, and spirals in towards the centre.' He waves a hand in the air to demonstrate. 'The corncrakes and their chicks get trapped in the middle, and eventually crushed.'

'How horrible.' I can't think what else to say.

Right on cue a corncrake calls nearby.

'All that's required for their future survival is for the farmer to make a different pattern – work from the centre outwards, and give the birds a chance to run towards cover.'

The corncrake is still calling, and it's as loud as if it was in the cloisters with us.

'They have the strangest call,' I say. 'I've never heard anything like it.'

'The females don't call, it's a male you can hear. You can hear them up to a mile away.'

'I can believe it,' I say. 'I hear them every night from my hotel bedroom.'

He laughs. 'I believe crofters used to throw things at them from their window in desperation. But these days it's a privilege to hear them really. Perhaps you'll even miss them when you're back home.'

'Maybe.' I smile. My thoughts turn to home and I shudder.

He struggles to his feet. I offer my arm but he refuses. Eventually he stands, but he seems unwilling to begin the effortful walk out of the abbey.

'Can I be of any assistance?' I ask. He seems so vulnerable, I'm worried about leaving him.

'No, but thank you. I'll be fine. Just a little slower these days.' He starts to jingle a few coins in his pocket, and I realise he'd probably rather not have an audience.

I thank him for telling me about the corncrakes and say goodbye. On my way back to the hotel I pass fields of sheep, all munching, heedless of the constant drizzle. The ewes have dull, pleasant faces, but the lambs are big and stocky, more like muscular teenage boys than cute babies. They butt each other and show their strength, little suspecting what it's all for. 'Keep eating, boys,' I say.

A large group of people approach, evidently just off the ferry for a day trip. They're talking loudly and snapping away with long-lensed cameras and smart phones. It must be obvious to the islanders who the tourists are: like migrating birds we arrive in spring and summer, huge flocks of us in our plumage of Gore-Tex and lace-up walking boots, full of chatter about beauty and remoteness.

'Isn't it tranquil!' they exclaim to each other.

When they've gone past, I stop to re-tie my bootlace, then peer over a low stone wall into a boggy meadow. A medium-sized, rather nondescript brown bird looks up at me, startled. Its eyes shine like beads of polished jet. It dashes into a clump of reeds.

A corncrake.

The bird itself was nothing special, but when it fixed its eyes on me, just for a second, it was like there was a connection between its consciousness and mine. A reminder that we share the same fabric of the world.

When I get back to the hotel room, David is sitting on the window seat reading a biography of St Columba. I say hello as if nothing happened earlier, as if abandoning him to my scone and pot of tea was perfectly normal behaviour. I think he's grateful for the pretence, he'll do anything to avoid confrontation. I decide to keep seeing the corncrake my secret.

'I'm going to have a shower before dinner – or do you want to go first?' I ask.

'No, that's fine. You go ahead.' He gives me a small smile. I almost feel sorry for him.

'I met an interesting man today,' I say. 'An elderly chap in tweed with shaggy white eyebrows. He told me about corncrakes.'

'I bet it was Sir Godrey Lyttelton.' David sounds excited. 'He spends every summer here – he was a military man but now he's a renowned ornithologist. I've got one of his books somewhere. He's the one who discovered that the male corncrake can call up to 20,000 times a night.'

I can never tell David anything he doesn't already know.

At dinner that evening the same dark-haired waiter is working. He's handsome – perhaps I could have an affair too. But the truth is I wouldn't know how to go about having one. The waiter barely looks at me. He doesn't know how my body aches to be touched again, or that I was proposed to by three men in less than a year when I was twenty. I don't know when men stopped noticing me, it must have been a gradual thing. I still look at them, but often I feel more maternal than anything else for the younger ones. How depressing. As for middle-aged men, well, they don't really interest me. I've already got one of those.

In the restaurant it's mostly couples, and one or two families with bored teenagers. David orders venison. The dense, dark meat has never agreed with me. I think of those bullying muscular sheep in the fields and ask for a rack of lamb.

The evening seems endless; it doesn't get dark here until eleven. We sit in the hotel lounge and read. Or more precisely, David reads and I brood. Later, he chats to some of the other guests. People always like him – he's easy to talk to, he knows the right things to say. A middle-aged Glaswegian couple are complaining about the weather.

'And they talk about that global warming!'

'Global warming doesn't mean we get a nice Mediterranean climate,' I say. 'The effects of climate change are unpredictable – overall there's a warming effect, but it's also likely to mean more storms, more wind, more rain. It doesn't mean you can start planting vineyards and wearing your bikini in Troon.'

The conversation goes a bit flat after my contribution. I do my best, but I'm awkward, I know it. I can't do small talk, I always take the conversation too seriously.

I decide to go up to bed for a rare moment of peace and privacy. Heaven knows it's hard to get much privacy in a marriage. I get into my pyjamas and try to read but my eyes slip over the words, so I turn out the light and listen to the corncrakes calling from the nearby meadows. When David comes to bed I keep well over to my side. I lie on the soft cotton sheet framing questions I don't want him to answer. *Do you still love her? Do you still love me? Do you miss her? Are you sorry it's over?* Even when I'm lying still I feel jittery, as if I'm pacing inside my own skin. All night the corncrakes keep me company. *Crex crex, crex crex.*

§

The next day we take the ferry back over to Mull so we can join a wildlife expedition. Mull seems huge compared to Iona, I've acclimatised already. The road skirts the mountains which are covered in grey scree and loom over the narrow road. Dozens of waterfalls come cascading down in milky streams. It's so different from the sweet flat greenness of Iona.

At the meeting point sixteen of us cram onto the minibus and after brief introductions we're on the road, or rather we're on Mull's endless loop of single track road. It's not raining yet but the sky is roiling with black clouds.

'Right folks, what do you want to see today?' asks Nigel, our guide.

'The Big Five,' someone calls out and I laugh.

'Don't laugh,' Nigel says to me. 'Scotland has a very special Big Five of her own. It might not be elephants and lions, but what does she have, folks?'

People call things out – it's like being at school. It turns out Scotland's Big Five consists of otters, red squirrels, red deer, harbour seals and golden eagles.

'We might see any of the Big Five today,' Nigel tells us. 'And we'll probably see a white-tailed eagle too, there are plenty of them around at the moment.'

Everyone oohs and ahs. After a mile or so Nigel swings the bus down a bumpy track and parks in a layby. He sets up two large spotting scopes on stands, though almost everyone has their own expensive-looking binoculars. I have David's second-best pair which still cost £200.

Nigel brings out his own binoculars. They're Swarovski and he looks nervous when anyone gets too close.

'Nice equipment, Nige,' someone quips. 'You win the lottery?'

We stand around while Nigel tells us that he saw two white-tailed eagles here last week and that the conditions are perfect for seeing them again. I shiver and wonder when he'll pass round the coffee and cake that were advertised on his website. We don't see any birds except a couple of gulls gliding overhead, probably on the lookout for cake too, and after twenty minutes we get back on the bus.

'Saw an otter at this spot last week,' Nigel tells us, pulling up on a verge beside a strip of sandy beach. 'Got to be nice and quiet for otters.' Needless to say everyone is chattering and rustling packets of boiled sweets or crisps. A pied wagtail makes his brisk little run across the sand, tail tap-tapping like a clockwork toy.

Most of the group seem to be from Hampshire or Surrey, but they travel all over Scotland every year looking for birds. The men are essentially all my husband – they have big cameras, big binoculars, and they talk of nothing but their Lists.

'Last I year I ticked a red-necked phalarope,' one of them says to David, who nods, evidently impressed.

'Was that in Shetland?' David asks. 'We're going there next year.'

News to me.

Another man asks David where we're staying. When he says Iona, the man instantly says, 'Oh, you must have seen a corncrake then.'

'We've heard plenty,' David says, unwilling to admit failure.

'Oh dear, they're shy bastards,' says the man, seeing through his hedging reply.

I smile to myself.

There's a Northern Irish girl here with her mum, and they're clearly not birders; in fact they don't seem to know anything at all about the natural world. Every bird we see the girl exclaims, 'Amaaaazing!' She asks what the big mottled birds are that we see beside the seagulls, and our guide tells her they're juvenile herring gulls. 'Amaaaazing!' she says.

Later, when we're eating our packed lunches, we talk about other holidays we've been on.

'Last year we went to Australia,' the Northern Irish girl says. 'We bungee-jumped and did a skydive from a plane. It was amaaaazing!'

I lean towards David and whisper, 'Her vocabulary is rather limited,' but he turns away.

'Have you ever bungee-jumped?'

I realise with a shock that the girl is addressing her question to me.

'Er, no. I haven't.' I try to convey some of the contempt I feel for this particular activity. I don't need to dangle over a ravine to know I'm alive, thanks.

'You should try it, it's – '

'Yes, I'm sure it's amazing,' I snap.

She gapes at me, then turns away.

And this is how the rest of the afternoon proceeds. At regular intervals we get out and stand in a layby, point our binoculars at a distant blob that Nigel thinks might be something hunched on a branch, but which turns out to be nothing much, and then we pile back into the bus. We stop at 'toilets' which means stopping near a wood so we can go behind the trees if we need to. I decide I can hold on.

There's much discussion about which birding apps people use. John from Brighton admits to using Merlin which appears to be a faux pas – it's for novices. Nigel prefers BirdsEye though it's not for beginners, as he tells shame-faced beginner John. 'You need to already know what you're looking at.'

'What's the point of it then?' I ask. 'Why do you need an app if you already know what you're seeing?'

'You use it to tick off the birds on your list,' he says. Obviously. Silly me. 'And it'll bring up all the birds you've not ticked yet, so you can see what you've got left, and it can divide your list up – World List, Regional List – it's brilliant.'

'Sounds it.'

David and I hardly speak for the entire expedition. The rain holds off and we see two golden eagles soaring above a pine forest. David is happy, he can tick that off. When we say goodbye to everyone at the end of the afternoon Nigel pats me on the shoulder.

'Take care, love. Hope you're feeling better soon.'

In the car I ask David if he knows what that was about.

'I told Nigel you were ill, to excuse your behaviour.'

'You did what?'

'You were embarrassing. What did you have to be so rude to Rebecca for?'

'Who's Rebecca?'

'The Northern Irish girl. And you were rude to Nigel. You were rude to everyone in fact. As usual.'

We're silent for the rest of the drive across Mull. It takes forever as David pulls into a passing place whenever there's a car remotely in view on the horizon, and allows speeding drivers to overtake us at every opportunity. When I met him I was fascinated by what a careful, patient driver he was. He was the only man I knew who didn't get angry when other drivers cut in front of him or ignored his right of way. Now his patience frustrates me, he seems slow and stupid. Why doesn't he care that these other drivers are rude and dangerous? I'm irritated by his big hands on the steering wheel, his bitten nails, the hole in his jumper at the elbow, his woolly hat knitted by his mother. How can the things that once filled you with tenderness fill you with rage?

§

The next morning is dreich again. David goes out alone, corncrake spotting. Their calls, which thrilled him at first, have become a source of irritation – he thinks they're taunting him. Later I go out too, dressed to the nines in waterproof trousers and an anorak. We're leaving Iona tomorrow and there are still places I haven't explored. I head north first, stopping briefly at the village shop for a packet of ginger biscuits, before squelching to the top of Dùn I. This is Iona's only hill, and it's only a few hundred feet high. The rain suddenly eases and the sun peers out between fast-moving clouds. To the east I can see Mull, its pink granite cliffs a blur in the low clouds. I know Staffa is to the north and the islands of Coll and Tiree are to the north-west, but I can't see them in this weather.

I open the biscuits and mechanically stuff them into my mouth, trying not to think about calories. I try not to think about a lot of things. Instead I look at the sea, the sky, the light – they never stop changing. I hear a droning: a helicopter is leaving the island, swaying like an injured insect. Then it steadies and zooms out of sight.

I decide to visit a beach to the west. I cross a deserted, scruffy golf course and half jump, half step into a wide, shallow burn to get there, but it's worth the wet feet. The beach is covered in birds that lift off as I approach – redshanks and ringed plovers mostly, and a dozen stocky oyster catchers calling *pee-peep!* in boisterous indignation at the disturbance. Further out to sea there's a group of shags on a rock, their black wings held out to dry; they look like vampires preparing to embrace their next fishy victim.

Seaweed is strewn across the beach in green and brown streamers, and every rock pool is rosetted with limpets. I sit on an outcrop to take the weight off my feet and dip my hand into the cool, clear water. My walking boots are rubbing now that my feet are wet – the boots are new and I didn't break them in properly. David told me to wear them round the house with two pairs of socks but I forgot. His walking boots are old and battered – I bet they're comfortable. Still, the pain is something to focus on. After all, Iona is a pilgrimage destination and pilgrims sometimes walk with bare feet, or deliberately put a stone in their shoe. There's nothing like pain to focus the mind, or at least to clear it of everything else.

I don't see David at any point which is odd, until I realise he's probably avoiding me. Maybe he took the boat over to Mull for the day again. Maybe he's gone home without me. My heart freezes over at the thought. Marriage is like an island where there are only two natives. Other people can never be more than visitors; they don't understand the history, the customs, the complicated codes of behaviour. There's endless potential for hurting each other. I can't bear to think he'll never be my sweetheart, my true love, again. But perhaps he hasn't been those things for a long time.

When I get back to our room I sit on the bed and remove my boots. The bathroom door is shut and the shower's running. I feel such relief:

he hasn't left me after all. Peeling my socks off is agony. My big toes are rubbed raw and my heels are bloody where the blisters have torn.

'Ouch,' is David's only comment when he comes out of the bathroom and sees my feet, but mingled with the 'I told you so' tone is a note of sympathy. Perhaps marriages have been saved by less. I am something like glad to see him.

That night at dinner we make conversation about normal things – his continued failure to see a corncrake (I keep my secret), his job, my job, friends we'll catch up with when we're back. We sit in the lounge afterwards and have a drink.

The hotel manager is doing her rounds, greeting people and apologising for the weather. I ask her about the helicopter I saw leaving Iona earlier.

'It was taking Sir Godfrey Lyttelton to Glasgow, he took a fall. Such a shame, he's a lovely gent. He's often in here in the evenings for a wee natter.'

'Will he be okay?' I ask.

'Oh yes. He lost his footing and broke his hip, but he's stable now.'

But I won't see him again. I won't be able to tell him I saw a corncrake. 'Will he come back to Iona this year, do you think?'

David gives me a 'Why do you want to know?' look.

'No, don't think he'll be returning at all. He needs looking after and there's no one to do that for him here. His nearest relative's his nephew in London, so I expect he'll go into a nursing home on the mainland. Sir Godfrey's been saying for years his nephew will put him in a home; seems he was right.'

'But he won't see the corncrakes again!' I say.

She looks puzzled and moves off to talk to other guests. David asks me why I'm so upset about Sir Godfrey, but I don't even know myself.

§

The last day. We packed most of our things last night and will be getting the boat to Mull after breakfast. Part of me is looking forward to getting home – being in my own house, walking around Edinburgh, opening the bedroom curtains and seeing the early morning light on the creamy stone buildings. Another part of me is dreading it. I wonder if I should suggest marriage counselling.

David's in the bathroom, but the door is ajar and I can see him shaving at the sink. Since last night things have been a tiny bit better between us, something of the old us is re-emerging and I feel hopeful. I hum as I open a jar of face moisturiser and smooth it over my skin. David appears at the bathroom door.

'I think we should have a trial separation when we get back,' he says. 'I'll move out, you can stay in the house.'

'Okay,' I say, and turn back to the mirror, my heart pounding against my ribcage. There are smears of white moisturising cream on my nose and chin. With the delicatest possible touch, as if my skin is made of cobwebs, I rub them away.

He goes back to shaving. I can see from here how his sandy hair is thinning and I feel an urge to go over to him and stroke where his scalp is showing. Suddenly I remember that ache you get from love. It has returned: at a low wattage, but there.

'But what if we separate and one of us gets ill? Or has a fall?' I call to him.

'What?' He steps back into the bedroom looking amazed, as though the way my mind works is one of the greatest mysteries of the world.

'Who would look after me then? Who would look after you?'

I run out of our room and go outside, down to the little beach. A few waders are on the sand, running in and out with the ebb of waves. If only we could touch the earth as lightly as they do. There's fragility everywhere I look. In the little wooden boats I see bobbing near sharp rocks. In birds' eggs, bracken tenderly tucked around them, futile against predator and storm. In the slender foxgloves battered by the wind, and most of all in us, in our brittle bones ready to shatter and our treacherous blood ready to spill at the slightest knock.

I watch the rain falling into the grey sea and listen to the corncrakes. Soon they will make their way to the abbey tower, launch themselves into the air, and make their unlikely flight to Africa. Meanwhile they're still asking their own unknowable questions. *Crex crex, crex crex, crex crex, crex crex.*

ST COLUMBA

Altus Prosator

ALTUS prosator vetustus dierum et ingenitus
erat absque origine primordii et crepidine
est et erit in saecula saeculorum infinita
cui est unigenitus Christus et sanctus spiritus
coaeternus in Gloria deitatis perpetua
non tres deos depromimus sed unum Deum dicimus
salva fidei in personis tribus gloriosissimis.

BONOS creavit angelos ordines et archangelos
principatum ac sedium potestatum virtutium
uti non esset bonitas otiosa ac majestas
trinitatis in omnibus largitatis muneribus
sed haberet caelestia in quibus privilegia
ostenderet magnopere possibili fatimine.

CAELI de regni apice stationis angelicae
claritate praefulgoris venustate speciminis
superbiendo ruerat Lucifer quem formaverat
apostataeque angeli eodem lapsu lugubri
auctoris cenodoxiae pervicacis invidiae
ceteris remanentibus in suis principatibus.

DRACO magnus taeterrimus terribilis et antiquus
qui fuit serpens lubricus sapientior omnibus
bestiis et animantibus terrae ferocioribus
tertiam partem siderum traxit secum in barathrum
locorum infernalium diversorumque carcerum
refugas veri luminis parasito praecipites.

The Maker on High

ANCIENT exalted seed-scatterer whom time gave no progenitor:
he knew no moment of creation in his primordial foundation
he is and will be all places in all time and all ages
with Christ his first-born only-born and the holy spirit co-borne
throughout the high eternity of glorious divinity:
three gods we do not promulgate one God we state and intimate
salvific faith victorious: three persons very glorious.

BENEVOLENCE created angels and all the orders of archangels
thrones and principalities powers virtues qualities
denying otiosity to the excellence and majesty
of the not-inactive trinity in all labours of bounty
when it mustered heavenly creatures whose well devised natures
received its lavish proffer through power-word for ever.

CAME down from heaven summit down from angelic limit
dazzling in his brilliance beauty's very likeness
Lucifer downfalling (once woke at heaven's calling)
apostate angels sharing the deadly downfaring
of the author of high arrogance and indurated enviousness
the rest still continuing safe in their dominions.

DAUNTINGLY huge and horrible the dragon ancient and terrible
known as the lubric serpent subtler in his element
than all the beasts and every fierce thing living earthly
dragged a third – so many – stars to his gehenna
down to infernal regions not devoid of dungeons
benighted ones hell's own parasite hurled headlong.

EXCELSUS mundi machinam praevidens et harmoniam
caelum et terram fecerat mare aquas condiderat
herbarum quoque germina virgultorum arbuscula
solem lunam ac sidera ignem ac necessaria
aves pisces et pecora bestias animalia
hominem demum regere protoplaustum praesagmine.

FACTIS simul sideribus aetheris luminaribus
conlaudaverunt angeli factura pro mirabili
immensae molis Dominum opificem caelestium
praeconio laudabili debito et immobili
concentuque egregio grates egerunt Domino
amore et arbitrio non naturae donario.

GRASSATIS primis duobus seductisque parentibus
secundo ruit diabolus cum suis satellitibus
quorum horrore vultuum sonoque volitantium
consternarentur homines metu territi fragiles
non valentes carnalibus haec intueri visibus
qui nunc ligantur fascibus ergastulorum nexibus.

HIC sublatus e medio deiectus est a Domino
cuius aeris spatium constipatur satellitum
globo invisibilium turbido perduellium
ne malis exemplaribus imbuti ac sceleribus
nullis unquam tegentibus saeptis ac parietibus
fornicarentur homines palam omnium oculis.

INVEHUNT nubes pontias ex fontibus brumalias
tribus profundioribus oceani dodrantibus
maris caeli climatibus caeruleis turbinibus
profuturas segitibus vineis et germinibus
agitatae flaminibus thesauris emergentibus
quique paludes marinas evacuant reciprocas.

EXCELLENT promethean armoury structuring world harmony
had created earth and heaven and wet acres of ocean
also sprouting vegetation shrubs groves plantations
sun moon stars to ferry fire and all things necessary
birds fish and cattle and every animal imaginable
but lastly the second promethean the protoplast human being.

FAST upon the starry finishing the lights high shimmering
the angels convened and celebrated for the wonders just created
the Lord the only artificer of that enormous vault of matter
with loud and well judged voices unwavering in their praises
an unexampled symphony of gratitude and sympathy
sung not by force of nature but freely lovingly grateful.

GUILTY of assault and seduction of our parents in the garden
the devil has a second falling together with his followers
whose faces set in horror and wingbeats whistling hollow
would petrify frail creatures into stricken fearers
but what men perceive bodily must preclude luckily
those now bound and bundled in dungeons of the underworld.

HE Zabulus was driven by the Lord from mid heaven
and with him the airy spaces were choked like drains with faeces
as the turgid rump of rebels fell but fell invisible
in case the grossest villains became willy-nilly
with neither walls nor fences preventing curious glances
tempters to sin greatly openly emulatingly.

IRRIGATING clouds showering wet winter from sea-fountains
from floods of the abysses three-fourths down through fishes
up to the skyey purlieus in deep blue whirlpools
good rain then for cornfields vineyard-bloom and grain-yields
driven by blasts emerging from their airy treasuring
dessicating not the land-marches but the facing sea-marshes.

KADUCA ac tyrannica mundique momentanea
regum praesentis gloria nutu Dei deposita
ecce gigantes gemere sub aquis magno ulcere
comprobantur incendio aduri ac supplicio
Cocytique Charybdibus strangulati turgentibus
Scyllis obtecti fluctibus eliduntur et scrupibus.

LIGATAS aquas nubibus frequenter cribrat Dominus
ut ne erumpant protinus simul ruptis obicibus
quarum uberioribus venis velut uberibus
pedetentim natantibus telli per tractus istius
gelidis ac ferventibus diversis in temporibus
usquam influunt flumina nunquam deficientia.

MAGNI Dei virtutibus appenditur dialibus
globus terrae et circulus abyssi magnae inditus
suffultu Dei iduma omnipotentis valida
columnis velut vectibus eundem sustenantibus
promontoriis et rupibus solidis fundaminibus
velut quibusdam basibus firmatus immobilibus.

NULLI videtur dubium in imis esse infernum
ubi habentur tenebrae vermes et dirae bestiae
ubi ignis sulphureus ardens flammis edacibus
ubi rugitus hominum fletus et stridor dentium
ubi Gehennae gemitus terribilis et antiquus
ubi ardor flammaticus sitis famisque horridus.

ORBEM infra ut legimus incolas esse novimus
quorum genu precario frequenter flectit Domino
quibusque impossibile librum scriptum revolvere
obsignatum signaculis septem de Christi monitis
quem idem resignaverat postquam victor exstiterat
explens sui praesagmina adventus prophetalia.

KINGS of the world we live in: their glories are uneven
brittle tyrannies disembodied by a frown from God's forehead:
giants too underwater groaning in great horror
forced to burn like torches cut by painful tortures
pounded in the millstones of underworld maelstroms
roughed rubbed out buried in a frenzy of flints and billows.

LETTING the waters be sifted from where the clouds are lifted
the Lord often prevented the flood he once attempted
leaving the conduits utterly full and rich as udders
slowly trickling and panning through the tracts of this planet
freezing if cold was called for warm in the cells of summer
keeping our rivers everywhere running forward for ever.

MAGISTERIAL are his powers as the great God poises
the earth ball encircled by the great deep so firmly
supported by an almighty robust nieve so tightly
that you would think pillar and column held it strong and solemn
the capes and cliffs stationed on solidest foundations
fixed uniquely in their place as if on immovable bases.

NO one needs to show us: a hell lies deep below us
where there is said to be darkness worms beasts carnage
where there are fires of sulphur burning to make us suffer
where men are gnashing roaring weeping wailing deploring
where groans mount from gehennas terrible never-ending
where parched and fiery horror feeds thirst and hunger.

OFTEN on their knees at prayer are many said to be there
under the earth books tell us they do not repel us
though they found it unavailing the scroll not unrolling
whose fixed seals were seven when Christ warning from heaven
unsealed it with the gesture of a resurrected victor
fulfilling the prophets' foreseeing of his coming and his decreeing.

PLANTATUM a prooemio paradisum a Domino
legimus in primordio Genesis nobilissimo
cuius ex fonte flumina quattuor sunt manantia
cuius etiam florido lignum vitae in medio
cuius non cadunt folia gentibus salutifera
cuius inerrabiles deliciae ac fertiles.

QUIS ad condictum Domini montem ascendit Sinai?
quis audivit tonitrua ultra modum sonantia
quis clangorem perstrepere inormitatis buccinae?
quis quoque vidit fulgura in gyro coruscantia
quis lampades et iacula saxaque collidentia
praeter Israhelitici Moysen iudicem populi?

REGIS regum rectissimi prope est dies Domini
dies irae et vindictae tenebrarum et nebulae
diesque mirabilium tonitruorum fortium
dies quoque angustiae maeroris ac tristitiae
in quo cessabit mulierum amor ac desiderium
hominumque contentio mundi huius et cupido.

STANTES erimus pavidi ante tribunal Domini
reddemusque de omnibus rationem affectibus
videntes quoque posita ante obtutus crimina
librosque conscientiae patefactos in facie
in fletus amarissimos ac singultus erumpemus
subtracta necessaria operandi materia.

TUBA primi archangeli strepente admirabili
erumpent munitissima claustra ac poliandria
mundi praesentis frigora hominum liquescentia
undique conglobantibus ad compagines ossibus
animabus aethralibus eisdem obviantibus
rursumque redeuntibus debitis mansionibus.

PARADISE was planted primally as God wanted
we read in sublime verses entering into Genesis
its fountain's rich waters feed four flowing rivers
its heart abounds with flowers where the tree of life towers
with foliage never fading for the healing of the nations
and delights indescribable abundantly fruitful.

QUIZ sacred Sinai: who is it has climbed so high?
Who has heard the thunder-cracks vast in the sky-tracts?
Who has heard the enormous bullroaring of the war-horns?
Who has seen the lightning flashing round the night-ring?
Who has seen javelins flambeaus a rock-face in shambles?
Only to Moses is this real only to the judge of Israel.

RUE God's day arriving righteous high king's assizing
dies irae day of the vindex day of cloud and day of cinders
day of the dumbfoundering day of great thundering
day of lamentation of anguish of confusion
with all the love and yearning of women unreturning
as all men's striving and lust for worldly living.

STANDING in fear and trembling with divine judgement assembling
we shall stammer what we expended before our life was ended
faced by rolling videos of our crimes however hideous
forced to read the pages of the conscience book of ages
we shall burst out into weeping sobbing bitter and unceasing
now that all means of action have tholed the last retraction.

The archangelic trumpet-blast is loud and great at every fastness
the hardest vaults spring open the catacombs are broken
the dead of the world are thawing their cold rigor withdrawing
the bones are running and flying to the joints of the undying
their souls hurry to meet them and celestially to greet them
returning both together to be one not one another.

VAGATUR ex climactere Orion caeli cardine
derelicto Virgilio astrorum splendidissimo
per metas Thetis ignoti orientalis circuli
girans certis ambagibus redit priscis reditibus
oriens post biennium Vesperugo in vesperum
sumpta in proplesmatibus tropicis intellectibus.

XRISTO de caelis Domino descendente celsissimo
praefulgebit clarissimum signum crucis et vexillum
tectisque luminaribus duobus principalibus
cadent in terram sidera ut fructus de ficulnea
eritque mundi spatium ut fornacis incendium
tunc in montium specubus abscondent se exercitus.

YMNORUM cantionibus sedulo tinnientibus
tripudiis sanctis milibus angelorum vernantibus
quattuorque plenissimis animalibus oculis
cum viginti felicibus quattuor senioribus
coronas admittentibus agni Dei sub pedibus
laudatur tribus vicibus Trinitas aeternalibus.

ZELUS ignis furibundus consumet adversarios
nolentes Christum credere Deo a Patre venisse
nos vero evolabimus obviam ei protinus
et sic cum ipso erimus in diversis ordinibus
dignitatum pro meritis praemiorum perpetuis
permansuri in Gloria a saeculis in saecula.

VAGRANT Orion driven from the crucial hinge of heaven
leaves the Pleiades receding most splendidly beneath him
tests the ocean boundaries the oriental quandaries
as Vesper circling steadily returns home readily
the rising Lucifer of the morning after two years mourning:
these things are to be taken as type and trope and token.

X spikes and flashes like the Lord's cross marching
down with him from heaven as the last sign is given
moonlight and sunlight are finally murdered
stars fall from dignity like fruits from a fig-tree
the world's whole surface burns like a furnace
armies are crouching in caves in the mountains.

YOU know then the singing of hymns finely ringing
thousands of angels advancing spring up in sacred dances
quartet of beasts gaze from numberless eyes in praise
two dozen elders as happiness compels them
throw all their crowns down to the Lamb who surmounts them
'Holy holy holy' binds the eternal trinity.

ZABULUS burns to ashes all those adversaries
who deny that the Saviour was Son to the Father
but we shall fly to meet him and immediately greet him
and be with him in the dignity of all such diversity
as our deeds make deserved and we without swerve
shall live beyond history in the state of glory.

translated from the Latin by Edwin Morgan

attributed to ST COLUMBA

Adiutor Laborantium

Adiutor laborantium,
Bonorum rector omnium,
Custos ad propugnaculum,
Defensorque credentium,
Exaltator humilium,
Fractor superbientium,
Gubernator fidelium,
Hostis impoenitentium,
Iudex cunctorum iudicum,
Castigator errantium,
Casta vita viventium,
Lumen et pater luminum,
Magna luce lucentium,
Nulli negans sperantium
Opem atque auxilium,
Precor ut me homunculum
Quassatum ac miserrimum
Remigantem per tumultum
Saeculi istius infinitum
Trahat post se ad supernum
Vitae portum pulcherrimum
Xristus; . . . infinitum
Ymnum sanctum in seculum
Zelo subtrahas hostium
Paradisi in gaudium.
    Per te, Christe Ihesu,
    qui vivis et regnas.

All Labourers' Helper

All labourers' helper,
Blessèd men's ruler,
Chief ramparts' warder,
Deep faith's defender,
Each small man's lifter,
Fashion-plates' humbler,
Great navigator,
Heretic-crusher,
Just judges' judger,
Keen sinners' punisher,
Light of good-livers,
Man's sanctifier,
New illuminator,
O endless giver,
Perfect in vigour,
Quicken my prayer;
Receive it, Master,
So, though I am no braver
Than the weakest rower
Under loud thunder's
Violent clamour,
Welcome me to the Father's
'X' – Christ the Keeper's
Yearned-for Cross. Saviour,
Zealously may you conquer
Per dominum nostrum
Forever and ever.

GEORGE BUCHANAN

from *The History of Scotland* (1582) *translated from the Latin by Mr Bond* (1827 edition)

Beyond Colonsay, to the north, lies Mull, twelve miles distant from Isla. This island is twenty-four miles in length, and as many in breadth; it is craggy, yet not wholly barren of corn. It hath many woods in it, and great herds of deer, and a port safe enough for ships; over against Icolmkill, it hath two large rivers full of salmon, besides other less streams not without fish; it hath also two lochs, in each of which are several islands, and castles on them all. The sea, breaking into it in divers places, makes four bays, all abounding with herrings. On the south-west is seated Calaman, or the island of Doves; in the north-east stands Erra; both these islands are commodious for cattle, corn, and fishing.

The island of Icolmkill is distant from them two miles; it is two miles long, and above a mile broad; fruitful in all things which that climate can produce, and famed for as many ancient monuments as could be well expected in such a country; but it was made yet more famous by the severe discipline and holiness of St. Columbus. It was beautified with two monasteries, one of monks, the other of nuns; with one curia, or (as they call it) a parish church, and with many chapels, some of them built by the munificence of the kings of Scotland, and others by the petty kings of the islands. In the old monastery of St. Columbus, the bishops of the islanders placed their see; their ancient mansion-house, which was before in the Isle of Man, being taken by the English. There still remains, however, among the ancient ruins, a churchyard, or burying-place, common to all the noble families which dwelt in the western islands. There are three tombs in it more eminent than the rest, at a small distance from one another, having little shrines, looking towards the east, built over them. In the west part of each is a stone with an inscription, declaring whose tomb it is; the middlemost hath one to this purport, – 'The tomb of the kings of Scotland'; for it is reported that no less than forty-eight monarchs were buried there: that on the right hand has this title, – 'The tomb of the kings of Ireland'; for four sovereigns of that nation are said to be interred there: that on the left side is inscribed: 'The tomb of the kings of Norway'; for report says, that eight sovereigns of that nation were entombed there. In the rest of the cemetery, the eminent families of the island have their tombs apart. There are six islands adjacent to it, small indeed, yet not unfruitful, which were given by ancient kings, or princes of the islands, to the nunnery of St. Columbus.

The island Soa, though it hath convenient pasturage for sheep, yet derives its greatest revenue from the sitting and hatching of sea fowl, and especially from their eggs. The next to that is Nun's island; then Rudana; after that Reringa; to which follows Skanny, distant half a mile from Mull; it hath one parish in it, but the parishioners live mostly in Mull. The shore abounds with rabbits. A mile from Skanny stands Eorsa. All these are under the jurisdiction of the monks of St. Columbus's monastery.

WILLIAM SHAKESPEARE

from *Macbeth, Act II, Scene IV*

Ross. Here comes the good Macduff.
How goes the world, sir, now?
Macduff. Why, see you not?
Ross. Is't known who did this more than bloody deed?
Macduff. Those that Macbeth hath slain.
Ross. Alas, the day!
What good could they pretend?
Macduff. They were suborned:
Malcolm and Donalbain, the king's two sons,
Are stol'n away and fled, which puts upon them
Suspicion of the deed.
Ross. 'Gainst nature still.
Thriftless ambition, that will ravin up
Thine own life's means! Then 'tis most like
The sovereignty will fall upon Macbeth.
Macduff. He is already named, and gone to Scone
To be invested.
Ross. Where is Duncan's body?
Macduff. Carried to Colme-kill,
The sacred storehouse of his predecessors
And guardian of their bones.

ROBERT CRAWFORD

Icolmkill

Road, stroll with me now
To the west-coast machair. Road,
Take my breath away.

*

It is a real place,
But its weather, its seasons
Are a Book of Hours.

*

As it was for saints,
So for us too, the world is
Data – given things.

*

Each ear of wheat hears.
You only have to listen
To each ear of wheat.

*

The weight of data
Makes everything bend here,
Makes us nod assent.

*

We are baptized now
Through our total immersion
In Loch Computer.

Lonely, I stand at
The Hermit's Cell and peer at
My hermit's cellphone.

*

Soon at the Four Roads,
Eye on the sea and fast clouds,
I will take the fifth.

ADOMNÁN

The Coof

From his writing hut Columba
Heard yelling over on Mull.
'That shouting coof destroys the stillness.
He's a man who will cuggle my ink.'

All day Columba's servant Diarmait
Guarded the inkhorn, but took his eye off it
Just as the man swept in, sleeves billowing,
To kiss the saint, and cuggled his ink.

ADOMNÁN

The Copyist

Baithéne asked a favour: 'Columba,
I want your sharp eye to check the text
Of this psalter.' Columba glanced up. 'Baithéne,
No need. Your transcription's perfect –
No superfluous detail, nothing missing,
Except, in just one verse, a single stroke.'
Later, in the writing hut, a shrewd monk,
Proofreading each passage line by line,
Found only a sole erratum, an absent 'I'.

ADOMNÁN

The Light House

While bad weather kept
Baithéne under the Sgurr
Of Eigg,
Columba slept
By the shore
On another island,
Locked, fasting
In a house all night.
At daybreak
As he woke,
Then all that long day
An intensely bright
Everlasting
Light
Surrounded him, and shone
Through the keyholes,
Between chinks
Round the doors
As if kindled
In a hearth
At the heart
Of that island house
While all day long
He sang
New songs
Never
Heard till then
And became aware
Of secrets hidden
Since before
The beginning
Of the world,
And mastered the art

Of how to handle
Reading obscure,
Difficult scriptures,
Making clear
Their hymnlike core,
Their simple
Inner candle.

ADOMNÁN

I

A lost
Life of St Brendan
Of Birr
Contains four
Puns
On the letter 'I':

Where a messenger
From Columba stands,
Men howk up a stone
Incised with a line,
A sign
To show
Where Columba must go:

'Go'
In Latin
Is the letter 'I'.

'Into'
In Irish
Is the letter 'I'.

The noun 'isle'
In Irish
Is the letter 'I',

And 'Iona'
In Irish
Is the letter 'I'.

So sly
St Brendan

Of Birr,
Said to the messenger,
'You'd better
Tell Columba
How I found
On this stone
Howked from the ground
His whole
Biography,
His hagiography
In the sum of just one
Letter:
'I'.

MICK IMLAH

The Prophecies

1 *Of the book which fell into the water-vessel*

ONE day, as he was staring into the hall-fire
with such sadness, that the serving brethren
redoubled their normal silence – he caught sight
in a corner of the youth Lugbe, from the clan Cummin,
reading a book, and suddenly said to him,
not in a threatening way, 'Take care, my son,
for it seems that the book you are reading is about
to fall into a vessel full of water.'

And so it proved: for when in time the boy
stood up to fetch a candle, he seemed to forget
the prophetic warning, and as he passed by
one of the saint's more senior men the book
slipped from under his arm, and lo! it was text-
down in the foot-bath, which was full of water.

2 *Similar, of the Thuringian inkhorn*

ONE day, when a shout went up on the far side
of the Sound of Hy, the saint, who had made for himself
an hour apart in his room, to meditate,
grew aware of the shout, and said, 'The man who is shouting
beyond the Sound is not of very sharp wit,
since when he comes knocking here today
for his food, or a spiritual lesson, he will surely
upset my Thuringian inkhorn, and spill the ink.'

This put his monks in a quandary, – whether
to bring the thing on, or to prevent it;
and some were busy, and some were standing still
the moment the shouter arrived: who in his haste
to embrace the saint, brushed the desk with a trailing
sleeve and we all had to write about it.

3 *Of the dead letter*

ONE day Baithéne, his old attendant, asked him:
'Could you spare a learned brother to read the psalter
your servant has written, and correct it?' To which
the saint replied: 'Why give my staff the trouble?
I daresay that in this psalter of yours, there is not
one word or letter too many; on the other hand,
look again at the work, and you will find
that everywhere the vowel 'i' is omitted!'

Now when Baithéne went back to the manuscript,
and checked it over, he found to his amazement
that in his absence some tick had gone over
his stuff and with a blue pencil scored out
every sentence in the first person, including
the entire intro and the acknowledgements.

4 *Of a future book*

Of course it got better, when he grew older
and sitting at supper was less apt to see
Judas in everyone's face at his shoulder:
'the wheels', as he put it, 'secure on the axle',
our wagon was 'fit to roam into the future'.
Thus, once, he emerged from a session, the dark
of his eyes rolled back from view – a trick he had –
and spoke of a small, black, impending book:

The Life of St Columba, Founder of Hy
by Adam something – many an abbot later –
in Penguin Classics, nineteen ninety-nine.
And now as he shared the vision he felt, he said,
a warm, delicious tingle and flush of the veins
as if he had been ravished by who knows whom.

DAVID KINLOCH

Between the Lines

Francis Campbell Boileau Cadell
'never indifferent to feminine charm'
did not marry, became a 'Bunty',
a playmate with a tartan face
who found aperitifs were 'necessary balm'
and made boys whisper at his approach:
'That's not a man, that's Mr Cadell!'

In shepherd trews, blue scarf,
yellow waistcoat or a kilt,
Uncle Bunty was a card;
in a white trenchcoat, collar
up, pipe and palette
clenched before a mirror,
he struck 'a gay and joyous note'.
A private in the trenches his uniform
was tailored privately.

The Somme was like Iona: a dreadful
dearth of baths: 'You either
stink or swim boom boom!'
Peploe sent a colour mag
to blot out mud and mud
yet Bunty wouldn't take commission
for anything but sketches
of the cocky Jacks and Tommies,
camerados in the lines.

The White Room, The White Teapot
Crème de Menthe, Carnations.
What explains his lust for white,
a creamy white, pursued across
the crunch of island beaches,
light's white: little bands
of spectra on the studio walls,
pink ladies, the odd pink man
who decorate the décor?

After the Great War everything was
flat. He took it at face value:
pleasure in a strand of sunlit carpet
linking joined but separate spaces,
the certain squareness of a room
saved from lumpenness
by an indefinable proportion.
He recalled the golden lining of a cape
pouring on a black and polished lake,

an orange blind with . . . something
blazing just behind. Once he painted
Able Seaman Vickers, twice
'a fine looking negro', often
his manservant Charles. And they were
full stops. Like the wink of ink
on Tommy's face, winks that spread
like ripples in Iona rock pools he never tried
to paint: going down and down
through emerald green

past the trench red of their sides.
And at the bottom there was death
again: flat and blank and white.

MEG BATEMAN

Peploe and Cadell in Iona

> 'I hope my Maker will credit me with the hours I have wasted watching the colours changing on the Sound' –
> Alexander Ritchie, quoted in E. Mairi MacArthur, *Iona Celtic Art: The Work of Alexander and Euphemia Ritchie*

Their interest held by a moment's light,
they brush pink shell-sand into a bay
where Adomnán saw eternity.

Foreground boulders make a still-life,
Beinn Mhòr, a backdrop of amethyst and jade,
their interest held by a moment's light.

Iona's so small they could climb Dùn Ì
and see a circlet of breaking waves
where Adomnán saw eternity.

Over lava sills and basalt dykes,
evening casts a shimmering veil,
their interest held by a moment's light.

Rose-flecked granite below opal sky,
the Treshnish Isles float away,
where Adomnán saw eternity.

The seabed below the tide
gleams aquamarine in a wash of paint,
their interest held by a moment's light
where Adomnán saw eternity.

ROBERT LOUIS STEVENSON

Dining at the Argyll Hotel with Sam Bough and Amy Sinclair, 5 August 1870, During the Franco-Prussian War

from a letter to his parents

At last, in comes the tureen and the handmaid lifts the cover. 'Rice Soup!' I yell, 'O no! none o' that for me!' – 'Yes,' says Bough, savagely, 'But Miss Amy didn't take me downstairs to eat salmon.' Accordingly he is helped. How his face fell. 'I imagine myself in the accident ward of the infirmary,' quoth he. It was, purely and simply, rice and water. After this, we have another weary pause, and then herrings in a state of mash and potatoes like iron. 'Send the potatoes out to Prussia for grape-shot,' was the suggestion. I dined off broken herrings and dry bread. At last 'the supreme moment comes', and the fowl in a lordly dish, is carried in. On the cover being raised, there is something so forlorn and miserable about the aspect of the animal that we both roar with laughter. Then Bough, taking up knife and fork, turns the 'swarry' over and over, shaking doubtfully his head. 'There's an aspect of quiet resistance about the beggar,' says he, 'that looks bad.' However, to work he falls until the sweat stands on his brow and a dismembered leg falls, dull and leaden-like, onto my dish. To eat it was simply impossible. Toughness was here at its farthest. I did not know before that flesh could be so tough. 'The strongest jaws in England,' says Bough piteously harpooning his dry morsel, 'couldn't eat this leg in less than twelve hours.' Nothing for it now, but to order boat and bill. 'That fowl,' says Bough to the landlady, 'is of a breed I know. I know the cut of its jib whenever it was put down. That was the grandmother of the cock that frightened Peter.' – 'I thought it was an historical animal,' says I, 'What a shame to kill it. It's as bad as eating Whittington's cat or the Dog of Montargis.' – 'Na – na it's no old,' says the landlady, 'but it eats hard.' – 'Eats!' I cry, 'where do you find that? Very little of that verb with us.' So with more raillery, we pay six shillings for our festival and run over to Earraid, shaking the dust of the Argyll Hotel from off our feet.

ROBERT LOUIS STEVENSON

The Islet

With my stepping ashore I began the most unhappy part of my adventures. It was half-past twelve in the morning, and though the wind was broken by the land, it was a cold night. I dared not sit down (for I thought I should have frozen) but took off my shoes and walked to and fro upon the sand, barefoot, and beating my breast with infinite weariness. There was no sound of man or cattle; not a cock crew, though it was about the hour of their first waking; only the surf broke outside in the distance, which put me in mind of my perils and those of my friend. To walk by the sea at that hour of the morning, and in a place so desert-like and lonesome, struck me with a kind of fear.

As soon as the day began to break I put on my shoes and climbed a hill – the ruggedest scramble I ever undertook – falling, the whole way, between big blocks of granite, or leaping from one to another. When I got to the top the dawn was come. There was no sign of the brig, which must have lifted from the reef and sunk. The boat, too, was nowhere to be seen. There was never a sail upon the ocean; and in what I could see of the land was neither house nor man.

I was afraid to think what had befallen my shipmates, and afraid to look longer at so empty a scene. What with my wet clothes and weariness, and my belly that now began to ache with hunger, I had enough to trouble me without that. So I set off eastward along the south coast, hoping to find a house where I might warm myself, and perhaps get news of those I had lost. And at the worst, I considered the sun would soon rise and dry my clothes.

After a little, my way was stopped by a creek or inlet of the sea, which seemed to run pretty deep into the land; and as I had no means to get across, I must needs change my direction to go about the end of it. It was still the roughest kind of walking; indeed the whole, not only of Earraid, but of the neighbouring part of Mull (which they call the Ross) is nothing but a jumble of granite rocks with heather in among. At first the creek kept narrowing as I had looked to see; but presently to my surprise it began to widen out again. At this I scratched my head, but still had no notion of the truth; until at last I came to a rising ground, and it burst upon me all in a moment that I was cast upon a little barren isle, and cut off on every side by the salt seas.

Instead of the sun rising to dry me, it came on to rain, with a thick mist; so that my case was lamentable.

I stood in the rain, and shivered, and wondered what to do, till it occurred to me that perhaps the creek was fordable. Back I went to the narrowest point and waded in. But not three yards from shore, I plumped in head over ears; and if ever I was heard of more, it was rather by God's grace than my own prudence. I was no wetter (for that could hardly be), but I was all the colder for this mishap; and having lost another hope was the more unhappy.

And now, all at once, the yard came in my head. What had carried me through the roost would surely serve me to cross this little quiet creek in safety. With that I set off, undaunted, across the top of the isle, to fetch and carry it back. It was a weary tramp in all ways, and if hope had not buoyed me up, I must have cast myself down and given up. Whether with the sea salt, or because I was growing fevered, I was distressed with thirst, and had to stop, as I went, and drink the peaty water out of the hags.

I came to the bay at last, more dead than alive; and at the first glance, I thought the yard was something farther out than when I left it. In I went, for the third time into the sea. The sand was smooth and firm, and shelved gradually down, so that I could wade out till the water was almost to my neck and the little waves splashed into my face. But at that depth my feet began to leave me, and I durst venture in no farther. As for the yard, I saw it bobbing very quietly some twenty feet beyond.

I had borne up well until this last disappointment; but at that I came ashore, and flung myself down upon the sands and wept.

The time I spent upon the island is still so horrible a thought to me, that I must pass it lightly over. In all the books I have read of people cast away, they have either their pockets full of tools, or a chest of things would be thrown upon the beach along with them, as if on purpose. My case was very different. I had nothing in my pockets but money and Alan's silver button; and being inland bred, I was as much short of knowledge as of means.

I knew indeed that shell-fish were counted good to eat; and among the rocks of the isle I found a great plenty of limpets, which at first I could scarcely strike from their places, not knowing quickness to be needful. There were, besides, some of the little shells that we call buckies; I think periwinkle is the English name. Of these two I made my whole diet, devouring them cold and raw as I found them; and so hungry was I, that at first they seemed to me delicious.

Perhaps they were out of season, or perhaps there was something wrong in the sea about my island. But at least I had no sooner eaten my first meal than I was seized with giddiness and retching, and lay for some time no better than dead. A second trial of the same food (indeed I had no other) did better with me, and revived my strength. But as long as I was on the island, I never knew what to expect when I had eaten; sometimes all was well, and sometimes I was thrown into a miserable sickness; nor could I distinguish what particular fish it was that hurt me.

All day it streamed rain; the island ran like a sop, there was no dry spot to be found; and when I lay down that night, between two boulders that made a kind of roof, my feet were in a bog.

The second day I crossed the island to all sides. There was no one part of it better than another; it was all desolate and rocky; nothing living on it but game birds which I lacked the means to kill, and the gulls that haunted the outlying rocks in a prodigious number. But the creek, or strait, that cut off the isle from the mainland of the Ross, opened out on the north into a bay, and the bay again opened into the Sound of Iona; and it was the neighbourhood of this place that I chose to be my home; though if I had thought upon the very name of home in such a spot, I must have burst out weeping.

I had good reasons for my choice. There was in this part of the isle a little hut of a house like a pig's hut, where fishers used to sleep when they came there upon their business; but the turf roof of it had fallen entirely in; so that the hut was of no use to me, and gave me less shelter than my rocks. What was more important, the shell-fish on which I lived grew there in great plenty; when the tide was out I could gather a peck at a time: and this was doubtless a convenience. But the other reason went deeper. I had become in no way used to the horrid solitude of the isle, but still looked round me on all sides (like a man that was hunted), between hope and fear that I might see some human creature coming. Now, from a little up the hillside over the bay, I could catch a sight of the great, ancient church and the roofs of the people's houses in Iona. And on the other hand, over the low country of the Ross, I saw smoke go up, morning and evening, as if from a homestead in a hollow of the land.

I used to watch this smoke, when I was wet and cold, and had my head half turned with loneliness; and think of the fireside and the company, till my heart burned. It was the same with the roofs of Iona. Altogether, this sight I had of men's homes and comfortable lives, although it put a point on my own sufferings, yet it kept hope alive, and helped me to eat my raw shellfish (which had soon grown to be a disgust) and saved me from the sense of horror I had whenever I was quite alone with dead rocks, and fowls, and the rain, and the cold sea.

I say it kept hope alive; and indeed it seemed impossible that I should be left to die on the shores of my own country, and within view of a church tower and the smoke of men's houses. But the second day passed; and though as long as the light lasted I kept a bright look-out for boats on the Sound or men passing on the Ross, no help came near me. It still rained, and I turned in to sleep, as wet as ever, and with a cruel sore throat, but a little comforted, perhaps, by having said goodnight to my next door neighbours, the people of Iona.

Charles the Second declared a man could stay outdoors more days in a year in the climate of England than in any other. This was very like a king, with a palace at his back and changes of dry clothes. But he must have had better luck on his flight from Worcester than I had on that miserable isle. It was the height of the summer; yet it rained for more than twenty-four hours, and did not clear until the afternoon of the third day.

This was the day of incidents. In the morning I saw a red deer, a buck with a fine spread of antlers, standing in the rain on the top of the island; but he had scarce seen me rise from under my rock, before he trotted off upon the other side. I supposed he must have swum the strait; though what should bring any creature to Earraid, was more than I could fancy.

A little after, as I was jumping about after my limpets, I was startled by a guinea-piece, which fell upon a rock in front of me and glanced off into the sea. When the sailors gave me my money again, they kept back not only about a third of the whole sum, but my father's leather purse; so that from that day out, I carried my gold loose in a pocket with a button. I now saw there must be a hole, and clapped my hand to the place in a great hurry. But this was to lock the stable door after the steed was stolen. I had left the shore at Queensferry with near on fifty pounds; now I found no more than two guinea-pieces and a silver shilling.

It is true I picked up a third guinea a little after, where it lay shining on a piece of turf. That made a fortune of three pounds and four shillings, English money, for a lad, the rightful heir of an estate, and now starving on an isle at the extreme end of the wild Highlands.

This state of my affairs dashed me still further; and indeed my plight on that third morning was truly pitiful. My clothes were beginning to rot; my stockings in particular were quite worn through, so that my shanks went naked; my hands had grown quite soft with the continual soaking; my throat was very sore, my strength had much abated, and my heart so turned against the horrid stuff I was condemned to eat, that the very sight of it came near to sicken me.

And yet the worst was not yet come.

There is a pretty high rock on the north-west of Earraid, which (because it had a flat top and overlooked the Sound) I was much in the habit of frequenting; not that ever I stayed in one place, save when asleep, my misery giving me no rest. Indeed I wore myself down with continual and aimless goings and comings in the rain.

As soon, however, as the sun came out, I lay down on the top of that rock to dry myself. The comfort of the sunshine is a thing I cannot tell. It set me thinking hopefully of my deliverance, of which I had begun to despair; and I scanned the sea and the Ross with a fresh interest. On the south of my rock, a part of the island jutted out and hid the open ocean, so that a boat could thus come quite near me upon that side, and I be none the wiser.

Well, all of a sudden, a coble with a brown sail and a pair of fishers aboard of it, came flying round that corner of the isle, bound for Iona. I shouted out, and then fell on my knees on the rock and reached up my hands and prayed to them. They were near enough to hear – I could even see the colour of their hair; and there was no doubt that they observed me, for they cried out in the Gaelic tongue, and laughed. But the boat never turned aside, and flew on, right before my eyes, for Iona.

I could not believe such wickedness, and ran along the shore from rock to rock, crying on them piteously; even after they were out of reach of my voice, I still cried and waved to them; and when they were quite gone I thought my heart would have burst. All the time of my troubles I wept only twice. Once, when I could not reach the yard, and now, the second time, when these fishers turned a deaf ear to my cries. But this time I wept and roared like a wicked child, tearing up the turf with my nails, and grinding my face in the earth. If a wish could kill men, these two fishers would never have seen morning, and I should likely have died upon my island.

When I was a little over my anger, I must eat again, but with such loathing of the mess as I could now scarce control. Sure enough, I should have done as well to fast, for my fishes poisoned me again. I had all my first pains; my throat was so sore I could scarce swallow; I had a fit of strong shuddering, which clucked my teeth together; and there came on me that dreadful sense of illness, which we have no name for either in Scots or English. I thought I should have died, and made my peace with God, forgiving all men, even my uncle and the fishers; and as soon as I had thus made up my mind to the worst, clearness came upon me: I observed the night was falling dry; my clothes were dried a good deal; truly, I was in a better case than ever before, since I had landed on the isle; and so I got to sleep at last, with a thought of gratitude.

The next day (which was the fourth of this horrible life of mine) I found my bodily strength run very low. But the sun shone, the air was sweet, and what I managed to eat of the shell-fish agreed well with me and revived my courage.

I was scarce back on my rock (where I went always the first thing after I had eaten) before I observed a boat coming down the Sound, and with her head, as I thought, in my direction.

I began at once to hope and fear exceedingly; for I thought these men might have thought better of their cruelty and be coming back to my assistance. But another disappointment, such as yesterday's, was more than I could bear. I turned my back, accordingly, upon the sea, and did not look again till I had counted many hundreds. The boat was still heading for the island. The next time I counted the full thousand, as slowly as I could, my heart beating so as to hurt me. And then it was out of all question. She was coming straight to Earraid!

I could no longer hold myself back, but ran to the sea-side and out, from one rock to another, as far as I could go. It is a marvel I was not drowned; for when I was brought to a stand at last, my legs shook under me, and my mouth was so dry, I must wet it with the sea-water before I was able to shout.

All this time the boat was coming on; and now I was able to perceive it was the same boat and the same two men as yesterday. This I knew by their hair, which the one had of a bright yellow and the other black. But now there was a third man along with them, who looked to be of a better class.

As soon as they were come within easy speech, they let down their sail and lay quiet. In spite of my supplications, they drew no nearer in, and what frightened me most of all, the new man tee-hee'd with laughter as he talked and looked at me.

Then he stood up in the boat and addressed me a long while, speaking fast and with many wavings of his hand. I told him I had no Gaelic; and at this he became very angry, and I began to suspect he thought he was talking English. Listening very close, I caught the word 'whateffer,' several times; but all the rest was Gaelic and might have been Greek and Hebrew for me.

'Whatever,' said I, to show him I had caught a word.

'Yes, yes – yes, yes,' says he, and then he looked at the other men, as much as to say, 'I told you I spoke English,' and began again as hard as ever in the Gaelic.

This time I picked out another word, 'tide.' Then I had a flash of hope. I remembered he was always waving his hand towards the mainland of the Ross.

'Do you mean when the tide is out – ?' I cried, and could not finish.

'Yes, yes,' said he. 'Tide.'

At that I turned tail upon their boat (where my adviser had once more begun to tee-hee with laughter), leaped back the way I had come, from one stone to another, and set off running across the isle as I had never run before. In about half an hour I came out upon the shores of the creek; and, sure enough, it was shrunk into a little trickle of water, through which I dashed, not above my knees, and landed with a shout on the main island.

A sea-bred boy would not have stayed a day on Earraid; which is only what they call a tidal islet, and except in the bottom of the neaps, can be entered and left twice in every twenty-four hours, either dry-shod, or at the most by wading. Even I, who had the tide going out and in before me in the bay, and even watched for the ebbs, the better to get my shell-fish – even I (I say) if I had sat down to think, instead of raging at my fate, must have soon guessed the secret, and got free. It was no wonder the fishers had not understood me. The wonder was rather that they had ever guessed my pitiful illusion, and taken the trouble to come back. I had starved with cold and hunger on that island for close upon one hundred hours. But for the fishers, I might have left my bones there in pure folly. And even as it was, I had paid for it pretty dear, not only in past sufferings, but in my present case; being clothed like a beggar-man, scarce able to walk, and in great pain of my sore throat.

I have seen wicked men and fools, a great many of both; and I believe they both get paid in the end; but the fools first.

ANON (Twelfth Century)

Meallach Liom Bheith I n-Ucht Oiléin

Meallach liom bheith I n-ucht oiléin
　　ar beinn cairrge,
go bhfaicinn ann ar a meince
　　féth na fairrge.

Go bhfaicinn a tonna troma
　　ós lear luchair,
amhail chanaid ceól dá nAthair
　　ar seól suthain.

Go bhfaicinn a trácht réidh rionnghlan
　　(ní dál dubha);
go gcloisinn guth na n-éan n-iongnadh,
　　seól go subha.

Go gcloisinn torm na dtonn dtana
　　ris na cairrge;
go gcloisinn nuall re taobh reilge,
　　fuam na fairrge.

Go bhfaicinn a healta ána
　　ós lear lionnmhar;
go bhfaicinn a míola mára,
　　mó gach n-iongnadh.

Go bhfaicinn a tráigh 's a tuile
　　ina réimim;
go madh é m'ainm, rún no ráidhim,
　　'Cúl re hÉirinn'.

ANON (Twelfth Century)

Delightful to Be on the Breast of an Island

Delightful it would be on the breast of an island,
    on a rocky clifftop,
from there I could often ponder
    the calm of the ocean.

I'd see her heavy billows
    on glittering surface,
as they sang thus to their Father
    in eternal surging.

I'd see her smooth clean bays and beaches
    (no mournful meeting);
I'd hear the call of wondrous seabirds,
    a cry of gladness.

I'd hear the thunder of the breakers
    against the headlands,
I'd hear a clamour beside the graveyard,
    the sound of the ocean.

I'd see her noble birdflocks
    on the teeming ocean;
I'd see her whales, the greatest
    of all wonders.

I'd see her ebbing and flooding
    in their order;
may my name be – I tell a secret –
    'Back towards Ireland'.

Go n-am-tíosadh congain cridhe
agá féaghadh;
go ro chaoininn m' ulca ile, –
annsa a réaladh.

Go ro bheannachainn an Coimdhe
con-ig uile,
neamh go muintir gráidh go ngloine,
tír, tráigh, tuile.

Go ro sgrúdainn aon na leabhar,
maith dom anmain;
seal ar sléachtain ar neamh n-ionmhain,
seal ar salmaibh.

Seal ag buain duilisg do charraig,
seal ar aclaidh,
seal ag tabhairt bhídh do bhochtaibh,
seal i gcarcair.

Seal ag sgrúdain flatha nimhe,
naomhdha an ceannach;
seal ar saothar ná badh forrach;
ro badh meallach!

My heart would be succoured
    by gazing at it,
I'd lament my every evil –
    hard to broadcast.

I would bless the Lord Almighty
    who maintains all:
heaven with its pure, loving orders,
    land, shore and water.

On some book I would ponder,
    for the soul beneficial;
a while beseeching beloved heaven,
    a while psalm-singing.

A while plucking dulse from the skerries,
    a while fishing,
a while giving food to the needy,
    a while in a rock-cell.

A while contemplating the prince of Heaven,
    holy the purchase;
a while toiling, nothing too taxing;
    it would be delightful.

translated from the Gaelic by Meg Bateman

attributed to ADOMNÁN

A Gaelic Quatrain

Má ro-m-thoiccthi écc i ndhÍ,
ba gabál di thrócari.
Nícon fettar fo nim glas
fóttán bad ferr fri tiugbás.

If on Iona I take my last breath,
My passing will be a merciful death.
No land I know beneath the blue sky
Offers a finer place to die.

La Chaluim-Chille / The Day of St Columba

from *Carmina Gadelica: Hymns and Incantations with Illustrative Notes on Words, Rites, and Customs, Dying and Obsolete: Orally Collected in the Highlands and Islands of Scotland and Translated into English by Alexander Carmichael* (1832–1912)

DIARDAOIN, Didaoirn – the day between the fasts – Thursday, was St Columba's Day – Diardaoin Chaluim-chille, St Columba's Thursday – and through him the day of many important events in the economy of the people. It was a lucky day for all enterprises – for warping thread, for beginning a pilgrimage, or any other undertaking. On Thursday eve the mother of a family made a bere, rye, or oaten cake into which she put a small silver coin. The cake was toasted before a fire of rowan, yew, oak, or other sacred wood. On the morning of Thursday the father took a keen cutting-knife and cut the cake into as many sections as there were children in the family, all the sections being equal. All the pieces were then placed in a 'ciosan' – a beehive basket – and each child blindfold drew a piece of cake from the basket in name of the Father, Son, and Spirit. The child who got the coin got the crop of lambs for the year. This was called 'sealbh uan' – lamb luck. Sometimes it was arranged that the person who got the coin got a certain number of the lambs, and the others the rest of the lambs among them. Each child had a separate mark, and there was much emulation as to who had most lambs, the best lambs, and who took best care of the lambs.

Maunday Thursday is called in Uist 'Diardaoin a brochain,' Gruel Thursday, and in Iona 'Diardaoin a brochain mhoir,' Great Gruel Thursday. On this day people in maritime districts made offerings of mead, ale, or gruel to the god of the sea. As the day merged from Wednesday to Thursday a man walked to the waist into the sea and poured out whatever offering had been prepared, chanting:

'A Dhe na mara
Cuir todhar 's an tarruin
Chon tachair an talaimh,
Chon bailcidh dhuinn biaidh.'

O God of the sea,
Put weed in the drawing wave
To enrich the ground,
To shower on us food.

Those behind the offerer took up the chant and wafted it along the sea-shore on the midnight air, the darkness of night and the rolling of the waves making the scene weird and impressive. In 1860 the writer conversed in Iona with a middle-aged man whose father, when young, had taken part in this ceremony. In Lewis the custom was continued till this [twentieth] century. It shows the tolerant spirit of the Columban Church and the tenacity of popular belief, that such a practice should have been in vogue so recently.

The only exception to the luck of Thursday was when Beltane fell on that day.

''D uair is Ciadaoineach an t-Samhain
Is iarganach fir an domhain,
Ach 's meirg is mathair dh' an mhac bhaoth
'D uair is Daorn dh' an Bhealltain.'

When the Wednesday is Hallowmas
Restless are the men of the universe;
But woe the mother of the foolish son
When Thursday is the Beltane.

LA CHALUIM-CHILLE

DAORN Chaluim-chille chaoimh
La chur chaorach air seilbh,
La chur ba air a laogh,
La chur aodach an deilbh.

La chur churach air sal,
La chur gais chon a meirgh,
La chon breith, la chon bais,
La chon ardu a sheilg.

La chur ghearran an eill,
La chur feudail air raon,
La chur urnuigh chon feum,
La m' eudail an Daorn.
    La m' eudail an Daorn.

THE DAY OF ST COLUMBA

THURSDAY of Columba benign,
Day to send sheep on prosperity,
Day to send cow on calf,
Day to put the web in the warp.

Day to put coracle on the brine,
Day to place the staff to the flag,
Day to bear, day to die,
Day to hunt the heights.

Day to put horses in harness,
Day to send herds to pasture,
Day to make prayer efficacious,
Day of my beloved, the Thursday,
    Day of my beloved, the Thursday.

Achlasan Chaluim-Chille / Saint John's Wort

from *Carmina Gadelica: Hymns and Incantations with Illustrative Notes on Words, Rites, and Customs, Dying and Obsolete: Orally Collected in the Highlands and Islands of Scotland and Translated into English by Alexander Carmichael* (1832–1912)

SAINT JOHN'S wort is known by various names, all significant of the position of the plant in the minds of the people: – 'achlasan Chaluim-chille,' armpit package of Columba; 'caod Chaluim-chille,' hail of Columba; 'seun Chaluim-chille,' charm of Columba; 'seud Chaluim chille,' jewel of Columba; 'allus Chaluim-chille,' glory of Columba; 'alla Mhoire,' noble plant of Mary; 'alla-bhi,' 'alla-bhuidhe,' noble yellow plant. Possibly these are pre-Christian terms to which are added the endearing names of Mary and Columba.

Saint John's wort is one of the few plants still cherished by the people to ward away second-sight, enchantment, witchcraft, evil eye, and death, and to ensure peace and plenty in the house, increase and prosperity in the fold, and growth and fruition in the field. The plant is secretly secured in the bodices of the women and in the vests of the men, under the left armpit. Saint John's wort, however, is effective only when the plant is accidentally found. When this occurs the joy of the finder is great, and gratefully expressed:

'Achlasan Chaluim-chille,
Gun sireadh, gun iarraidh!
Dheoin Dhia agus Chriosda
Am bliadhna chan fhaigheas bas.'

Saint John's wort, Saint John's wort,
Without search, without seeking!
Please God and Christ Jesu
This year I shall not die.

It is specially prized when found in the fold of the flocks, auguring peace and prosperity to the herds throughout the year. The person who discovers it says:

'Alla bhi, alla bhi,
Mo niarach a neach dh' am bi,
An ti a gheobh an cro an ail,
Cha bhi gu brath gun ni.'

Saint John's wort, Saint John's wort,
Happy those who have thee,
Whoso gets thee in the herd's fold,
Shall never be without kine.

There is a tradition among the people that Saint Columba carried the plant on his person because of his love and admiration for him who went about preaching Christ, and baptizing the converted, clothed in a garment of camel's hair and fed upon locusts and wild honey.

ACHLASAN CHALUIM-CHILLE

ACHLASAIN Chaluim-chille,
Gun sireadh, gun iarraidh,
Achlasain Chaluim-chille,
Fo m' righe gu siorruidh!

Air shealbh dhaona,
Air shealbh mhaona,
Air shealbh mhianna,
Air shealbh chaora,
Air shealbh mhaosa,
Air shealbh iana,
Air shealbh raona,
Air shealbh mhaora,
Air shealbh iasga,
Air shealbh bhliochd is bhuar,
Air shealbh shliochd is shluagh,
Air shealbh bhlar is bhuadh,
Air tir, air lir, air cuan,
Trid an Tri ta shuas,
Trid an Tri ta nuas,

Trid an Tri ta buan,
Achlasain Chaluim-chille,
Ta mis a nis da d' bhuain,
    Ta mis a nis da d' bhuain.

ST COLUMBA'S PLANT

PLANTLET of Columba,
Without seeking, without searching,
Plantlet of Columba,
Under my arm for ever!

For luck of men,
For luck of means
For luck of wish (?),
For luck of sheep,
For luck of goats,
For luck of birds,
For luck of fields,
For luck of shell-fish,
For luck of fish,
For luck of produce and kine,
For luck of progeny and people,
For luck of battle and victory,
On land, on sea, on ocean,
Through the Three on high,
Through the Three a-nigh,
Through the Three eternal,
Plantlet of Columba,
I cull thee now,
    I cull thee now.

SEAMUS HEANEY

Gravities

High-riding kites appear to range quite freely,
Though reined by strings, strict and invisible.
The pigeon that deserts you suddenly
Is heading home, instinctively faithful.

Lovers with barrages of hot insult
Often cut off their nose to spite their face,
Endure a hopeless day, declare their guilt,
Re-enter the native port of their embrace.

Blinding in Paris, for his party-piece
Joyce named the shops along O'Connell Street
And on Iona Colmcille sought ease
By wearing Irish mould next to his feet.

FIONA MACLEOD

The Sin-Eater

SIN.

Taste this bread, this substance: tell me
Is it bread or flesh?

[*The Senses approach.*]

THE SMELL.

Its smell
Is the smell of bread.

SIN.

Touch, come. Why tremble?
Say what's this thou touchest?

THE TOUCH.

Bread.

SIN.

Sight, declare what thou discernest
In this object.

THE SIGHT.

Bread alone.

CALDERON,
Los Encantos de la Culpa.

A wet wind out of the south mazed and mooned through the sea-mist that hung over the Ross. In all the bays and creeks was a continuous weary lapping of water. There was no other sound anywhere.

Thus was it at daybreak: it was thus at noon: thus was it now in the darkening of the day. A confused thrusting and falling of sounds through the silence betokened the hour of the setting. Curlews wailed in the mist: on the seething limpet-covered rocks the skuas and terns screamed, or uttered hoarse, rasping cries. Ever and again the prolonged note of the oyster-catcher shrilled against the air, as an echo flying blindly along a blank wall of cliff. Out of weedy places, wherein the tide sobbed with long, gurgling moans, came at intervals the barking of a seal.

Inland, by the hamlet of Contullich, there is a reedy tarn called the Loch-a-chaoruinn.[1] By the shores of this mournful water a man moved. It was a slow, weary walk that of the man Neil Ross. He had come from

Duninch, thirty miles to the eastward, and had not rested foot, nor eaten, nor had word of man or woman, since his going west an hour after dawn.

At the bend of the loch nearest the clachan he came upon an old woman carrying peat. To his reiterated question as to where he was, and if the tarn were Feur-Lochan above Fionnaphort that is on the strait of Iona on the west side of the Ross of Mull, she did not at first make any answer. The rain trickled down her withered brown face, over which the thin grey locks hung limply. It was only in the deep-set eyes that the flame of life still glimmered, though that dimly.

The man had used the English when first he spoke, but as though mechanically. Supposing that he had not been understood, he repeated his question in the Gaelic.

After a minute's silence the old woman answered him in the native tongue, but only to put a question in return.

'I am thinking it is a long time since you have been in Iona?'

The man stirred uneasily.

'And why is that, mother?' he asked, in a weak voice hoarse with damp and fatigue; 'how is it you will be knowing that I have been in Iona at all?'

'Because I knew your kith and kin there, Neil Ross.'

'I have not been hearing that name, mother, for many a long year. And as for the old face o' you, it is unbeknown to me.'

'I was at the naming of you, for all that. Well do I remember the day that Silis Macallum gave you birth; and I was at the house on the croft of Ballyrona when Murtagh Ross – that was your father – laughed. It was an ill laughing that.'

'I am knowing it. The curse of God on him!'

''Tis not the first, nor the last, though the grass is on his head three years agone now.'

'You that know who I am will be knowing that I have no kith or kin now on Iona?'

'Ay; they are all under grey stone or running wave. Donald your brother, and Murtagh your next brother, and little Silis, and your mother Silis herself, and your two brothers of your father, Angus and Ian Macallum, and your father Murtagh Ross, and his lawful childless wife, Dionaid, and his sister Anna – one and all, they lie beneath the green wave or in the brown mould. It is said there is a curse upon all who live at Ballyrona. The owl builds now in the rafters, and it is the big sea-rat that runs across the fireless hearth.'

'It is there I am going.'

'The foolishness is on you, Neil Ross.'

'Now it is that I am knowing who you are. It is old Sheen Macarthur I am speaking to.'

'*Tha mise* . . . it is I.'

'And you will be alone now, too, I am thinking, Sheen?'

'I am alone. God took my three boys at the one fishing ten years ago; and before there was moonrise in the blackness of my heart my man went. It was after the drowning of Anndra that my croft was taken from me. Then I crossed the Sound, and shared with my widow sister, Elsie McVurie: till *she* went: and then the two cows had to go: and I had no rent: and was old.'

In the silence that followed, the rain dribbled from the sodden bracken and dripping loneroid. Big tears rolled slowly down the deep lines on the face of Sheen. Once there was a sob in her throat, but she put her shaking hand to it, and it was still.

Neil Ross shifted from foot to foot. The ooze in that marshy place squelched with each restless movement he made. Beyond them a plover wheeled, a blurred splatch in the mist, crying its mournful cry over and over and over.

It was a pitiful thing to hear: ah, bitter loneliness, bitter patience of poor old women. That he knew well. But he was too weary, and his heart was nigh full of its own burthen. The words could not come to his lips. But at last he spoke.

'Tha mo chridhe goirt,' he said, with tears in his voice, as he put his hand on her bent shoulder; 'my heart is sore.'

She put up her old face against his.

''S tha e ruidhinn mo chridhe,' she whispered; 'it is touching my heart you are.'

After that they walked on slowly through the dripping mist, each dumb and brooding deep.

'Where will you be staying this night?' asked Sheen suddenly, when they had traversed a wide, boggy stretch of land; adding, as by an afterthought – 'Ah, it is asking you were if the tarn there were Feur-Lochan. No; it is Loch-a-chaoruinn, and the clachan that is near is Contullich.'

'Which way?'

'Yonder: to the right.'

'And you are not going there?'

'No. I am going to the steading of Andrew Blair. Maybe you are for knowing it? It is called le-Baile-na-Chlais-nambuidheag.'[2]

'I do not remember. But it is remembering a Blair I am. He was Adam, the son of Adam, the son of Robert. He and my father did many an ill deed together.'

'Ay, to the stones be it said. Sure, now, there was, even till this weary day, no man or woman who had a good word for Adam Blair.'

'And why that . . . why till this day?'

'It is not yet the third hour since he went into the silence.'

Neil Ross uttered a sound like a stifled curse. For a time he trudged wearily on.

'Then I am too late,' he said at last, but as though speaking to himself. 'I had hoped to see him face to face again, and curse him between the eyes. It was he who made Murtagh Ross break his troth to my mother, and marry that other woman, barren at that, God be praised! And they say ill of him, do they?'

'Ay, it is evil that is upon him. This crime and that, God knows; and the shadow of murder on his brow and in his eyes. Well, well, 'tis ill to be speaking of a man in corpse, and that near by. 'Tis Himself only that knows, Neil Ross.'

'Maybe ay and maybe no. But where is it that I can be sleeping this night, Sheen Macarthur?'

'They will not be taking a stranger at the farm this night of the nights, I am thinking. There is no place else for seven miles yet, when there is the clachan, before you will be coming to Fionnaphort. There is the warm byre, Neil, my man; or, if you can bide by my peats, you may rest, and welcome, though there is no bed for you, and no food either save some of the porridge that is over.'

'And that will do well enough for me, Sheen; and Himself bless you for it.'

And so it was.

. . . .

After old Sheen Macarthur had given the wayfarer food – poor food at that, but welcome to one nigh starved, and for the heartsome way it was given, and because of the thanks to God that was upon it before even spoon was lifted – she told him a lie. It was the good lie of tender love.

'Sure now, after all, Neil, my man,' she said, 'it is sleeping at the farm I ought to be, for Maisie Macdonald, the wise woman, will be sitting by the corpse, and there will be none to keep her company. It is there I must be going; and if I am weary, there is a good bed for me just beyond the dead-board, which I am not minding at all. So, if it is tired you are sitting by the peats, lie down on my bed there, and have the sleep; and God be with you.'

With that she went, and soundlessly, for Neil Ross was already asleep, where he sat on an upturned *claar*, with his elbows on his knees, and his flame-lit face in his hands.

The rain had ceased; but the mist still hung over the land, though in thin veils now, and these slowly drifting seaward. Sheen stepped wearily along the stony path that led from her bothy to the farm-house. She stood still once, the fear upon her, for she saw three or four blurred yellow gleams moving beyond her, eastward, along the dyke. She knew what they were – the corpse-lights that on the night of death go between the bier and the place of burial. More than once she had seen them before the last hour, and by that token had known the end to be near.

Good Catholic that she was, she crossed herself, and took heart. Then, muttering:

Crois nan naoi aingeal leam
'O mhullach mo chinn
Gu craican mo bhonn

(The cross of the nine angels be about me,
From the top of my head
To the soles of my feet),

she went on her way fearlessly.

When she came to the White House, she entered by the milk-shed that was between the byre and the kitchen. At the end of it was a paved place, with washing-tubs. At one of these stood a girl that served in the house, – an ignorant lass called Jessie McFall, out of Oban. She was ignorant, indeed, not to know that to wash clothes with a newly dead body near by was an ill thing to do. Was it not a matter for the knowing that the corpse could hear, and might rise up in the night and clothe itself in a clean white shroud?

She was still speaking to the lassie when Maisie Macdonald, the deid-watcher, opened the door of the room behind the kitchen to see who it was that was come. The two old women nodded silently. It was not till Sheen was in the closed room, midway in which something covered with a sheet lay on a board, that any word was spoken.

'Duit sìth mòr, Beann Macdonald.'

'And deep peace to you, too, Sheen; and to him that is there.'

'Och, ochone, mise 'n diugh; 'tis a dark hour this.'

'Ay; it is bad. Will you have been hearing or seeing anything?'

'Well, as for that, I am thinking I saw lights moving betwixt here and the green place over there.'

'The corpse-lights?'

'Well, it is calling them that they are.'

'I *thought* they would be out. And I have been hearing the noise of the planks – the cracking of the boards, you know, that will be used for the coffin tomorrow.'

A long silence followed. The old women had seated themselves by the corpse, their cloaks over their heads. The room was fireless, and was lit only by a tall wax death-candle, kept against the hour of the going.

At last Sheeen began swaying slowly to and fro, crooning low the while. 'I would not be for doing that, Sheen Macarthur,' said the deid-watcher in a low voice, but meaningly; adding, after a moment's pause, '*The mice have all left the house.*'

Sheen sat upright, a look half of terror half of awe in her eyes.

'God save the sinful soul that is hiding,' she whispered.

Well she knew what Maisie meant. If the soul of the dead be a lost soul it knows its doom. The house of death is the house of sanctuary; but before the dawn that follows the death-night the soul must go forth, whosoever or whatsoever wait for it in the homeless, shelterless plains of air around and beyond. If it be well with the soul, it need have no fear: if it be not ill with the soul, it may fare forth with surety; but if it be ill with the soul, ill will the going be. Thus is it that the spirit of an evil man cannot stay, and yet dare not go; and so it strives to hide itself in secret places anywhere, in dark channels and blind walls; and the wise creatures that live near man smell the terror, and flee. Maisie repeated the saying of Sheen; then, after a silence, added –

'Adam Blair will not lie in his grave for a year and a day because of the sins that are upon him; and it is knowing that, they are, here. He will be the Watcher of the Dead for a year and a day.'

'Ay, sure, there will be dark prints in the dawn-dew over yonder.'

Once more the old women relapsed into silence. Through the night there was a sighing sound. It was not the sea, which was too far off to be heard save in a day of storm. The wind it was, that was dragging itself across the sodden moors like a wounded thing, moaning and sighing.

Out of sheer weariness, Sheen twice rocked forward from her stool, heavy with sleep. At last Maisie led her over to the niche-bed opposite, and laid her down there, and waited till the deep furrows in the face relaxed somewhat, and the thin breath laboured slow across the fallen jaw.

'Poor old woman,' she muttered, heedless of her own grey hairs and greyer years; 'a bitter, bad thing it is to be old, old and weary. 'Tis the sorrow, that. God keep the pain of it!'

As for herself, she did not sleep at all that night, but sat between the living and the dead, with her plaid shrouding her. Once, when Sheen gave a low, terrified scream in her sleep, she rose, and in a loud voice cried, '*Sheeach-ad! Away with you!*' And with that she lifted the shroud from the dead man, and took the pennies off the eyelids, and lifted each lid; then, staring into these filmed wells, muttered an ancient incantation that would compel the soul of Adam Blair to leave the spirit of Sheen alone, and return to the cold corpse that was its coffin till the wood was ready.

The dawn came at last. Sheen slept, and Adam Blair slept a deeper sleep, and Maisie stared out of her wan, weary eyes against the red and stormy flares of light that came into the sky.

When, an hour before sunrise, Sheen Macarthur reached her bothy, she found Neil Ross, heavy with slumber, upon her bed. The fire was not out, though no flame or spark was visible; but she stooped and blew at the heart of the peats till the redness came, and once it came it grew. Having done this, she kneeled and said a rune of the morning, and after that a prayer, and then a prayer for the poor man Neil. She could pray no more because of the tears. She rose and put the meal and water into the pot for the porridge to be ready against his awaking. One of the hens that was there came and pecked at her ragged skirt. 'Poor beastie,' she said. 'Sure, that will just be the way I am pulling at the white robe of the Mother o' God. 'Tis a bit meal for you, cluckie, and for me a healing hand upon my tears. O, och, ochone, the tears, the tears!'

It was not till the third hour after sunrise of that bleak day in the winter of the winters, that Neil Ross stirred and arose. He ate in silence. Once he said that he smelt the snow coming out of the north. Sheen said no word at all.

After the porridge, he took his pipe, but there was no tobacco. All that Sheen had was the pipeful she kept against the gloom of the Sabbath. It was her one solace in the long weary week. She gave him this, and held a burning peat to his mouth, and hungered over the thin, rank smoke that curled upward.

It was within half-an-hour of noon that, after an absence, she returned.

'Not between you and me, Neil Ross,' she began abruptly, 'but just for the asking, and what is beyond. Is it any money you are having upon you?'

'No.'

'Nothing?'

'Nothing.'

'Then how will you be getting across to Iona? It is seven long miles to Fionnaphort, and bitter cold at that, and you will be needing food, and then the ferry, the ferry across the Sound, you know.'

'Ay, I know.'

'What would you do for a silver piece, Neil, my man?'

'You have none to give me, Sheen Macarthur; and, if you had it, it would not be taking it I would.'

'Would you kiss a dead man for a crown-piece – a crown-piece of five good shillings?'

Neil Ross stared. Then he sprang to his feet.

'It is Adam Blair you are meaning, woman! God curse him in death now that he is no longer in life!'

Then, shaking and trembling, he sat down again, and brooded against the dull red glow of the peats.

But, when he rose, in the last quarter before noon, his face was white.

'The dead are dead, Sheen Macarthur. They can know or do nothing. I will do it. It is willed. Yes, I am going up to the house there. And now I am going from here. God Himself has my thanks to you, and my blessing too. They will come back to you. It is not forgetting you I will be. Good-bye.'

'Good-bye, Neil, son of the woman that was my friend. A south wind to you! Go up by the farm. In the front of the house you will see what you will be seeing. Maisie Macdonald will be there. She will tell you what's for the telling. There is no harm in it, sure: sure, the dead are dead. It is praying for you I will be, Neil Ross. Peace to you!'

'And to you, Sheen.'

And with that the man went.

When Neil Ross reached the byres of the farm in the wide hollow, he saw two figures standing as though awaiting him, but separate, and unseen of the other. In front of the house was a man he knew to be Andrew Blair; behind the milk-shed was a woman he guessed to be Maisie Macdonald.

It was the woman he came upon first.

'Are you the friend of Sheen Macarthur?' she asked in a whisper, as she beckoned him to the doorway.

'I am.'

'I am knowing no names or anything. And no one here will know you, I am thinking. So do the thing and begone.'

'There is no harm to it?'

'None.'

'It will be a thing often done, is it not?'

'Ay, sure.'

'And the evil does not abide?'

'No. The . . . the . . . person . . . the person takes them away, and . . .'

'*Them?*'

'For sure, man! Them . . . the sins of the corpse. He takes them away; and are you for thinking God would let the innocent suffer for the guilty? No . . . the person . . . the Sin-Eater, you know . . . takes them away on himself, and one by one the air of heaven washes them away till he, the Sin-Eater, is clean and whole as before.'

'But if it is a man you hate . . . if it is a corpse that is the corpse of one who has been a curse and a foe . . . if . . .'

'*Sst!* Be still now with your foolishness. It is only an idle saying, I am thinking. Do it, and take the money and go. It will be hell enough for Adam Blair, miser as he was, if he is for knowing that five good shillings of his money are to go to a passing tramp because of an old, ancient silly tale.'

Neil Ross laughed low at that. It was for pleasure to him.

'Hush wi' ye! Andrew Blair is waiting round there. Say that I have sent you round, as I have neither bite nor bit to give.'

Turning on his heel, Neil walked slowly round to the front of the house. A tall man was there, gaunt and brown, with hairless face and lank brown hair, but with eyes cold and grey as the sea.

'Good day to you, an' good faring. Will you be passing this way to anywhere?'

'Health to you. I am a stranger here. It is on my way to Iona I am. But I have the hunger upon me. There is not a brown bit in my pocket. I asked at the door there, near the byres. The woman told me she could give me nothing – not a penny even, worse luck, – nor, for that, a drink of warm milk. 'Tis a sore land this.'

'You have the Gaelic of the Isles. Is it from Iona you are?'

'It is from the Isles of the West I come.'

'From Tiree? . . . from Coll?'

'No.'

'From the Long Island . . . or from Uist . . . or maybe from Benbecula?'

'No.'

'Oh well, sure it is no matter to me. But may I be asking your name?'

'Macallum.'

'Do you know there is a death here, Macallum?'

'If I didn't, I would know it now, because of what lies yonder.'

Mechanically Andrew Blair looked round. As he knew, a rough bier was there, that was made of a dead-board laid upon three milking-stools. Beside it was a *claar*, a small tub to hold potatoes. On the bier was a corpse, covered with a canvas sheeting that looked like a sail.

'He was a worthy man, my father,' began the son of the dead man, slowly; 'but he had his faults, like all of us. I might even be saying that he had his sins, to the Stones be it said. You will be knowing, Macallum, what is thought among the folk . . . that a stranger, passing by, may take away the sins of the dead, and that, too, without any hurt whatever . . . any hurt whatever.'

'Ay, sure.'

'And you will be knowing what is done?'

'Ay.'

'With the bread . . . and the water . . . ?'

'Ay.'

'It is a small thing to do. It is a Christian thing. I would be doing it myself, and that gladly, but the . . . the . . . the passer-by who . . .'

'It is talking of the Sin-Eater you are?'

'Yes, yes, for sure. The Sin-Eater as he is called – and a good Christian act it is, for all that the ministers and the priests make a frowning at it – the Sin-Eater must be a stranger. He must be a stranger, and should know nothing of the dead man – above all, bear him no grudge.'

At that Neil Ross's eyes lightened for a moment.

'And why that?'

'Who knows? I have heard this, and I have heard that. If the Sin-Eater was hating the dead man he could take the sins and fling them into the sea, and they would be changed into demons of the air that would harry the flying soul till Judgement Day.'

'And how would that thing be done?'

The man spoke with flashing eyes and parted lips, the breath coming swift. Andrew Blair looked at him suspiciously; and hesitated, before, in a cold voice, he spoke again.

'That is all folly, I am thinking, Macallum. Maybe it is all folly, the whole of it. But, see here, I have no time to be talking with you. If you will take the bread and the water you shall have a good meal if you want it, and . . . and . . . yes, look you, my man, I will be giving you a shilling too, for luck.'

'I will have no meal in this house, Anndra-mhic-Adam; nor will I do this thing unless you will be giving me two silver half-crowns. That is the sum I must have, or no other.'

'Two half-crowns! Why, man, for one half-crown . . .'

'Then be eating the sins o' your father yourself, Andrew Blair! It is going I am.'

'Stop, man! Stop, Macallum. See here: I will be giving you what you ask.'

'So be it. Is the . . . Are you ready?'

'Ay, come this way.'

With that the two men turned and moved slowly towards the bier.

In the doorway of the house stood a man and two women; farther in, a woman; and at the window to the left, the serving-wench, Jessie McFall, and two men of the farm. Of those in the doorway, the man was Peter, the half-witted youngest brother of Andrew Blair; the taller and older woman was Catreen, the widow of Adam, the second brother; and the thin, slight woman, with staring eyes and drooping mouth, was Muireall, the wife of Andrew. The old woman behind these was Maisie Macdonald.

Andrew Blair stooped and took a saucer out of the *claar*. This he put upon the covered breast of the corpse. He stooped again, and brought forth a thick square piece of new-made bread. That also he placed upon the breast of the corpse. Then he stooped again, and with that he emptied a spoonful of salt alongside the bread.

'I must see the corpse,' said Neil Ross simply.

'It is not needful, Macallum.'

'I must be seeing the corpse, I tell you – and for that, too, the bread and the water should be on the naked breast.'

'No, no, man; it . . .'

But here a voice, that of Maisie the wise woman, came upon them, saying that the man was right, and that the eating of the sins should be done in that way and no other.

With an ill grace the son of the dead man drew back the sheeting. Beneath it, the corpse was in a clean white shirt, a death-gown long ago prepared, that covered him from his neck to his feet, and left only the dusky yellowish face exposed.

While Andrew Blair unfastened the shirt and placed the saucer and the bread and the salt on the breast, the man beside him stood staring fixedly on the frozen features of the corpse. The new laird had to speak to him twice before he heard.

'I am ready. And you, now? What is it you are muttering over against the lips of the dead?'

'It is giving him a message I am. There is no harm in that, sure?'

'Keep to your own folk, Macallum. You are from the West you say, and we are from the North. There can be no messages between you and a Blair of Strathmore, no messages for *you* to be giving.'

'He that lies here knows well the man to whom I am sending a message' – and at this response Andrew Blair scowled darkly. He would fain have sent the man about his business, but he feared he might get no other.

'It is thinking I am that you are not a Macallum at all. I know all of that name in Mull, Iona, Skye, and the near isles. What will the name of your naming be, and of your father, and of his place?'

Whether he really wanted an answer, or whether he sought only to divert the man from his procrastination, his question had a satisfactory result.

'Well, now, it's ready I am, Anndra-mhic-Adam.'

With that, Andrew Blair stooped once more and from the *claar* brought a small jug of water. From this he filled the saucer.

'You know what to say and what to do, Macallum.'

There was not one there who did not have a shortened breath because of the mystery that was now before them, and the fearfulness of it. Neil Ross drew himself up, erect, stiff, with white, drawn face. All who waited, save Andrew Blair, thought that the moving of his lips was because of the prayer that was slipping upon them, like the last lapsing of the ebb-tide. But Blair was watching him closely, and knew that it was no prayer which stole out against the blank air that was around the dead.

Slowly Neil Ross extended his right arm. He took a pinch of the salt and put it in the saucer, then took another pinch and sprinkled it upon the bread. His hand shook for a moment as he touched the saucer. But there was no shaking as he raised it towards his lips, or when he held it before him when he spoke.

'With this water that has salt in it, and has lain on thy corpse, O Adam mhic Anndra mhic Adam Mòr, I drink away all the evil that is upon thee . . . '

There was throbbing silence while he paused.

'. . . And may it be upon me and not upon thee, if with this water it cannot flow away.'

Thereupon, he raised the saucer and passed it thrice round the head of the corpse sun-ways; and, having done this, lifted it to his lips and drank as much as his mouth would hold. Thereafter he poured the remnant over his left hand, and let it trickle to the ground. Then he took the piece of bread. Thrice, too, he passed it round the head of the corpse sun-ways.

He turned and looked at the man by his side, then at the others, who watched him with beating hearts.

With a loud clear voice he took the sins.

'Thoir dhomh do ciontachd, O Adam mhic Anndra mhic Adam Mòr! Give

me thy sins to take away from thee! Lo, now, as I stand here, I break this bread that has lain on thee in corpse, and I am eating it, I am, and in that eating I take upon me the sins of thee, O man that was alive and is now white with the stillness!'

Thereupon Neil Ross broke the bread and ate of it, and took upon himself the sins of Adam Blair that was dead. It was a bitter swallowing, that. The remainder of the bread he crumbled in his hand, and threw it on the ground, and trod upon it. Andrew Blair gave a sigh of relief. His cold eyes lightened with malice.

'Be off with you, now, Macallum. We are wanting no tramps at the farm here, and perhaps you had better not be trying to get work this side Iona; for it is known as the Sin-Eater you will be, and that won't be for the helping, I am thinking! There: there are the two half-crowns for you . . . and may they bring you no harm, you that are *Scapegoat* now!'

The Sin-Eater turned at that, and stared like a hill-bull. *Scapegoat!* Ay, that's what he was. Sin-Eater, Scapegoat! Was he not, too, another Judas, to have sold for silver that which was not for the selling? No, no, for sure Maisie Macdonald could tell him the rune that would serve for the easing of this burden. He would soon be quit of it.

Slowly he took the money, turned it over, and put it in his pocket.

'I am going, Andrew Blair,' he said quietly, 'I am going now. I will not say to him that is there in the silence, *A chuid do Pharas da!* – nor will I say to you, *G'un gleidheadh Dia thu*, – nor will I say to this dwelling that is the home of thee and thine, *G'un beannaic-headh Dia an tigh!*'[3]

Here there was a pause. All listened. Andrew Blair shifted uneasily, the furtive eyes of him going this way and that, like a ferret in the grass.

'But, Andrew Blair, I will say this: when you fare abroad, *Droch caoidh ort!* And when you go upon the water, *Gaoth gun direadh ort!* Ay, ay, Anndra-mhic-Adam, *Dia ad aghaidh 's ad aodann . . . agus bas dunach ort! Dhonas 's dholas ort, agus leat-sa!*'[4]

The bitterness of these words was like snow in June upon all there. They stood amazed. None spoke. No one moved.

Neil Ross turned upon his heel, and, with a bright light in his eyes, walked away from the dead and the living. He went by the byres, whence he had come. Andrew Blair remained where he was, now glooming at the corpse, now biting his nails and staring at the damp sods at his feet.

When Neil reached the end of the milk-shed he saw Maisie Macdonald there, waiting.

'These were ill sayings of yours, Neil Ross,' she said in a low voice, so that she might not be overheard from the house.

'So, it is knowing me you are.'

'Sheen Macarthur told me.'

'I have good cause.'

'That is a true word. I know it.'

'Tell me this thing. What is the rune that is said for the throwing into the sea of the sins of the dead? See here, Maisie Macdonald. There is no money of that man that I would carry a mile with me. Here it is. It is yours, if you will tell me that rune.'

Maisie took the money hesitatingly. Then, stooping, she said slowly the few lines of the old, old rune.

'Will you be remembering that?'

'It is not forgetting it I will be, Maisie.'

'Wait a moment. There is some warm milk here.'

With that she went, and then, from within, beckoned to him to enter.

'There is no one here, Neil Ross. Drink the milk.'

He drank; and while he did so she drew a leather pouch from some hidden place in her dress.

'And now I have this to give you.'

She counted out ten pennies and two farthings.

'It is all the coppers I have. You are welcome to them. Take them, friend of my friend. They will give you the food you need, and the ferry across the Sound.'

'I will do that, Maisie Macdonald, and thanks to you. It is not forgetting it I will be, nor you, good woman. And now, tell me, is it safe that I am? He called me a 'scapegoat'; he, Andrew Blair! Can evil touch me between this and the sea?'

'You must go to the place where the evil was done to you and yours – and that, I know, is on the west side of Iona. Go, and God preserve you. But here, too, is a Sian that will be for the safety.'

Thereupon, with swift mutterings she said this charm: an old, familiar Sian against Sudden Harm:

'Sian a chuir Moire air Mac ort,
Sian ro' marbhadh, sian ro' lot ort,
Sian eadar a' chlioch 's a' ghlun,
Sian nan Tri ann an aon ort,

O mhullach do chinn gu bonn do chois ort:
Sian seachd eadar a h-aon ort,
Sian seachd eadar a dha ort,
Sian seachd eadar a tri ort,
Sian seachd eadar a ceithir ort,
Sian seachd eadar a coig ort
Sian seachd eadar a sia ort,
Sian seachd paidir nan seach paidir dol deiseil ri diugh
narach ort, ga do ghleidheadh bho bheud 's bho
mhi-thapadh!'

Scarcely had she finished before she heard heavy steps approaching.

'Away with you,' she whispered, repeating in a loud, angry tone, 'Away with you! *Seachad! Seachad!*'

And with that Neil Ross slipped from the milk-shed and crossed the yard, and was behind the byres before Andrew Blair, with sullen mien and swift, wild eyes, strode from the house.

It was with a grim smile on his face that Neil tramped down the wet heather till he reached the high road, and fared thence as through a marsh because of the rains there had been.

For the first mile he thought of the angry mind of the dead man, bitter at paying of the silver. For the second mile he thought of the evil that had been wrought for him and his. For the third mile he pondered over all that he had heard and done and taken upon him that day.

Then he sat down upon a broken granite heap by the way, and brooded deep till one hour went, and then another, and the third was upon him.

A man driving two calves came towards him out of the west. He did not hear or see. The man stopped: spoke again. Neil gave no answer. The drover shrugged his shoulders, hesitated, and walked slowly on, often looking back.

An hour later a shepherd came by the way he himself had tramped. He was a tall, gaunt man with a squint. The small, pale-blue eyes glittered out of a mass of red hair that almost covered his face. He stood still, opposite Neil, and leaned on his *cromak*.

'*Latha math leat*,' he said at last: 'I wish you good day.'

Neil glanced at him, but did not speak.

'What is your name, for I seem to know you?'

But Neil had already forgotten him. The shepherd took out his snuff-mull, helped himself, and handed the mull to the lonely wayfarer. Neil mechanically helped himself.

'*Am bheil thu 'dol do Fhionphort?*' tried the shepherd again: 'Are you going to Fionnaphort?'

'*Tha mise 'dol a dh' I-challum-chille*,' Neil answered, in a low, weary voice, and as a man adream: 'I am on my way to Iona.'

'I am thinking I know now who you are. You are the man Macallum.'

Neil looked, but did not speak. His eyes dreamed against what the other could not see or know. The shepherd called angrily to his dogs to keep the sheep from straying; then, with a resentful air, turned to his victim.

'You are a silent man for sure, you are. I'm hoping it is not the curse upon you already.'

'What curse?'

'Ah, *that* has brought the wind against the mist! I was thinking so!'

'What curse?'

'You are the man that was the Sin-Eater over there?'

'Ay.'

'The man Macallum?'

'Ay.'

Strange it is, but three days ago I saw you in Tobermory, and heard you give your name as Neil Ross to an Iona man that was there.'

'Well?'

'Oh, sure, it is nothing to me. But they say the Sin-Eater should not be a man with a hidden lump in his pack.'[5]

'Why?'

'For the dead know, and are content. There is no shaking off any sins, then – for that man.'

'It is a lie.'

'Maybe ay and maybe no.'

'Well, have you more to be saying to me? I am obliged to you for your company, but it is not needing it I am, though no offence.'

'Och, man, there's no offence between you and me. Sure, there's Iona in me, too; for the father of my father married a woman that was the granddaughter of Tomais Macdonald, who was a fisherman there. No, no; it is rather warning you I would be.'

'And for what?'

'Well, well, just because of that laugh I heard about.'

'What laugh?'

'The laugh of Adam Blair that is dead.'

Neil Ross stared, his eyes large and wild. He leaned a little forward. No word came from him. The look that was on his face was the question.

'Yes: it was this way. Sure, the telling of it is just as I heard it. After you ate the sins of Adam Blair, the people there brought out the coffin. When they were putting him into it, he was as stiff as a sheep dead in the snow – and just like that, too, with his eyes wide open. Well, someone saw you trampling the heather down the slope that is in front of the house, and said, "It is the Sin-Eater!" With that, Andrew Blair sneered, and said – "Ay, 'tis the scapegoat he is!" Then, after a while, he went on: "The Sin-Eater they call him: ay, just so: and a bitter good bargain it is, too, if all's true that's thought true!" And with that he laughed, and then his wife that was behind him laughed, and then . . .'

'Well, what then?'

'Well, 'tis Himself that hears and knows if it is true! But this is the thing I was told: After that laughing there was a stillness and a dread. For all there saw that the corpse had turned its head and was looking after you as you went down the heather. Then, Neil Ross, if that be your true name, Adam Blair that was dead put up his white face against the sky, and laughed.'

At this, Ross sprang to his feet with a gasping sob.

'It is a lie, that thing!' he cried, shaking his fist at the shepherd. 'It is a lie!'

'It is no lie. And by the same token, Andrew Blair shrank back white and shaking, and his woman had the swoon upon her, and who knows but the corpse might have come to life again had it not been for Maisie Macdonald, the deid-watcher, who clapped a handful of salt on his eyes, and tilted the coffin so that the bottom of it slid forward, and so let the whole fall flat on the ground, with Adam Blair in it sideways, and as likely as not cursing and groaning, as his wont was, for the hurt both to his old bones and his old ancient dignity.'

Ross glared at the man as though the madness was upon him. Fear and horror and fierce rage swung him now this way and now that.

'What will the name of you be, shepherd?' he stuttered huskily.

'It is Eachainn Gilleasbuig I am to ourselves; and the English of that for those who have no Gaelic is Hector Gillespie; and I am Eachainn mac Ian mac Alasdair of Strathsheean that is where Sutherland lies against Ross.'

'Then take this thing – and that is, the curse of the Sin-Eater! And a bitter bad thing may it be upon you and yours.'

And with that Neil the Sin-Eater flung his hand up into the air, and then leaped past the shepherd, and a minute later was running through the frightened sheep, with his head low, and a white foam on his lips, and his eyes red with blood as a seal's that has the death-wound on it.

On the third day of the seventh month from that day, Aulay Macneill, coming into Balliemore of Iona from the west side of the island, said to old Ronald MacCormick, that was the father of his wife, that he had seen Neil Ross again, and that he was 'absent' – for though he had spoken to him, Neil would not answer, but only gloomed at him from the wet weedy rock where he sat.

The going back of the man had loosed every tongue that was in Iona. When, too, it was known that he was wrought in some terrible way, if not actually mad, the islanders whispered that it was because of the sins of Adam Blair. Seldom or never now did they speak of him by his name, but simply as 'The Sin-Eater.' The thing was not so rare as to cause this strangeness, nor did many (and perhaps none did) think that the sins of the dead ever might or could abide with the living who had merely done a good Christian charitable thing. But there was a reason.

Not long after Neil Ross had come again to Iona, and had settled down in the ruined roofless house on the croft of Ballyrona, just like a fox or a wild-cat, as the saying was, he was given fishing-work to do by Aulay Macneill, who lived at Ard-an-teine, at the rocky north end of the *machar* or plain that is on the west Atlantic coast of the island.

One moonlit night, either the seventh or the ninth after the earthing of Adam Blair at his own place in the Ross, Aulay Macneill saw Neil Ross steal out of the shadow of Ballyrona and make for the sea. Macneill was there by the rocks, mending a lobster-creel. He had gone there because of the sadness. Well, when he saw the Sin-Eater, he watched.

Neil crept from rock to rock till he reached the last fang that churns the sea into yeast when the tide sucks the land just opposite.

Then he called out something that Aulay Macneill could not catch. With that he springs up, and throws his arms above him.

'Then,' says Aulay when he tells the tale, 'it was like a ghost he was.

The moonshine was on his face like the curl o' a wave. White! there is no whiteness like that of the human face. It was whiter than the foam about the skerry it was; whiter than the moon shining; whiter than . . . well, as white as the painted letters on the black boards of the fishing-cobles. There he stood, for all that the sea was about him, the slip-slop waves leapin' wild, and the tide making, too, at that. He was shaking like a sail two points off the wind. It was then that, all of a sudden, he called in a womany, screamin' voice –

' "I am throwing the sins of Adam Blair into the midst of ye, white dogs o' the sea! Drown them, tear them, drag them away out into the black deeps! Ay, ay, ay, ye dancin' wild waves, this is the third time I am doing it, and now there is none left; no, not a sin, not a sin!

' "O-hi, O-ri, dark tide o' the sea,
I am giving the sins of a dead man to thee!
By the Stones, by the Wind, by the Fire, by the Tree,
From the dead man's sins set me free, set me free!
Adam mhic Anndra mhic Adam and me,
Set us free! Set us free!' "

'Ay, sure, the Sin-Eater sang that over and over; and after the third singing he swung his arms and screamed –

' "And listen to me, black waters an' running tide,
That rune is the good rune told me by Maisie the wise,
And I am Neil the son of Silis Macallum
By the black-hearted evil man Murtagh Ross,
That was the friend of Adam mac Anndra, God against him!' "

And with that he scrambled and fell into the sea. But, as I am Aulay mac Luais and no other, he was up in a moment, an' swimmin' like a seal, and then over the rocks again, an' away back to that lonely roofless place once more, laughing wild at times, an' muttering an' whispering.'

It was this tale of Aulay Macneill's that stood between Neil Ross and the isle-folk. There was something behind all that, they whispered one to another.

So it was always the Sin-Eater he was called at last. None sought him. The few children who came upon him now and again fled at his approach, or at the very sight of him. Only Aulay Macneill saw him at times, and had word of him.

After a month had gone by, all knew that the Sin-Eater was wrought to madness because of this awful thing: the burden of Adam Blair's sins would not go from him! Night and day he could hear them laughing low, it was said.

But it was the quiet madness. He went to and fro like a shadow in the grass, and almost as soundless as that, and as voiceless. More and more the name of him grew as a terror. There were few folk on that wild west coast of Iona, and these few avoided him when the word ran that he had knowledge of strange things, and converse, too, with the secrets of the sea.

One day Aulay Macneill, in his boat, but dumb with amaze and terror for him, saw him at high tide swimming on a long rolling wave right into the hollow of the Spouting Cave. In the memory of man, no one had done this and escaped one of three things: a snatching away into oblivion, a strangled death, or madness. The islanders know that there swims into the cave, at full tide, a Mar-Tarbh, a dreadful creature of the sea that some call a kelpie; only it is not a kelpie, which is like a woman, but rather is a sea-bull, offspring of the cattle that are never seen. Ill indeed for any sheep or goat, ay, or even dog or child, if any happens to be leaning over the edge of the Spouting Cave when the Mar-Tarbh roars: for, of a surety, it will fall in and straightway be devoured.

With awe and trembling Aulay listened for the screaming of the doomed man. It was full tide, and the sea-beast would be there.

The minutes passed, and no sign. Only the hollow booming of the sea, as it moved like a baffled blind giant round the cavern-bases: only the rush and spray of the water flung up the narrow shaft high into the windy air above the cliff it penetrates.

At last he saw what looked like a mass of seaweed swirled out on the surge. It was the Sin-Eater. With a leap, Aulay was at his oars. The boat swung through the sea. Just before Neil Ross was about to sink for the second time, he caught him and dragged him into the boat.

But then, as ever after, nothing was to be got out of the Sin-Eater save a single saying: '*Tha e lamhan fuar: Tha e lamhan fuar!*' – 'It has a cold, cold hand!'

The telling of this and other tales left none free upon the island to look upon the 'scapegoat' save as one accursed.

It was in the third month that a new phase of his madness came upon Neil Ross.

The horror of the sea and the passion for the sea came over him at the same happening. Oftentimes he would race along the shore, screaming wild names to it, now hot with hate and loathing, now as the pleading of a man with the woman of his love. And strange chants to it, too, were upon his lips. Old, old lines of forgotten runes were overheard by Aulay Macneill, and not Aulay only: lines wherein the ancient sea-name of the island, *Ioua*, that was given to it long before it was called Iona, or any other of the nine names that are said to belong to it, occurred again and again.

The flowing tide it was that wrought him thus. At the ebb he would wander across the weedy slabs or among the rocks: silent, and more like a lost duinshee than a man.

Then again after three months a change in his madness came. None knew what it was, though Aulay said that the man moaned and moaned because of the awful burden he bore. No drowning seas for the sins that could not be washed away, no grave for the live sins that would be quick till the day of the Judgment!

For weeks thereafter he disappeared. As to where he was, it is not for the knowing.

Then at last came that third day of the seventh month when, as I have said, Aulay Macneill told old Ronald MacCormick that he had seen the Sin-Eater again.

It was only a half-truth that he told, though. For, after he had seen Neil Ross upon the rock, he had followed him when he rose, and wandered back to the roofless place which he haunted now as of yore. Less wretched a shelter now it was, because of the summer that was come, though a cold, wet summer at that.

'Is that you, Neil Ross?' he had asked, as he peered into the shadows among the ruins of the house.

'That's not my name,' said the Sin-Eater; and he seemed as strange then and there, as though he were a castaway from a foreign ship.

'And what will it be, then, you that are my friend, and sure knowing me as Aulay mac Luais – Aulay Macneill that never grudges you bit or sup?'

'I am Judas.'

'And at that word,' says Aulay Macneill, when he tells the tale, 'at that word the pulse in my heart was like a bat in a shut room. But after a bit I took up the talk.

'"Indeed," I said; "and I was not for knowing that. May I be so bold as to ask whose son, and of what place?"

'But all he said to me was, "*I am Judas.*"

'Well, I said, to comfort him, "Sure, it's not such a bad name in itself, though I am knowing some which have a more home-like sound." But no, it was no good.

'"I am Judas. And because I sold the Son of God for five pieces of silver . . ."'

'But here I interrupted him and said, – "Sure, now, Neil – I mean, Judas – it was eight times five." Yet the simpleness of his sorrow prevailed, and I listened with the wet in my eyes.

'"I am Judas. And because I sold the Son of God for five silver shillings, He laid upon me all the nameless black sins of the world. And that is why I am bearing them till the Day of Days."'

And this was the end of the Sin-Eater; for I will not tell the long story of Aulay Macneill, that gets longer and longer every winter: but only the unchanging close of it.

I will tell it in the words of Aulay.

'A bitter, wild day it was, that day I saw him to see him no more. It was late. The sea was red with the flamin' light that burned up the air betwixt Iona and all that is west of West. I was on the shore, looking at the sea. The big green waves came in like the chariots in the Holy Book. Well, it was on the black shoulder of one of them, just short of the ton o' foam that swept above it, that I saw a spar surgin' by.

'"What is that?" I said to myself. And the reason of my wondering was this: I saw that a smaller spar was swung across it. And while I was watching that thing another great billow came in with a roar, and hurled the double spar back, and not so far from me but I might have gripped it. But who would have gripped that thing if he were for seeing what I saw?

'It is Himself knows that what I say is a true thing.

'On that spar was Neil Ross, the Sin-Eater. Naked he was as the day he was born. And he was lashed, too – ay, sure, he was lashed to it by ropes round and round his legs and his waist and his left arm. It was the Cross he was on. I saw that thing with the fear upon me. Ah, poor drifting wreck that he was! *Judas on the Cross:* It was his *eric!*

'But even as I watched, shaking in my limbs, I saw that there was life in him still. The lips were moving, and his right arm was ever for swinging this way and that. 'Twas like an oar, working him off a lee shore: ay, that was what I thought.

'Then, all at once, he caught sight of me. Well he knew me, poor man, that has his share of heaven now, I am thinking!

'He waved, and called, but the hearing could not be, because of a big surge o' water that came tumbling down upon him. In the stroke of an oar he was swept close by the rocks where I was standing. In that flounderin', seethin' whirlpool I saw the white face of him for a moment, an' as he went out on the re-surge like a hauled net, I heard these words fallin' against my ears, –

'"*An eirig m'anama* . . . In ransom for my soul!"

'And with that I saw the double-spar turn over and slide down the back-sweep of a drowning big wave. Ay, sure, it went out to the deep sea swift enough then. It was in the big eddy that rushes between Skerry-Mòr and Skerry-Beag. I did not see it again – no, not for the quarter of an hour, I am thinking. Then I saw just the whirling top of it rising out of the flying yeast of a great, black-blustering wave, that was rushing northward before the current that is called the Black-Eddy.

'With that you have the end of Neil Ross: ay, sure, him that was called the Sin-Eater. And that is a true thing; and may God save us the sorrow of sorrows.

'And that is all.'

1 *Contullich: i.e.* Ceann-nan-tulaich, 'the end of the hillocks.' *Loch-a-chaoruinn* means the loch of the rowan-trees.

2 The farm in the hollow of the yellow flowers.

3 (1) *A chuid do Pharas da!* 'His share of heaven be his.' (2) *G'un gleidheadh Dia thu*, 'May God preserve you.' (3) *G'un beannaicheadh Dia an tigh!* 'God's blessing on this house.'

4 (1) *Droch caoidh ort!* 'May a fatal accident happen to you' (*lit.* 'bad moan on you'). (2) *Gaoth gun direadh ort!* 'May you drift to your drowning (*lit.* 'wind without direction on you'). (3) *Dia ad aghaidh*, etc., 'God against thee and in thy face . . . and may a death of woe be yours . . . Evil and sorrow to thee and thine!'

5 *i.e.* With a criminal secret, or an undiscovered crime.

FIONA MACLEOD

The Sun-Chant of Cathal

O hot yellow fire that streams out of the sky, sword-white and golden,
Be a flame upon the monks that are praying in their cells in Iona!
Be a fire in the veins of Colum, and the hell that he preacheth be his,
And be a torch to the men of Lochlin that they discover the isle and
 consume it!

For I see this thing, that the old gods are the gods that die not:
All else is a seeming, a dream, a madness, a tide never ebbing.
Glory to thee, O Grian, lord of life, first of the gods, Allfather,
Swords and spears are thy beams, thy breath a fire that consumeth!

And upon this isle of A-rinn send sorrow and death and disaster,
Upon one and all save Ardanna, who gave me her bosom,
Upon one and all send death, the curse of a death slow and swordless,
From Molios of the Cave to Mûrta and Diarmid my doomsmen!

ADOMNÁN

Acts

Another
Amongst Columba's acts
Among the Picts:
A translator
Interpreted his preaching,
Reaching out
To a rich man
Whose family
And servants
Were baptized;
But soon
The man's son
Fell ill.
Wizards came:
'You fool,
There's no doubt
This boy is ill
Because you had him baptized.
His illness
Is the raw sickness
Of Christ.'

Too late
Columba came back.
The shock
Of the dead boy
Made him cry;
But he took
His cold hand,
Urging him,
'Stand.'
And when the boy's eyes
Opened

In terrified surprise
And he talked
Excitedly
Then walked
Out
Of the house,
A shout
Went up
Among those Picts
Who could not read
The Book of Acts
But saw
Right then
The saint's own
Straightforward acts
Raise the dead.

ADOMNÁN

Among the Picts

Among the Picts:
'Broichan,
Wizard,
Free that slave,
That Irish girl.
She too
Is human.
If you
Will not
Free that Irish
Slave,
You will not live.'

He picked up a chuckie
From the Ness.
'This blessed stone
Will be lucky
For the sick,
But, Broichan,
An unlucky
Cup
Is going to shatter
In your hand.'
Later
Broichan suffered
A stroke.
A glass vessel broke
In his hand.
He began
To choke,
Muttering
'Let the slave girl go.'

So Columba sent
Two men who went
To the Pictish king
Explaining,
'Dip
This lucky stone
Deep
In a cup
Once she has gone
And so give
Broichan
Fresh hope
He may live.'

So the girl went free
And that stone,
When dipped
In a cup,
Floated
Like an apple
Or a nut.
Then Broichan
Had not
Long to wait
Before his thrapple
Healed,
And his stroke
Eased and was gone.

Afterwards, remembering the cleric,
The wizard smiled
With pleasure
At how that lucky stone
So soon
Became a treasure,
A relic.

ADOMNÁN

Broichan

Broichan
And his tall
Wizards
Stood in a gale
By Loch Ness:
'Now, Columba,
Confess
How our power
In this mist
Controls
The weather
And makes you
Unable to sail.'
But Columba
Put his trust
In God
And said
Nothing at all,
But sailed
On
In a sudden
Miraculous calm
Till the sun shone
And Broichan
Was gone.

SAMUEL JOHNSON

In the Morning Our Boat Was Ready

In the morning our boat was ready: it was high and strong. Sir *Allan* victualled it for the day, and provided able rowers. We now parted from the young Laird of *Col*, who had treated us with so much kindness, and concluded his favours by consigning us to Sir *Allan*. Here we had the last embrace of this amiable man, who, while these pages were preparing to attest his virtues, perished in the passage between *Ulva* and *Inch Kenneth*.

Sir *Allan*, to whom the whole region was well known, told us of a very remarkable cave, to which he would show us the way. We had been disappointed already by one cave, and were not much elevated by the expectation of another.

It was yet better to see it, and we stopped at some rocks on the coast of *Mull*. The mouth is fortified by vast fragments of stone, over which we made our way, neither very nimbly nor very securely. The place, however, well repaid our trouble. The bottom, as far as the flood rushes in, was encumbered with large pebbles, but as we advanced was spread over with smooth sand. The breadth is about forty-five feet: the roof rises in an arch, almost regular, to a height which we could not measure; but I think it about thirty feet.

This part of our curiosity was nearly frustrated; for though we went to see a cave, and knew that caves are dark, we forgot to carry tapers, and did not discover our omission till we were wakened by our wants. Sir *Allan* then sent one of the boatmen into the country, who soon returned with one little candle. We were thus enabled to go forward, but could not venture far. Having passed inward from the sea to a great depth, we found on the right hand a narrow passage, perhaps not more than six feet wide, obstructed by great stones, over which we climbed and came into a second cave, in breadth twenty-five feet. The air in this apartment was very warm, but not oppressive, nor loaded with vapours. Our light showed no tokens of a feculent or corrupted atmosphere. Here was a square stone, called, as we are told, *Fingal's Table*.

If we had been provided with torches, we should have proceeded in our search, though we had already gone as far as any former adventurer, except some who are reported never to have returned; and, measuring our way back, we found it more than a hundred and sixty yards, the eleventh part of a mile.

Our measures were not critically exact, having been made with a walking pole, such as it is convenient to carry in these rocky countries, of which I guessed the length by standing against it. In this there could be no great errour, nor do I much doubt but the Highlander, whom we employed, reported the number right. More nicety however is better, and no man should travel unprovided with instruments for taking heights and distances.

There is yet another cause of errour not always easily surmounted, though more dangerous to the veracity of itinerary narratives, than imperfect mensuration. An observer deeply impressed by any remarkable spectacle, does not suppose, that the traces will soon vanish from his mind, and having commonly no great convenience for writing, defers the description to a time of more leisure, and better accommodation.

He who has not made the experiment, or who is not accustomed to require rigorous accuracy from himself, will scarcely believe how much a few hours take from certainty of knowledge, and distinctness of imagery; how the succession of objects will be broken, how separate parts will be confused, and how many particular features and discriminations will be compressed and conglobated into one gross and general idea.

To this dilatory notation must be imputed the false relations of travellers, where there is no imaginable motive to deceive. They trusted to memory, what cannot be trusted safely but to the eye, and told by guess what a few hours before they had known with certainty. Thus it was that *Wheeler* and *Spon* described with irreconcilable contrariety things which they surveyed together, and which both undoubtedly designed to show as they saw them.

When we had satisfied our curiosity in the cave, so far as our penury of light permitted us, we clambered again to our boat, and proceeded along the coast of *Mull* to a headland, called *Atun*, remarkable for the columnar form of the rocks, which rise in a series of pilasters, with a degree of regularity, which Sir *Allan* thinks not less worthy of curiosity than the shore of *Staffa*.

Not long after we came to another range of black rocks, which had the appearance of broken pilasters, set one behind another to a great depth. This place was chosen by Sir *Allan* for our dinner. We were easily accommodated with seats, for the stones were of all heights, and refreshed ourselves and our boatmen, who could have no other rest till we were at *Icolmkill*.

The evening was now approaching, and we were yet at a considerable distance from the end of our expedition. We could therefore stop no more to make remarks in the way, but set forward with some degree of eagerness. The day soon failed us, and the moon presented a very solemn and pleasing scene. The sky was clear, so that the eye commanded a wide circle: the sea was neither still nor turbulent: the wind neither silent nor loud. We were never far from one coast or another, on which, if the weather had become violent, we could have found shelter, and therefore contemplated at ease the region through which we glided in the tranquillity of the night, and saw now a rock and now an island grow gradually conspicuous and gradually obscure. I committed the fault which I have just been censuring, in neglecting, as we passed, to note the series of this placid navigation.

We were very near an island, called *Nun's Island*, perhaps from an ancient convent. Here is said to have been dug the stone that was used in the buildings of *Icolmkill*. Whether it is now inhabited we could not stay to inquire.

At last we came to *Icolmkill*, but found no convenience for landing. Our boat could not be forced very near the dry ground, and our Highlanders carried us over the water.

We were now treading that illustrious Island, which was once the luminary of the *Caledonian* regions, whence savage clans and roving barbarians derived the benefits of knowledge, and the blessings of religion. To abstract the mind from all local emotion would be impossible, if it were endeavoured, and would be foolish, if it were possible. Whatever withdraws us from the power of our senses; whatever makes the past, the distant, or the future predominate over the present, advances us in the dignity of thinking beings. Far from me and from my friends, be such frigid philosophy as may conduct us indifferent and unmoved over any ground which has been dignified by wisdom, bravery, or virtue. That man is little to be envied, whose patriotism would not gain force upon the plain of *Marathon*, or whose piety would not grow warmer among the ruins of *Iona*!

We came too late to visit monuments: some care was necessary for ourselves. Whatever was in the Island, Sir *Allan* could command, for the inhabitants were *Macleans*; but having little they could not give us much. He went to the headman of the Island, whom Fame, but Fame delights in amplifying, represents as worth no less than fifty pounds. He was perhaps proud enough of his guests, but ill prepared for our entertainment; however, he soon produced more provision than men not luxurious require. Our lodging was next to be provided. We found a barn well stocked with hay, and made our beds as soft as we could.

In the morning we rose and surveyed the place. The churches of the two convents are both standing, though unroofed. They were built of unhewn stone, but solid, and not inelegant. I brought away rude measures of the buildings, such as I cannot much trust myself, inaccurately taken, and obscurely noted. Mr *Pennant's* delineations, which are doubtless exact, have made my unskilful description less necessary.

The episcopal church consists of two parts, separated by the belfry, and built at different times. The original church had, like others, the altar at one end, and tower at the other; but as it grew too small, another building of equal dimension was added, and the tower then was necessarily in the middle.

That these edifices are of different ages seems evident. The arch of the first church is *Roman*, being part of a circle; that of the additional building is pointed, and therefore *Gothick*, or *Saracenical*; the tower is firm, and wants only to be floored and covered.

Of the chambers or cells belonging to the monks, there are some walls remaining, but nothing approaching to a complete apartment.

The bottom of the church is so incumbered with mud and rubbish, that we could make no discoveries of curious inscriptions, and what there are have been already published. The place is said to be known where the black stones lie concealed, on which the old Highland Chiefs, when they made contracts and alliances, used to take the oath, which was considered as more sacred than any other obligation, and which could not be violated without the blackest infamy. In those days of violence and rapine, it was of great importance to impress upon savage minds the sanctity of an oath, by some particular and extraordinary circumstances. They would not have recourse to the black stones, upon small or common occasions, and when they had established their faith by this tremendous sanction, inconstancy and treachery were no longer feared.

The chapel of the nunnery is now used by the inhabitants as a kind of general cow-house, and the bottom is consequently too miry for examination. Some of the stones which covered the later abbesses have inscriptions, which might yet be read, if the chapel were cleansed. The roof of this, as of all the other buildings, is totally destroyed, not only because timber quickly decays when it is neglected, but because in an island utterly destitute of wood, it was wanted for use, and was consequently the first plunder of needy rapacity.

The chancel of the nuns' chapel is covered with an arch of stone, to which time has done no injury; and a small apartment communicating with the choir, on the north side, like the chapterhouse in cathedrals, roofed with stone in the same manner, is likewise entire.

In one of the churches was a marble altar, which the superstition of the inhabitants has destroyed. Their opinion was, that a fragment of this stone was a defence against shipwrecks, fire, and miscarriages. In one corner of the church the bason for holy water is yet unbroken.

The cemetery of the nunnery was, till very lately, regarded with such reverence, that only women were buried in it. These reliques of veneration always produce some mournful pleasure. I could have forgiven a great injury more easily than the violation of this imaginary sanctity.

South of the chapel stand the walls of a large room, which was probably the hall, or refectory of the nunnery. This apartment is capable of repair. Of the rest of the convent there are only fragments.

Besides the two principal churches, there are, I think, five chapels yet standing, and three more remembered. There are also crosses, of which two bear the names of St *John* and St *Matthew*.

A large space of ground about these consecrated edifices is covered with grave-stones, few of which have any inscription. He that surveys it, attended by an insular antiquary, may be told where the Kings of many nations are buried, and if he loves to sooth his imagination with the thoughts that naturally rise in places where the great and powerful lie mingled with the dust, let him listen in submissive silence; for if he asks any questions, his delight is at an end.

Iona has long enjoyed, without any very credible attestation, the honour of being reputed the cemetery of the *Scottish* Kings. It is not unlikely, that, when the opinion of local sanctity was prevalent, the Chieftains of the Isles, and perhaps some of the *Norwegian* or *Irish* princes were reposited in this venerable enclosure. But by whom the subterraneous vaults are peopled is now utterly unknown. The graves are very numerous, and some of them undoubtedly contain the remains of men, who did not expect to be so soon forgotten.

Not far from this awful ground, may be traced the garden of the monastery: the fishponds are yet discernible, and the aqueduct, which supplied them, is still in use.

There remains a broken building, which is called the Bishop's house, I know not by what authority. It was once the residence of some man above the common rank, for it has two stories and a chimney. We were shewn a chimney at the other end, which was only a nich, without perforation, but so much does antiquarian credulity, or patriotick vanity prevail, that it was not much more safe to trust the eye of our instructor than the memory.

There is in the Island one house more, and only one, that has a chimney: we entered it, and found it neither wanting repair nor inhabitants; but to the farmers, who now possess it, the chimney is of no great value; for their fire was made on the floor, in the middle of the room, and notwithstanding the dignity of their mansion, they rejoiced, like their neighbours, in the comforts of smoke.

It is observed, that ecclesiastical colleges are always in the most pleasant and fruitful places. While the world allowed the monks their choice, it is surely no dishonour that they chose well. The Island is remarkably fruitful. The village near the churches is said to contain seventy families, which, at five in a family, is more than a hundred inhabitants to a mile. There are perhaps other villages; yet both corn and cattle are annually exported.

But the fruitfulness of *Iona* is now its whole prosperity. The inhabitants are remarkably gross, and remarkably neglected: I know not if they are visited by any Minister. The Island, which was once the metropolis of learning and piety, has now no school for education, nor temple for worship, only two inhabitants that can speak *English*, and not one that can write or read.

The people are of the clan of *Maclean*; and though Sir *Allan* had not been in the place for many years, he was received with all the reverence due to their Chieftain. One of them being sharply reprehended by him, for not sending him some rum, declared after his departure, in Mr *Boswell's* presence, that he had no design of disappointing him, *for*, said he, *I would cut my bones for him; and if he had sent his dog for it, he should have had it.*

When we were to depart, our boat was left by the ebb at a great distance from the water, but no sooner did we wish it afloat, than the islanders gathered round it, and, by the union of many hands, pushed it down the beach; every man who could contribute his help seemed to think himself happy in the opportunity of being, for a moment, useful to his Chief.

We now left those illustrious ruins, by which Mr *Boswell* was much affected, nor would I willingly be thought to have looked upon them without some emotion. Perhaps, in the revolutions of the world, *Iona* may be sometime again the instructress of the Western Regions.

ADOMNÁN

Dùn I

Perched on Dùn I,
Gazing north
On a clear day,
Columba saw a drab, grey
Storm-cloud, rising
Over the sea
Towards Arisaig,
And Silnan heard him say,
'Silnan,
That cloud brings fear
And plague
To folk and beasts. Today
It will pass us by
Here on Iona, but tonight,
Crossing over
The sea,
It will blight
Ireland from Dublin to the River
Delvin. It'll cause
Sores filled with pus
On human skin
And the udders of cows,
And at its height
Will kill
All its victims;
Yet still
We must
Trust
The mercy of God –
We must
Send relief.
So get food,
Silnan. Leave.

Wave
Goodbye
To Dùn I.
For, yes,
My son,
If life goes on
You will need
To feed
The sick
With this bread
I bless
In the name of God.

You must dip
This bread
In water
So every daughter,
Every son,
Every cow
And sheep
Wetted
By each precious drop
Of this water
Will discover
How to heal.

On this clear day
Gazing north
From Dùn I,
I say,
Silnan,
Go now.
I know now
All
Will be well.'

ADOMNÁN

Forecast

That morning Baithéne set sail from Iona for Tiree,
Blown there by strong winds from the south.
That evening Colmán set sail from Iona for Ireland,
Blown there by strong winds from the north.
Columba, praying, forecast those winds.
'The faithful stay one with the weather.'

ADOMNÁN

Iona Fragments

Whittling a stick with a favourite knife,
A servant cut his knee and died.

*

When a monk dipped a bronze basin in a spring,
Afterwards the spring filled with blood.

*

While Columba chanted the forty-third psalm
His voice in the air became thunder.

ADOMNÁN

Blessing

In the writing hut,
Copying,
When asked
To bless an implement,
He went on with his task,
Eyes down,
But waved his pen
In blessing.
Then,
When he had done
Copying,
He laid down that pen
And asked,
'What did I bless?'
'A knife.'
'Well, may that knife
Never take life
Or hurt
Anyone.'
And so,
Though
A butcher in the yard
Tried hard
To slit
A beast's throat
With that knife,
It would do no harm,
And even
When melted down
Its metal
Unsettled
The blacksmiths,
For if they made

Any sharp thing
Out of it
Then the charm
That the saint had spoken
With his blessing pen
In the writing hut
Stayed
Unbroken
In that blessed nib-like
Blade.

ADOMNÁN

Pilgrim

Sit
Away
Above the shore
Near the machair.
At the ninth hour
A guest
Will arrive
Exhausted
From the west,
A grey
Heron
Blasted
By the wind,
That will land,
Collapsing, on the shore.
Carry it
To a house nearby.

Don't let it die
Bereft.
Feed it.
Look after it
For three days
And three nights
Till at last,
Stronger,
And no longer
A pilgrim guest,
It will rise,
Take flight,
And fly

Home, west,
To the sweetness
I have known
In the island
Of Ireland –
To my own
Blest
Homeland
I have left.

LOUISE IMOGEN GUINEY

Columba and the Stork

The cliffs of Iona were red, with the moon to lee,
A finger of rock in the infinite wind and the sea;
And white on the cliffs as a volley of spray down-flying,
The beautiful stork of Eiré indriven and dying.

I stole from the choir; I fed him, I bathed his breast,
Till in late sunshine he lifted his wing to the west.
Oh, the bells of the Abbey were calling clearer and bolder,
And I feared the pale admonishing face at my shoulder.

Columb the saint's! but I said, with mine arm in air,
(Of that banished body and homesick spirit aware,)
'The bird is of Eiré; out of the storm I bore him;
And lo, he is free, with the valleys of Eiré before him.'

Of the man that was Eiré-born, and in exile yet,
This is the reproach I had, and cannot forget,
This is the reproach I had, and never another:
'Blessed art thou, to have lightened the heart of my brother!'

ALICE THOMPSON

Hologram

When Orla went out looking for mussels on the South Beach, she knew very well that mussels could only be found on the North Beach. But she wanted more time away from the small wooden hut where her family unintentionally crowded her out. She wanted an isolated place where she had all the time in the world.

Orla was very fine and precise and fair because of her Norse ancestry. Her skin was pale like paper. Her hands and feet were thin and oulined clearly by her bones. Her veins showed through her fine skin like lines of purple ink as if she had been drawn into existence.

Arriving at the South Beach, Orla was surprised to see a nun sitting cross-legged on a rock, her back to her. Orla watched as the nun carefully undid her wimple and placed it on the ground. Her golden hair was the same colour as the sand.

Hearing Orla approach, the nun quickly turned round. Orla could see clearly that her face was contorted and tear-stained.

'What's wrong?' Orla asked her, gently.

'I keep telling them it is not a good idea.'

'Telling whom?'

'The voices in my head. But they are insisting I document everything.'

'What do you mean?'

The nun's tears stopped and her eyes turned stony.

'You are too young too understand.'

The nun seized her wimple and leapt up and ran back up the beach in the direction of the nunnery. Was it her imagination or had Orla seen whip marks on the nun's legs and arms?

The sea looked flat and calm and gave nothing away. The sea was perfectly itself, its colour the slate grey of neolithic rock. All that remained of the nun now were her footprints in the sand by the shore line. Orla watched the footprints slowly fill with water.

The nuns were not popular on the island. They were resented when they first arrived, thought not to be needed. The Augustinian nunnery was established at the same time as the Benedictine monastery and lay just south of it. There was hidden rivalry between the denominations. It was thought unfair by the villagers that the Lord of the Isles favoured the nunnery over the monastery. The nunnery had a chapter house with stone seats, a chapel with an aisle on the North side, a refectory and kitchen on the South, all grouped round an enclosure. There were mutterings amongst the villagers that the nuns should be exiled to the women's island where Columba over half a century ago had put all the women of Iona. The huts with straw roofs nestled in the shadow of the monastery. The heavy stone building of the monastery was just another form of rock.

The rumours about the nuns had started up a few months ago. Orla overheard her mother talk about how the nuns were becoming increasingly isolated from the rest of the island. The nuns had always scared Orla a little. She saw them walking along the path up to the nunnery in their long dark robes, thin and different.

Over time their contact with the villagers grew increasingly inconsistent. The nuns prayed all day and tended their garden but ventured out of the nunnery enclosure less and less.

'What is happening?' Orla wondered to her father.

'It is as if they are looking more and more inwards. Their religion has become about sacred texts and spoken words. It is as if the pleasure of their inward spiritual life has distracted them from real life.'

The nuns were so different from the laughing, outgoing monks. The monks were always doing things. It was said that one was writing up the history of Iona in fine illumination. Orla had heard about the exquisite detail of the intricate marginalia in these manuscripts. Orla's father made up pigments for the monks and he had recently been asked to produce an increasing variety of colours. Orla helped by picking red berries from the bushes until her fingers and palms turned scarlet. She boiled the water and dropped the seeds into the cauldron. The carmine colours swirled in the water. She used the same method for drawing purple from the lichen. It took two weeks of seeping in the water before the pigments were ready. For the ink for the text, she broke up oak galls and placed them in a pot with gum and water. Oak, ash, birch and hazel trees all grew on Iona. Her father would then take the pigments up to the monastery in clay pots.

The monks seemed authoritative and strong – but the nuns – they seemed like ghosts from the other side.

The villagers began to avoid the vicinity of the nunnery. There was the unspoken acceptance, as there is in a small community, that certain actions were taboo. Nothing was said. The forbidden was communicated through behaviour and silence and disapproval. However the freakish aura of the nuns didn't seem Godless but part of God. The dark Old Testament side, so their darkness and difference was also valued in a strange way. God created everything, everything was entitled. Iona, place of dreams, of circles and crosses.

It was not a place where one could draw straight lines or reduce it to a binary system. The symmetry of nature could be reduced to mathematical codes but when you looked at the reality of nature, Iona was all shimmering seas and greying sand and coarse sand dunes pierced by the remnants and currency of religions. The religious buildings all seemed intrinsic to the island. There seemed no distinction between organic rock and religious totem. God was ingrained everywhere, was a part of nature as existence itself. The Island mapped out the word of God.

As long as nothing happened regarding the nunnery, as long as the interior quality of their existence never became apparent or invaded the villagers' daily life, everything was fine.

Orla was exploring another small beach a few days later when she saw Latin words indented in the sand. She couldn't read Latin so she didn't understand what the writing said. It seemed taken from a religious text. The script was lined and exquisite with little delicate marginalia drawings. It was as if the beach had been turned into a page of text. The figurative skill it must have taken to write and draw this page on the sand amazed her. It also horrified her. It seemed to lack all function. And this impoverished community depended on function, out of necessity. She remembered one of her father's favourite sayings, *'Sin is what is unnecessary'*. To her surprise one word on the sand – CREDO – suddenly filled with black ink, as if the beach was bleeding colour. And she could suddenly, miraculously understand what the word meant: *I believe.*

She looked out at the sunset. The colours seemed so red and lurid, more blood-like than she had ever seen. The colours of the landscape were becoming more and more hallucinatory.

The nun with her golden hair looked out at the gannets squawking on the rocks below her arched window. She wanted to capture the birds on paper, to add to the text. The voices in her head were telling her to recreate the world of Iona on paper, all of its natural beauty and history. The island was too beautiful to be apprehended directly. By putting it on vellum she mediated the ecstasy she felt by looking at the natural world. An ecstasy that felt irreligious. Writing and drawing reduced her emotions about reality to the comprehensible. And it was a way of paying homage to God to recreate his creation in this manner.

Orla allowed happiness into herself. She was unusual in this capacity for joy. It was as if others stopped joy coming into themselves. Set up obstacles which Orla did not do. She would run naked into the sea. Laugh with her two younger siblings. It was almost as if in some way her joy was a cry for help, a call for arms against death, *take me if you dare*, an armory against death itself. Death which had surrounded her from an early age. Her mother had died in childbirth a few years ago when Orla was nine. She had lost another sibling recently to fever. Death lurked everywhere, between the straw roofs of the huts, the bones of dead animals and in the ashes of the fire.

Death was another part of the family. But no one mentioned or addressed it directly. Only the wise woman in the hut would talk to death, try and make sense of it, cure illnesses with herbs and mead as the monks and nuns did, but with pagan rather than Christian incantations. Orla was scared of the wise woman's direct connection to death. Everyone else tried to ignore death in various ways, but Orla noticed, as people reached middle age, death lurking behind their salty eyes or in the black corners of their thin lips. It was the monks and the nuns who seemed to own death, make it their own and say that it did not really exist, it was a figment of our imagination, if only we believed in God.

'We can't stay here long,' the Abbess said.

'Why not?' asked the nun with the golden hair.

'They don't like us here.'

'It is because we are women.'

'Well, there is nothing we can do about that.'

'I don't understand. We heal and cure the sick.'

'But they also die in our arms. The villagers associate us with death. And have you not noticed how the colours on the island are changing?'

'What do you mean?'

'The colours on the island are becoming more lurid. The grass is the colour of emerald green. The sky the colour of lapis lazuli. The yellow corn looks golden. I used to think,' the Abbess continued, 'it is the light because we are so far North. The way the sunlight travels through the clear air.'

It was accepted that at puberty the girls on Iona, for a brief period of time, were blessed with certain telepathic gifts. And Orla felt she could hear Iona talking to her. That it was whispering to her that it was restless, that it was too beautiful and charismatic to be understood fully by the villagers that lived here. There were still bonfires at Halloween, animal sacrifices, omens read in the entrails. The islanders moved from one set of beliefs to the other seamlessly, as if they were two different sides to the same transparent coin. Christianity lived side by side with these pagan beliefs. Hadn't Columba all those years ago soothed stormy seas? When the first warm drops of menstrual blood began, Orla felt warm and brimming with hot potential and full of prophecy, like Columba. She could hear voices on the island saying to her that things on the island were not as they should be, that someone on the island was doing irretrievable harm, that some kind of truth was being written down that should remain unwritten.

Learning and information belonged to the monks on the island, alone. They could access the books, read the texts and communicate them to others if they wished. A room above the chapter house housed the library of Iona. Father John had recently been given the privilege of writing down the history of Iona. He would disappear for hours into his dormitory cell to work at his lectern.

One day, Father Andrew entered his cell, holding goose quills and pigments. To his surprise, Father John was lying in his bed, looking up at the ceiling. The vellum on the lectern was completely blank. There were no traces of a manuscript, at all.

'You have written nothing!' Father Andrew exclaimed.

'Sin is what is unneccesary.'

'What do you mean?'

'Someone else is already writing down a history of Iona.'

'But no one in the monastery would have the requisite skills. They may be able to help with the drawings and the text but no one could manage on their own except you.'

'This person does not live in the monastery.'

'How do you know this is happening then?'

Father John lifted up the hem of his garment. His legs were covered in written script, and images of buildings being destroyed and manuscripts torn up were painted on his skin.

'Is this the writing of the future? This destruction to our monastery and manuscripts? What have you *done*?'

'I have done nothing but pray to God. Words keep appearing day and night all over my mortal flesh. I can feel the pen scratching into my skin. I know someone else on the island is writing its story.'

'So while you have been up here, you have not written a word?'

'I tried, but in vain. The harder I tried, the more quickly this strange text appeared on my skin. Look at the ink. It is the purple black shade you get from the oak gall on the oaks that grow here. It is the ink used for these manuscripts'.

Orla looked out over the sea at the lines of pale colour, the beige shades of the sand. Now outlines were beginning to form round the rocks and sea as if they were being contained by a line of ink. Was it only she who was seeing it? She asked Dreya, her friend who was stumpy like a log and had black curly hair that fell over her slanted eyes and whose skin was as rough to touch as lichen.

'Of course I can see the lines, Orla! There must be some kind of natural explanation for it that we don't understand.'

Orla walked along the causeway that led from the monastery to the hermit's cell. It was where Columba had used to pray. Orla sat crosslegged in the circle of stones, the only remains of the hermit's cell. She could see Tiree in the distance, partially covered by mist. It started to rain. The clouds grew overcast. There seemed to be violence in the air. She looked up to see what she thought were two huge clouds in the sky. She could make out they were huge figures grappling with each other in the darkening clouds. Their giant heads were butting each other like bullocks. Their arms and legs, in huge monstrous form, wrestled and kicked.

Orla cut herself on the bush while picking berries for the pigments; a deep thorn pierced her hand, which she could not pull out. She left it there, too distracted to care. The next morning she noticed the skin around it had grown red and inflamed. Worried, her father took her to the wise woman. The three of them sat down cross-legged in a triangle on the floor of her large circular hut. The fire in the corner of the hut burned fiercely and hot on all their faces.

The woman took out small stones, rubbed smooth, with markings on them and flung them on the floor. They landed in front of Orla and her father where they sat opposite her. Orla watched as the wise woman stared hard at how they had fallen, examined which markings were visible. She drew lines in the earth floor that matched the markings, then drew lines to join them, making an interconnected pattern.

'What do they mean,' Orla blurted out before she could stop herself and her father gave her a hard look to reprimand her for her impatience.

Finally, the wise woman spoke. 'They say, "*Death is no wonder.*"'

And then she rubbed out the marks with the palm of her hands. She stood up stiffly, her old tattered clothes flapping around her thick-set body like the ragged wings of a buzzard. Her face was hollowed out, as if her reading of the future took away all vitality. She smelt of the sea, Orla thought. Orla and her father quickly stood to their feet, too. Orla wanted to escape the claustrophobic hut but she felt faint and staggered to one side. The wise woman quickly grabbed her thin shoulders and steadied her.

'Take her to the Tobar na H-Aoise,' she said to Orla's father.

A vision of the future was compelling the golden haired nun to complete the illuminated manuscript. As if by writing down the island and its history, communicating it, she could somehow make sense of our place in the world. She wrote of Columba, his consorting with kings, his vivid, exacting visions. She wrote of the story of his miraculous knowledge of the missing 'I' from Baithéne's psalter, before the final version had been read. She always wondered where that missing 'I' had gone. She drew an 'I' in the marginalia of the text. Blue, with added decorations that swirled around the single letter elaborately like the bleeding of pigment into water. She worked late into the night, until her fingers ached. The future meant the present to Columba, so clearly could he apprehend it. She wrote, *To one who marvelled at his visionary powers – Columba made the reply, 'Heaven has granted to some to see on occasion on their mind, clearly and surely, the whole of earth and sea and sky.'*

A sentence a day was rapid work. Each letter became a work of art. The nun wondered about time. Was it fluid like water. Or ice? Why should it flow only in one direction? What was time made of? Sometimes when she was working hard by candelight, the moon shining through the window, she felt she could touch time, that it was sharp and glittery, an object she could rotate like any other thing. It was of many dimensions. It had substance.

The swelling of Orla's hand would not subside. Her father tried not to show his anxiety but his studied indifference to her was a mask, so as not to let the inflammation grow worse. But Orla knew in her heart that the poison from the thorn was seeping through her. She was becoming a phantom. All she had left to leave on the world were traces of her, information, a hologram of what she had been.

In the early hours of the morning Orla and her father went to the Well of the Age, as the wise woman had advised. The healing pool lay at the northern edge of the island out of sight of the path, below an overhanging rock. Father and daughter waited for dawn as the sun lit up the dark sky, waited for the first moment the pool was touched by the sun's rays. Light illuminated its dark water and Orla dipped her hand in the icy water, where the thorn had pricked it, but the sore flesh hurt terribly and she pulled her hand immediately out. 'Keep it in longer,' her father insisted, but she couldn't.

That night Orla became delirious. She vividly dreamt of tiptoeing into the nunnery's cloister. She was looking for the nun with the golden hair. She suddenly became certain of which room the nun was in. Orla approached her room and quietly entered. She saw the nun working at her lectern and Orla approached her from behind and looked over her shoulder. She was drawing a map of Iona, colouring the sea in.

'You are making the colours too bright,' she said, 'the sea is never that blue'.

The nun turned, her face impassive. 'Haven't you seen the sea ever look like that? At certain times of day it really is that colour. In a certain light. You just have to look.'

'It's not realistic,' Orla insisted. 'You have made everything look too bright and intense'. She felt impatient with the nun, the way she was tampering with reality.

The nun just looked preternaturally calm and benign, so different from how she had been on the beach, Orla thought with a shock.

'It's just a matter of perspective.' She reached out and took Orla's hand. The nun's hand felt cool and some verdigris came off onto Orla's hand.

'Touch this.'

Orla tentatively touched the edge of the white page. Her hand went straight through.

She gasped. 'It's not real.'

'It's a hologram. An illusion. Like all of this'. The nun glanced outside through the window.

Orla followed her gaze through the small arched window to see all of the landscape shimmering, out of focus, pin pricks of multifarious coloured lights, as if the world had turned to stained glass.

Orla's fever refused to abate. In desperation, her father took her to the monastery. There were rumours that the monks had recently acquired new medical knowledge – monastic mauscripts translated from the Arabic. These new texts contained information from antique Greek authors such as Aristotle.

Father Andrew laid Orla down on a bed in the hospital. A deformed man was lying next to her. His face and his limbs were inflamed and the skin taut red over the swellings, like wood that had been swollen by water. His eyes were slits beneath the engorged eyelids.

'Are you going to be here long?' he asked.

'I don't think so,' Orla replied. She didn't like to look at his hideous form. He was lying propped up on his bed and it was difficult to know if he could see anything, anyway.

'What is wrong with you?' she asked, curiosity getting the better of her.

'They think the devil has got into me.'

'And has he?'

'Well if he has, he's not telling me anything. You will probably see me soon being carried down the Street of the Dead.'

She laughed. 'Columba could expel malignant spirits. You should visit his tomb. It's just next to the cloister wall.'

'Or visit *Sithean Mor* just to hedge my bets!'

'Columba also went to the fairy mound. He was visited there by a band of Holy Angels who flew down at high speed and stood by him while he prayed.'

'You know a lot about him. Yet he died so long ago!'

She didn't reply. Where was this knowledge coming from? She didn't understand. It was as if images were coming unbidden into her mind.

Father Andrew gave her a herbal potion. It tasted vile and bitter, unlike any drink she had had before. The monk laughed at her grimaces.

'It's only rosemary for the infection and other things'.

The monk uttered some prayers over her. The herbal treatments were only manifestations of their religious medicines.

Her fever subsided.

'Thank you, Father,' her father said. He gave the monks all the coins he had saved.

Father Andrew looked at her with sparkling eyes.

'Death is no wonder,' he said.

She saw her father looking worried.

'But will I survive?' she asked the monk.

'We shall see. I prayed for you. God will be with you.'

Her father put his arm around her as they left the monastery.

'Look how much better you are!'

She looked at him trying to introduce further well-being into her eyes.

'You know Columba could return the dead to life,' she said.

The nun looked at the blue made from the flower woad and the yellow from the arsenic powder. She carefully started to paint one of the visions of St Columba, of the angel coming down. The colours were so bright as she mixed them in the pot, adding one pigment after another, onto the vellum, that her eyes began to hurt in the candlelight. But the colours were luminous in the evening light. She suddenly felt the whole room was aglow with the blue and yellow light, that she was drowning in their intense hues. She collapsed to the ground as the blue and yellow light swirled around her, the pigments colouring the whole room in blue and gold, her garments and skin, so the room was like an image from the marginalia.

Orla returned to the South Beach when she saw the angel standing on the same rock where the golden-haired nun had sat before. He had huge wings and was holding in his hand a book of glass. His robe was blue and yellow. She wondered if the book listed the appointment of kings. But as she approached the angel, he disappeared, not by flying away but by disappearing into the air, particle by particle, like he was an image made up a series of dots.

The fever returned but this time even more virulently. When her father finally realised his daughter was dying, he took her on the boat to Fingal's cave. Orla was gradually feeling more detached from the natural world, as if she could not sense it anymore. Joy was being replaced by an objective sense of omnipotence. As if it didn't matter whether she lived or died. It was arbitrary. It was not a sadness, it was a sense of leaving life behind. Was it a kind of spiritual awakening? Orla was too young to know whether it was or not.

Towers of basalt formed columns all around them as her father rowed the boat over the calm water into the entrance of the cave. The cave was as cavernous as a huge cathedral. As she lay on the floorboards of the boat, she looked up at her father's face. How thin he looked now, grief beginning to be etched on his angular features, the indifference no longer holding.

'Columba had powers of prophecy, you know,' she whispered to her father, 'he could see the present and the future at the same time.'

She sat up with difficulty in the boat to look back at Iona for the last time. Orla touched her body. It felt oddly papery. Now everything around them seemed white, except for splashes of bright colour.

Iona now was a phantom of a place, like a hologram, that took the form of an illuminated manuscript. A manuscript that depicted in words and imagery the story of the whole island: information stored for eternity. Orla saw the Druids worshipping beneath the oaks, Columba arriving in his coracle, his retreat to Elachnave, the invasion of the Danish pirates, the monastery and the nunnery in flames, red as the setting sun.

ALAN DEARLE

The Iona Machine

From at least the early Middle Ages Iona has been a place of *scientia* – of knowledge. More particularly, it has been a place where the communication of knowledge has been bound up with a knowledge of technologies of communication. Columban monks who copied and illuminated sacred texts, and who created on Iona the manuscript which is now called *The Book of Kells*, wrote in the international language of their era: Latin. No one who looks at *The Book of Kells* can doubt the sophistication of their communication technology. What they produced stands at the intersection of *ars* and *scientia*, of art and knowledge.

Nowadays, the word *scientia* suggests its English derivative, science; and it may seem odd, in our age of machines, to think of Iona as a scientific place. Yet just as medieval Iona was connected by boat and by writing with locations near and far, so today Iona is at once a small Scottish island and a focus for international attention, a place at the centre of networks of people that stretch around the globe. Iona can stand for remoteness, but also for connectedness; and to think of it as somehow set apart from our age of science is to misunderstand its nature as a present-day place – a site whose inhabitants (and many of whose visitors) have just as much of an interest in science and technology as do people elsewhere.

The story of the Iona Machine begins in 2010 some seventy-five miles south of Iona on the north coast of Antrim at a place known as the Giant's Causeway or Clochán an Aifir. I was there with my family to visit the 40,000 interlocking basalt columns that the Irish giant Finn MacCool is said to have strode across in order to return to Ireland after defeating his Scottish rival. The Causeway lies at the bottom of a high cliff. To the north is nothing but sea until, if you sail as Columba once did, you reach the shores of Iona. The Giant's Causeway site is protected by the National Trust who have installed the usual collection of information boards about the folk legends and the local geology. However, when I visited the Causeway, the information on these boards was quickly exhausted by my fifteen-year-old daughter: all too soon she started asking questions I could not answer. Like many people in such challenging circumstances, my usual reaction is to pull out my phone and Google for the required information. However, at the Giant's Causeway my inquisitive daughter and I were at the bottom of a cliff, surrounded by sea on one side in a sparsely populated part of the county. There was no wifi, no 3G, no available communications technology and no source of further information. For me as a scientist this situation raised two immediate questions: 1. why not? and, 2. what could be done about it?

I soon realised that the *why not* question is dictated by economics – it is not cost effective to deploy expensive communications infrastructure where there is not enough demand. In recent years, reports such as *Spreading the Benefits of Digital Participation*, produced in April 2014 by the Royal Society of Edinburgh, have emphasised the importance of Scotland-wide access to modern knowledge technologies. Yet a Scottish Government report entitled *Mobile Performance and Coverage in Scotland* published in April 2013 revealed that 75% of the Western Isles and 50% of the Highland region did not have any 2 or 3G data coverage. Unless subsidised by government grants, it is unlikely there will ever be anything like full data coverage in these areas – it is simply not economically viable. The same logic applies at the Giant's Causeway and many other areas of cultural, historic or environmental interest.

The next question – what could be done about it? This is where things get interesting. I am a computer scientist, and computer scientists like to apply technology to tricky problems. The question I asked myself was, 'Could an (economically viable) data service be provided to supply data in sites like Iona or the Giant's Causeway where there are no infrastructure facilities including power?' And so the germ of something that could be called the Iona Machine was born.

'Qraqrbox' – this Iona Machine – was also partially inspired by a European research project called Global Smart Spaces (Gloss). In 2001 A. Munro, P. Welen and A. Wilson published online through the Gloss Consortium a paper on 'Interaction Archetypes'. Undertaken at the very start of the twenty-first century, the Gloss project was unfortunately years ahead of its time; it was hindered by the (poor) technology that was then available. Back in those days there were no iPhones or iPads, and the Internet of Things hadn't been thought of yet. Despite those drawbacks, Gloss aimed to support interaction amongst people, artefacts and places while taking account of both context and movement on a global scale. The project identified three metaphors which could be implemented as services, and which were known as *Trails*, *Radar* and *Hearsay*.

Whether on Iona or in Yellowstone National Park, trails are an ancient method of finding your way around in an area, regardless of whether that area is known or unknown. In the Gloss project trails were used to represent the movement of people or artefacts, to conceptualise future movements, to record past movements and to represent paths through space and time. A simple example of a trail is an ordered sequence of *places* (coordinates, regions or locations) along with some optional additional information.

As originally described by Munro, Welen and Wilson, Radar is a tool that will give you 'an overview beyond the immediate environment. With this tool you will be able to locate low and high densities, crowds and groups in a larger area . . . this can help you find the special gap of freedom, the emptiness, one sometimes lacks in a public environment. This instrument can search the streets and spaces for one on a hunt for either noise or silence.' Put more simply, a radar service permits the user to find things that they cannot otherwise see – this may be people, artefacts, or even perhaps the past.

In the same Gloss project paper Munro, Welen and Wilson describe hearsay like this: 'Hearsay is an intimate, sensitive tool that will be there to allow the user to pick up small notes in the environment left for them. It will make sure that only that user will find the message left for them if the context is right . . . Posted or left in the global environment, the message waits at the same place to be delivered at the right time for whom it's left for. A mail where time is not an option but the context is.'

Before returning to Qraqrbox, my putative Iona machine, one last Gloss concept needs to be mentioned – location. Location is central to the provision of contextual services. Without location there is no way of knowing where somebody is standing or what they are looking at and it is consequently impossible to deliver appropriate contextual information to them. The location of a user can be determined in many ways including the electronic, satellite-based GPS (global positioning system), proximity tags and various forms of beacons (such as iBeacon which is becoming popular). However, the first Qraqrbox prototype relied upon barcode-based QR (quick response) codes: if somebody is able to scan a QR code and you know where that code has been placed, then you have a pretty accurate idea of where the user is. This approach is low cost (in terms of power usage) and does not require any infrastructure other than a passive printed code.

The three metaphors of Trails, Radar and Hearsay along with location are all, in part, embodied in what I'm calling here my Iona machine, but whose official name is Qraqrbox. Qraqrbox is a low powered server which delivers contextual information in places where there are no infrastructure facilities including power. That is perhaps a little bit technical, so another way of thinking about it is as delivering a *puddle of internet* where there is no internet. A user standing within that puddle, can have appropriate contextual information delivered to their mobile device (typically a smart phone).

In addition to having no internet services, many sites of interest in Scotland – from St Columba's Bay to the Nevis Gorge – do not have any power. Therefore, returning to 2010 when I came back from the Giant's Causeway to my lab in St Andrews, the question puzzling me and my computer science colleagues was, 'Could we build a box that could run 24/7 in Scotland 365 days of the year without any external power and deliver a puddle of internet?' In order to answer this question, we made use of 'maker culture'. To paraphrase the Wikipedia entry on this phenomenon, it's a contemporary subculture representing a technology-based extension of DIY and hacking culture which is concerned with the creation of new technological devices. In line with this approach, our first attempt at building an Iona machine involved hacking a domestic wifi router like the one many readers have in their homes. In our case our first target was a MR3220 router manufactured by TP-Link. A bit of soldering to attach an SD card provided some permanent storage needed for web content and a real operating system (OpenWRT – a variation of Linux). Once a light-weight web server was installed (lighttpd), we had created a simple low-power, wifi-based web server.

The next problem was how to provide electrical power. This was solved using a solar-panel backed up by a relatively large car battery. The addition of some electronics to manage the charging and de-charging of the battery enclosed in a weather-proof plastic enclosure satisfied the requirements. One of these servers operated successfully on the roof of the University of St Andrews computer science building for about a year. This was our first hardware proof of the concept. Our platform could deliver web pages to connected devices in a 50 metre radius and ran happily on sunlight for 365 days of the year, even in Scotland.

Hardware does not a system make; an operational system needs software. In our case we needed software to provide some of the Gloss project's abstractions – in particular Trails and Places. We also needed some way for users to have content delivered to them and for the delivery of content to be triggered. Our next step was to develop *Apps*. The apps (one for iPhone and one for Android) contained a QR scanner with which a user could scan a QR code. The QR code was decoded in the phone and a request was sent to the Qraqrbox server which sent data back to the app. The data received was interpreted by the app and presented to the user. This information was typically either information about a Place or a Trail.

In 2012 the world of computing changed (as it does every year). That year a small device called the Raspberry Pi was launched. Although originally developed to teach computer science in schools, it found a myriad of other uses. The Raspberry Pi is a credit-card-sized computer that contains a fast low-power ARM processor, a reasonable amount of memory, a slot for an SD card and the ability to plug in a wifi antenna. Its ability to function as a full-blown desktop computer that can drive a screen and a keyboard was of no interest to us. Instead, we were interested in using it to power our Iona machines or Qraqrboxes; and since the Pi ran a modern variation of Linux, it was immediately clear that our days of hacking wireless routers were over. The Pi became the centre of the next generation of Qraqrboxes.

The following year (2013) Qraqrbox was used to support the St Andrews international poetry festival, StAnza. At StAnza a Trail was created in 13 locations in St Andrews. At each place on this Poetry Trail a QR code was located which allowed a user to hear a poem about the place and get information about the author. For example, at St Andrews Castle you could listen to a poem written and read by Gill Andrews. The idea of delivering more information via the spoken word quickly grew. When in a beautiful location who wants to read information on a tiny screen? It is much nicer to be read to. It is even nicer to have poetry read to you by the author of the poems. By going to www.qraqrbox.com/#/trail/stt you can listen to all the poems yourself, should you wish.

The other development that StAnza gave rise to is the idea of the connected/disconnected Internet. This is an idea that has been explored further in the Royal Society of Edinburgh and Scottish Government-supported project called Loch Computer, whose theme is remoteness and connectedness in the digital age, and much of which has the island of Iona as its focus. Loch Computer brought together scientists, digital humanities professionals, artists, and several of the poets and writers in this book. It also created a website with texts, photographs and interviews at www.lochcomputer.weebly.com. Anyhow, the StAnza Poetry Trail did not use a low-power web server – there was no need, since St Andrews is a place blessed with dense high-speed networking. The StAnza Poetry Trail content was delivered via the connected internet. From this project came the realisation that information hosted on low-powered, stand-alone boxes could be replicated on the normal internet that we use every day; or, flipping this idea around, Qraqrboxes could be used to infill contextual information where there is no other infrastructure. Qraqrbox, this 'Iona machine', lets us be remote and yet stand, even in the back of beyond, in a puddle of internet; but it also lets us relive that remoteness while physically disconnected from it by virtue of internet connectedness: the same experience is available in the wild or at home.

The world has gone mad for apps: everyone and every organisation wants one. When you are living in a connected world, apps are great: you can get a micro weather forecast, find out when the next high tide is or the time of the next ferry. However, when you are in a disconnected world apps are not so good. There are two different problems: if you have no internet connection where does the content come from? If you are reading this, then you know this answer: from an Iona machine, a Qraqrbox. However, what if you don't have the app? You are stuck: if, for instance, you are standing on a part of Iona where you can't get an internet connection, then you can't download an app because you don't have a connection, and you can't connect to a Qraqrbox without an app. The solution is to go app-free: and that is what we did in 2015. Currently when you connect to a Qraqrbox using your browser, you get contextual information about the Place you are in along with some software. This software (a sort of 'mini-app') even includes a QR code reader to let you scan QR codes.

Having said something about Qraqrbox, let's consider how it might change visits to somewhere comparatively remote and disconnected like the island of Iona. Visitors arriving by ferry after the ten-minute trip from Fionnphort in Mull would see the Iona Machine located at the ferry slipway. They would connect to the box using their smartphones and information and software would be downloaded into their browser according to their own specific interests. Those interested in history might get information about Columba and might see the Port of the Coracle where he and his followers came ashore in 563 highlighted on a map. A nature lover might have the Spouting Cave highlighted on a map and be told about how periodically water spouts rise into the air from it. Music lovers might be directed towards the northern tip of the island where they could look towards the geological wonders of Staffa which so inspired Felix Mendelssohn; perhaps, thanks to their Iona Machine, they might be accompanied by some music. Maybe the reader of this book might be interested in Loch Staoineig – the physical location said to have inspired 'Loch Computer' – and might want to experience its ever-changing shimmering surface and listen to one of the more eloquent pieces of prose read by one of the authors of the book in which this present text appears . . .

QUEEN VICTORIA

On Visiting Staffa

from her Journal, 17 August 1847

At three we anchored close before *Staffa*, and immediately got into the barge with Charles, the children and the rest of our people, and rowed towards the cave. As we rounded the point, the wonderful basaltic formation came in sight. The appearance it presents is most extraordinary; and when we turned the corner to go into the renowned *Fingal's Cave*, the effect was splendid, like a great entrance into a vaulted hall: it looked almost awful when we entered, and the barge heaved up and down on the swell of the sea. It is very high, but not longer than 227 feet, and narrower than I expected, being only 40 feet wide. The sea is immensely deep in the cave. The rocks, under water, were all colours – pink, blue, and green – which had a most beautiful and varied effect. It was the first time the British standard with a Queen of Great Britain, and her husband and children, had ever entered *Fingal's Cave*, and the men gave three cheers, which sounded very impressive there. We backed out, and then went on a little further to look at the other cave, not of basaltic formation, and at the point called *The Herdsman*. The swell was beginning to get up, and perhaps an hour later we could not have gone in.

We returned to the yacht, but Albert and Charles landed again at *Staffa*. They returned in three-quarters of an hour, and we then went on to *Iona*; here Albert and Charles landed, and were absent an hour. I and the ladies sketched. We saw from the yacht the ruins of the old Cathedral of *St. Oran*. When Albert and Charles returned, they said the ruins were very curious, there had been two monasteries there, and fine old crosses and tombs of ancient kings were still to be seen. I must see it some other time.

ANON

A Traditional Gaelic Prophecy

Seachd bliadna roimh'n brhaà
Thig muir thar *Eirin* re aon tra'
Sthar *Ile* ghu irm ghlais
Ach Snàmhaidh *I Colum* clairich.

Seven years before the awful day,
  When time shall be no more,
A watery deluge will o'er sweep
  Hibernia's mossy shore:
The green clad Isla too shall sink,
  While with the great and good,
Columba's happy isle will rear
  Her towers above the flood.

Gaelic text and English 'Imitation' from T. Garnett,
Observations on a Tour through the Highlands and Part of the Western Isles of Scotland, particularly Staffa and Icolmkill (1800).

KENNETH STEVEN

Iona Poems

After the storm
blue sky comes back –
a whole field of sunlight.

*

A little glen
opens its winter dark
into the riches of orchids.

*

The marble quarry
is never where you want it to be –
I'm sure they move it in winter.

ROBERT CRAWFORD

The Marble Quarry

For the second time in fifty years
I come to the Marble Quarry.
Last time, a boy, I came with my father.
Now I am here with my son.
Afternoon heat streams from the marble,
White light chipped from the earth.
At the quarry's hoist and jetty
Underwater abandoned altars,
Veined slabs, shine through the waves.
We eye up shards among the scarred,
Discarded blocks. I tell my son
How my dad handed me a monumental
Offcut, heavy as an unfinished temple.
We scour what's left. I pick a piece
That fits my hand, and hand it to him
Gingerly. It fits his hand too.

AMY CLAMPITT

Westward

for Anthony Kemp

Distance is dead. At Gatwick, at Heathrow
the loud spoor, the grinding tremor,
manglings, accelerated trade routes

in reverse: the flyblown exotic place,
the heathen shrine exposed. A generation
saw it happen: the big-eyed, spindling

overleapers of the old slow silk route
shiver in terylene at Euston, grimed
caravansary of dispersal, where a lone

pigeon circles underneath the girders,
trapped in the breaking blur of sound waves –
a woman's sourceless voice interminably

counting off the terminals, a sibyl's
lapful of uncertainties. There's trouble
to the north, the trains are late: from

knotted queues the latest émigrés
of a spent Commonwealth look up: so many,
drawn toward what prospect, from what

point of origin? Bound for Iona in
the Western Isles, doleful, unlulled
by British Rail, lying awake I listen

to the clicking metronome as time
runs out, feeling the old assumptions,
aired, worm-tunneled, crumble,

thinking of the collapse of distance:
Proust's paradise of the unvisited,
of fool's-gold Eldorado. At Glasgow

there's still trouble, but the train
to Oban's running. Rain seeps in;
past the streaked, streaming pane,

a fir-fringed, sodden glimpse, the
verberation of a name: Loch Lomond.
'Really?' The callow traveler opposite

looks up, goes back to reading – yes,
it really is Thucydides: hubris,
brazen entitlements, forepangs of

letting go, all that. At Oban, a wet
trek to the ferry landing, where a
nun, or the daft counterfeit of one

(time runs out, the meek grow jaded,
shibboleths of piety no guarantee):
veil and wimple above dank waterproof,

nun-blue pantsuit protruding – lugs
half a dozen satchels ('tinned things
you can't get up here'), has misplaced

her ticket, is so fecklessly egregious
it can't (or could it, after all?) be
contraband. From Craignure, Isle of Mull,

a bus jolts westward, traversing, and
it's still no picnic, the slow route
Keats slogged through on that wet

walking tour: a backward-looking
homage, not a setting forth, as for
his brother George, into the future:

drowned Lycidas, whether beyond the
stormy . . . And of course it rained,
the way it's doing as I skitter up

the cleated iron of the gangway at
Fionnphort; Iona, an indecipherable
blur, a slosh of boots and oilskins,

once landed on, is even wetter.
Not that it always rains: tomorrow
everything will be diaphanous

as the penumbra of a jellyfish:
I'll ride to Staffa over tourmaline
and amethyst without a wrinkle;

will stand sun-warmed above the bay
where St. Columba made his pious landfall,
the purple, ankle-deep, hung like a mantle

on the starved shoulder of the moor.
Heather! I'd thought, the year I first
set foot, in Maine, among the blueberries'

belled, pallid scurf; then – But there's
no heather *here*. Right to begin with:
botanically, they're all one family.

I saw that pallor, then, as an attenuation
in the west: the pioneers, the children's
children of the pioneers, look up from

the interior's plowed-under grassland,
the one homeland they know no homeland
but a taken-over turf: no sanction, no cover

but the raveled sleeve of empire: and yearn
for the pristine, the named, the fabulous,
the holy places. But from this island –

its nibbled turf, sheep trails, rabbit
droppings, harebells, mosses' brass-
starred, sodden firmament, the plink

of plover on that looped, perennial,
vast circumnavigation: at ground level
an incessant whimpering as everything,

however minuscule, joins the resistance
to the omnipresent wind – the prospect
is to the west. Here at the raw edge

of Europe – limpet tenacities, the tidal
combings, purplings of kelp and dulse,
the wrack, the blur, the breakup

of every prospect but turmoil, of
upheaval in the west – the retrospect
is once again toward the interior:

backward-looking, child of the child
of pioneers, forward-slogging with
their hooded caravels, their cattle,

and the fierce covered coal of doctrine
from what beleaguered hearth-fire of
the Name, they could not speculate,

such was the rigor of the Decalogue's
Thou Shalt Not – I now discover that
what looked, still looks, like revelation

was not hell-fire, no air-splintering
phosphorous of injunction, no Power,
no force whatever, but an opening

at the water's edge: a little lake,
world's eye, the mind's counterpart,
an eyeblink of reflection wrung from

the unreflecting seethe and chirr and
whimper of the prairie, the wind-
stirred grass, incognizant incognito

(all flesh being grass) of the mind's
resistance to the omnipresence of what
moves but has no, cannot say its name.

There at the brim of an illumination
that can't be entered, can't be lived in –
you'd either founder, a castaway, or drown –

a well, a source that comprehends, that
supersedes all doctrine: what surety,
what reprieve from drowning, is there,

other than in names? The prairie eyeblink,
stirred, grows murmurous – a murderous,
a monstrous world rimmed by the driftwood

of embarkations, landings, dooms, conquests,
missionary journeys, memorials: Columba
in the skin-covered wicker of that coracle,

lofting these stonily decrepit preaching
posts above the heathen purple; in their
chiseled gnarls, dimmed by the weatherings

of a millennium and more, the braided syntax
of a zeal ignited somewhere to the east,
concealed in hovels, quarreled over,

portaged westward: a basket weave, a
fishing net, a weir to catch, to salvage
some tenet, some common intimation for

all flesh, to hold on somehow till
the last millennium: as though the routes,
the ribbonings and redoublings, the

attenuations, spent supply lines, frayed-
out gradual of the retreat from empire, all
its castaways, might still bear witness.

SARA LODGE

The Grin Without the Cat

I was so young when I met him. Only seventeen. I was doing a project at school that required me to write about a painting and, being both contrary and ambitious, I chose a sculpture. Darius Dacre's latest work was on display at Tate Modern and I took the train in from Leamington Spa to see it on my own – so self-conscious that I stared at my pale face in the window throughout the journey. ScratchCard was a gallery-sized piece of red plastic covered in black wax, which Dacre had scratched all over with burins and nails and chisels, gouging out the wax to make marks that looked like cave art, or blackboard graffiti. Scrolling rings and waves and violent dashes and injuries to the surface. It fascinated me in the original sense of the word: 'to deprive of the power of escape'. I stayed in the gallery for three hours, watching how Dacre's work amused some and disconcerted others. Viewers were invited to mount the scaffold to add their own mark, rubbing away at a surface that, when exposed, revealed a pattern of tiny skulls spelling out 'You Are Not a Winner'. I was seventeen, but I got it.

I was thinking about death a lot then. All the glamorous people I knew were dead and death itself seemed the ultimate way of forcing people to speak to the hand. Most adults were warped and mouldy with compromise. They were bothered about strange spills on the sofa (not me!), and who would want turkey at Christmas (not me!), and what that odd ticking noise was that the car made when we reached 50. I didn't want to reach 50. It seemed improbable and faintly disgusting, like scorpions mating.

So I wrote a long essay for Year 12 about 'Dacre and Death', which got a 20 out of 20: a mark hitherto regarded as impossible by our class. And I sent it to him. Like the smug implacable little lemon pip I was. I wrote to the Tate, told them to forward it to Dacre, and proposed to meet him sometime to discuss it.

Six months later, I was in my first year studying History of Art at

Cambridge and had almost forgotten this indiscretion when my parents forwarded me an envelope containing a postcard of a badly stuffed walrus. In a capitalised biro scrawl, as of a shaky hand leaning heavily on the pen, it read:

Imogen Grimshaw
I will see you dead
on the stroke of four pm
on Feb four
Dacre

There was a sticker with an address in SE28. I couldn't have been more excited if you had force-fed me jellybeans and put my jeans on vibrate. Indeed this thought had occurred to me, since Dacre's most famous work, 'Shock and Augury' was all about electricity. It was the only one of his sculptures that everyone had heard of. *Daily Mail* cartoons still used the tagline 'That's Offal' to represent any kind of modern art. It was so simple as to be almost abstract in form. A bull's heart, liver and spleen in a vitrine; round it an electric walkway, delivering 200 volts at random intervals to individuals whose movement triggered the unseen sensors. Some people got shocked, but most didn't. People queued for hours to experience this strange artistic Russian roulette.

I took a long time to decide to wear black. Pencil skirt. Boots to make me look taller than five-foot-two. Poloneck to accentuate the cheekbones (my only good feature, I thought at the time) at which my mousey, fine hair was cropped. Rimless glasses. Eyeliner and no lipstick. I thought of this as French dressing, though I'd only ever spent a week in Paris on a school trip.

'Be careful,' my friend Joan warned me.

'I think he's innocent.'

'He may not have done it, but he's not innocent.'

He was living in a tower block in Greenwich. I got there an hour early and ended up drinking water in a pub whose carpet smelled of puke. Nauseously nervous, I climbed the dirty stairs to his flat and knocked. Eventually the door was opened by a black woman with tangerine hair wearing an apron.

'Yes?'

'I have a meeting with Darius Dacre.'

'He's gone out', she said, 'I don't know when he'll be back. Sometimes he forgets.'

'I do not forget,' said a lugubrious Scots voice behind us.

He was 80. It was the same big, fleshy face with the challenging eyes and the cigarette dripping out of the mouth's corner that you see in the famous black and white photograph by Jane Bown. But the shock of hair was completely white and, as he drew level, I could see the eczema that made one temple red and flaky and the strong, liver-spotted hand extended to me had nails as yellow and horn-like as neglected toenails.

He ushered me into a sitting-room that was small, cluttered, and disappointingly ordinary save for the view of the Thames. On a sideboard was a silver-framed wedding photograph of Dacre (sideburns, huge lapels) and Lou Bourden (minidress, dreamy smile). One window gave onto a metal balcony. (Oh god, I thought, this must be the same flat that she fell from. *He hasn't moved.*) There were no sculptures, unless you counted the cactus coatstand.

'Do you want a tea?'

I accepted; sat down on the sofa, resting my cup-free arm on a white powder puff cushion. To my alarm, the cushion sprang away from me with a yowl and a scalding spurt of tea napalmed my nylons.

'That's Sir. He can be a wee bit funny with strangers.'

Sir was huge. Over 30 pounds from the jink of his whiskers to the muscular query of his tail. He hunched on the battered leather spine of the couch, like a Chinese dragon considering which canton to torch.

I undid my briefcase, bought specially for the occasion, and withdrew a sheaf of notes, girlishly embellished with pink highlighter pen.

Dacre snorted. My hand was shaking.

'I wanted to ask you about violence . . . in your work.'

'And will you?'

'Sorry?'

'Will you ask me? Do you think?'

At that moment the cat suddenly jumped onto my lap, swishing its large tail in my face before settling itself to distribute white hairs across my best black woollen skirt.

'I was wondering where the violence comes from? Is it an attempt to force the viewer to respond or (I was breathless, because I was reading from my notes) is it portraying the ruthless dystopia of modern life?'

He looked interested. Then I realised that he was observing the cat, which had settled down and was using my left hand rather as a cow might use a fence, to rub its head against.

'There is violence. Yes.' His voice was gentle. 'But there is violence in everything. A rose is very violent, in its way. Is it not?'

A loud vibration emanated from the cat like a faulty fridge. I tried not to sneeze. Its heavy raised haunches partially obscured my notes.

'Do you have a philosophy?'

'No.'

He was still standing, still smoking. Pale blue linen jacket; open white shirt; jeans. Very straight for 80, but smoke had leathered the bags under his eyes and his shaving was uneven. He had hairs in his ears.

He might have been laughing at me; it was hard to tell. He was studiously polite.

'In a *Times* interview you quote Paul Valéry: "modern artists want the grin without the cat . . . the sensation of life without the boredom of conveyance." Does that mean that, for you, the effect of the work is the real art?'

'Did I say that?'

'Why do you destroy the greater number of your works? From perfectionism, or to increase the value of those you choose to keep?'

He thought. He shrugged.

There was much more in this vein. Each question met with quiet consideration and gnomic rebuff.

Meanwhile, Sir had cramponed his claws into my tights and was rhythmically kneading my knees. It was agony. I tried to ignore him. Dacre had turned to the kitchen counter and was fishing in a drawer. I went on.

'In the piece, WELCOME, you present a doormat that is woven from your dead mother's hair. Is that a comment on how women of that generation were oppressed, or does it express some of the anger that you felt when she left shortly after you were . . .'

The cat bit me, springing onto the floor with a graceful bound. It was so sudden that it took me a moment to understand the origin of the twin holes on the inside of my wrist, which were only now reddening and beginning to bleed.

I didn't cry out. I just pulled the sleeve of my poloneck down to cover the wound.

'Why did you invite me if you aren't prepared to answer my questions?'

Dacre looked up; smiled with polite concern.

'For the same reason you came here. I was interested to see you, just. To see if my imagining of you was in any way correct.'

I didn't meet him again. Every few months I sent him a postcard, of something taxidermic. A mummified crocodile in the British Museum. Two Victorian frogs in a glass case, dressed as gentlemen and duelling with miniature épées. It was a kind of shared joke. I got three back, which I have framed and now keep above my bed. I wrote that I was working on him. He replied that various doctors were doing the same.

I stayed on in Cambridge, sliding noiselessly from a BA into a PhD. Who would be my topic but Dacre? There was the advantage that competition in the field was narrow. He had been judicially acquitted; but academic distaste hovered around his achievement. Despite being lionized in Venice and legionised in Paris, he did not receive a knighthood. The level of alcohol in Louise Bourden's blood pointed to an accident. But there was the scratch on Dacre's face and the neighbour who claimed that she had heard the sounds of a fight and someone screaming 'No!' (Dacre said in court it was him) before the body hit the street, detonating a dirge of car alarms across the docklands.

By my final year, I was preparing to write up my doctorate and he was in a hospice, with failing kidneys. His death coincided with the Queen's (an irony that would have delighted him), so the obits were last page, subdued, implying that his sculpture had been a phase in art that was passé long before he died. I disagreed. It was melancholy to think of the end of Dacre's output and of our taxidermic correspondence. But in the grate of my sadness was an ember of excitement. A PhD thesis must have a strong hook if it is to be published. Dacre's death was just the hook I needed.

When the letter arrived, I was disbelieving. I'd thought I was merely a casual acquaintance in his last days. Not so, apparently. Old and contrary and friendless, he had left his money to his cleaner. To me, he had left a different kind of legacy. I was permitted to live in his Scottish studio rent-free while completing my work on him, on condition that I cared for his ageing cat.

'Are there other conditions?' asked Joan.

'No. Well, not difficult ones. No access to outhouse. No naked flames. Fair enough.'

'It sounds really remote.'

'There's a ferry every half hour. In summer.'

'How long will you go for?'

'Six months. However long it takes to write up.'

'You'll go mad.'

'Rent free,' I repeated. 'I'll be immersed in his world. No distractions. Don't you see, it's perfect?'

It took me three days to get there. In the same time, I could have travelled to Australia. First a train to Peterborough, then five hours to Edinburgh where I stayed overnight. Then to Glasgow and a six hour train journey over moors and through mountains to Oban. Then, the next day, a ferry to Mull, a long taxi ride, and another ferry to what I joked with Joan was Three Mile Island. Iona: a three-mile-long scurf of thin turf, rock and sand. I heaved my rucksack off the boat in September sunshine, the straps harrowing my shoulders, amongst a crowd of 50-something tourists in Gore-Tex. I had brought so many books and files with me that my wheeled suitcase toppled over every few yards like an embarrassing drunk.

The studio was a wind-worn 1960s box of glass and wood set apart from the scatter of other buildings on the north-west side of the island. The wheels of the suitcase clattered. Otherwise, just the 'WHY, why, why?' of gulls, the repeated hush of the sea. The door stuck. I had to force it open with my shoulder.

Mess and smell assaulted me. An upended roll of green carpet; tubes of epoxy; planks; bottles of turps, a Newton's cradle on which dust lay thick; a whetstone. Musty cigarette smoke clung about the orange curtains, mingling with the ammonia of ageing human and cat. Just one large room with a green velvet sofa and a big industrial metal desk, where Dacre had eaten, worked on his computer, and made art. To the rear, shelves of materials, a bird's skull and feathers from the beach. To the side: a spartan kitchen and a draughty bathroom. Up some steep open wooden stairs was a narrow gallery where the bed was. I lay down, exhausted, hot sweat turning chill, feeling the pleasant weightlessness of a body newly unburdened. I was floating in travellers' limbo, catching up with my own blood as it coursed northward to my brain, when something heavy landed on my chest.

'Fuck,' I said.

His nose was inches from my nose. He treadmilled my breasts: his big white whiskery face and intense eyes shoved into my own. A drop of his saliva fell on my cheek. Disgusted, I sat up sharply, forcing him to jump to the floor. He stalked to the wardrobe, then sat and stared at me. His eyes were pale green seaglass with thin black ellipses of pupil.

'Hello, Sir,' I said. 'Poor thing. You must be hungry.'

In Fionnphort I had bought a pint of milk, tea bags, and Whiskas. I nearly tripped over Sir as he dove for the metal ashtray I had grabbed as the nearest thing to a cat bowl. He ate in stealthy snatches, gulping loudly. Then he gave me a dirty look, went to the door, delicately finessed it open with his paw, and disappeared. It was seven o'clock and still sunny. Light struck the sea like inspiration, moving rapidly as cloud-thoughts formed and altered and regrouped.

Over builder's tea, I took stock. I don't know what I had expected, but it wasn't this. The wardrobe still had smoky jackets and shirts hanging in it; the drawers were stiff with stuff. There were faded paperbacks face-down like corpses in the bathroom, dead wasps and shelves with whisky bottles, a few fingers still intact. Whatever it was that made Dacre who he was, was here, if I could only understand it properly. I had the keys to the keys. My skin prickled with excitement, tempered with unease. As desert dwellers love water I love having my own room clean and clear. Here the smell of Dacre was already seeping into my pores, my sweater picking up cat hairs.

It was vital to be professional, to impose discipline on the space, the cat, the material. I took pictures: over 100, of every angle and surface. Then I cleaned the bathroom and draped my neatly folded towels on the rack. Like a new girlfriend moving into her lover's apartment, ('something I have never done,' I thought bitterly) and then noted how inappropriate that comparison was. I unpacked my notes and made space for them on the desk, upended some fish boxes that Dacre had piled in a corner and improvised a bookcase for my academic books: *Art and Transgression*; *Surrealism and the Path to Modernity*; *The Chic of Shock*. This was my workspace now. I switched on Dacre's computer – but all I got was a grey screen that reminded me of cigarette smoke, a white box hovering in the middle of it like the very symbol of irrecoverable absence. I thought of Dacre's self-designed memorial. It was a stone near Greenwich docks, down which saltwater flowed, gradually erasing the legend 'exsculpo exculpat': 'I sculpt, it exonerates me'. I tried typing exsculpo exculpat; the box didn't move. The screen reflected my pinched face back at me. I switched it off.

Sir woke me at 6 a.m., with an angry 'MAO', demanding to be fed. Chairman Mao, I thought. Full of nervous energy, I took a brisk stroll around the island. Tussocky, muted landscape. Piles of seaweed on the beach like green rubber tagliatelle. A couple of hotels, a few shops. It wasn't Cambridge, but I would survive here. When the shops opened I bought spaghetti and a fresh mackerel. Soon, I vowed, I would have him eating out of my hand.

I settled down to write. My thesis was called *Violent Designs: The Making of Darius Dacre*. The first chapter, 'Twist', was about Dacre's first exhibition in 1967. Provocatively, he'd called it 'Old Rope'. My difficulty was that none of the work survived, even in photographs. 'Complex hanging knots, for which there is no conceivable artistic purpose or excuse.' John Canaday had written in the *New Review*. Could one argue that the hanging knots were overblown representations of male genitals; that Dacre was literally showing his youthful *cojones*? Too reductive? 'Dacre's brilliance lay . . . '

I heard, rather than saw, the cat return. He dragged the fish onto the sofa and proceeded to eat it, eye first. When he was done, he washed. My throat constricted. He stepped over to the desk, tail swishing, and sniffed my knuckles, lapped the salt off them with tiny, precise licks. I stroked him very gingerly from head to rump, feeling the crackle of static from his luxuriant fur. Fine white dander drifted in the air. I sneezed. He leaped up, landing in my lap like a two-volume encyclopaedia, then attempting to jump onto the keyboard: 'xt^p'

'We're going to get along. You are a very fine animal. Yes you are.'

A purr arose from his belly as he studied my writing or, perhaps, the light reflecting off my screen.

Chapter two was called 'Shock'. It was the one that was nearest to completion, except that my supervisor, whom I saw more often on television than in reality, had written in red pen in the margin 'Yes. But what is *new* about your account?' After his first exhibition, Dacre had moved to Paris and lived off canapés. The society hostess Margot Winstanley reported that when bored at a dinner, he stood up and peed with devastating accuracy into the floral centrepiece. He began making pieces that took this spirit of performed outrage into the art gallery. 'Missing You' (1972) was a knife-throwing machine that was exhibited in Berlin but destroyed by customs officials in New York. It was around this time that Dacre began to embrace the idea that the artwork should if possible involve its own destruction. 'Butcher's' (1979) resembled a Dutch still life, with a bunch of pheasants hung by the heels; hares; a stag on a hook. The meat rotted over the month it was in the Barbican: the sealed vitrine becoming increasingly green. 'In 1980 Dacre declared that he did not want to be collected, publicly or privately,' I wrote. 'His best-known remark "Art dies in galleries – it loses its smell" conveys his passion for showing not metaphorically but actually the process of death and dissolution by creating sculpture that decomposes itself. Among these tableaux mortes is 'Butcher's' – a title that refers self-referentially to the process of looking and the aggression it can embody or displace.'

Sir lay on the sofa, unblinking. There was something stoned about his expression. As if I were purely abstract, like a painting on his wall.

That night, I dreamed about a party to which I wasn't invited. The hostess, seeing me, gave a scream so piercing that I was in a rictus of horrified attention – when suddenly I came awake and realised that the shriek had persisted. It was on the roof: a low gurgling moan rising to a bloodcurdling wail. The Cat. Mating? Fighting? 3.23 a.m.; pitch dark. I pulled on my jumper, my trousers without underwear, stormed downstairs and threw open the kitchen door. Silence. Just cold, rain, and sea.

I read until dawn – my feet freezing, my mind full of the thoughts of failure that breed in darkness – then slept heavily until eleven. When I staggered downstairs feeling as if I had glue in my eyes, there was another unfamiliar noise, a kind of chugging, as of water stuck in a blocked pipe. I entered the kitchen just as the cat threw up on the tiles.

Writing that day was impossible. My head throbbed as if I had a hangover. I decided to catalogue the studio methodically, going through each drawer and cupboard. Opening the first drawer of Dacre's steel desk felt like putting my hand into a trap. I pulled out pens, centimes, batteries, endless books of matches. There were bank statements, receipts, nameless metal components. What was I looking for? Words. I wanted a notebook, a diary, letters. Scholars, like neglected wives, are always looking for words as ammunition to fire back at their subject. Dacre was giving me nothing. I tried the cupboards, under the bed. After endless prying, I excavated a postcard of a dog turd in a hotdog bun (Jake and Dinos Chapman?) on the reverse of which was scribbled in Dacre's distinctive small caps, REMEMBER: THIS IS SHIT.

It is an odd sound, laughing on your own in an empty house; my voice sounded high and girlish in my own ears. I inventoried the studio shelves: tools, pieces of driftwood, a few thrillers. I itemised the kitchen. The conclusion of my extensive research was . . . Dacre didn't cook. Surely there must be a smoking gun amongst all this mess? Alas, the only thing smoking was me. Tired and irritable, I had gone to the shop and got some tobacco and Rizlas. Roll-ups were a bad schoolgirl habit I had kicked at Cambridge; now, however, the need for something other than cleaning and typing to occupy my twitching fingers was overwhelming. Obeying the house rule, I stood out on the stoop to smoke, facing away from the sharp sea wind, fine hair twisting into knots that no hairbrush would resolve.

As I sat at the desk later that evening, I doodled faces on my thesis plan. It had all seemed so straightforward on the aerial map: I would argue that Dacre was a master of the art of visual theatre, like Beckett. Then I would talk about the shock installations as a reaction to 1980s capitalism, its naked aggression. Chapter 3, 'Silence', would handle the 1990s, after the grotesque publicity of the trial and his eventual acquittal. Chapter 4, 'Movement', was to be about Dacre's final phase of making: his obsession with pendulums, automata, laser beams, sculptures that were made of chased light. But now I was in the thicket of argument, the landscape was hostile and I couldn't see any path through. Because, in the end, there was only one question about Darius Dacre: did he murder his wife?

A week passed, then two, then three. It was as if my laptop had developed a force field. Every time I sat down to write, I ricocheted away from the table. I went to fetch a glass of water or a roll-up and when I got to the kitchen, there was the cat – sidling into the open fridge or leaping up to the counter or wanting in as I was going out: elusive as a thought that haunts the back of your mind but can't be pinned down. I began to play with him, as if he were not the distraction but the object of my study. I would take a shoelace and drag it very gently along the floor at the periphery of his vision. The cat ignored me. I whipped the shoelace faster and faster. The cat watched lazily. At last, fixing the lace in his sights, he sprang up and bit my wrist, hard. Then he carried away the lace and killed it in a corner. At night, when I undressed, he watched me intently. Self-consciously slipping off my bra, I tugged on my French grey pyjamas facing the wall. But after I was in bed, there was no way I could prevent him from leaping up to stand over me, drooling and paddling. Sometimes I woke with a start, imagining that he was lying over my face, his thick white fur stifling my nose and mouth.

Nonetheless, I stayed. I didn't want to let anybody know that I was failing. When I walked around the island, it seemed as if people instinctively drew back to give me room; not unkindly, but as if I were a wave rather than a person. In that state between idling and drowning, a strange thought drifted towards me. One afternoon, I switched on Dacre's computer yet again and got the grey smoky screen and the white box. I stared at it for hours, listening to the rain titter against the glass, vaguely afraid of – what? Then I typed: THIS IS SHIT. There was a pause. The screen changed to blue. I was in.

I opened folder after folder. I gaped. Here were photographs of things that didn't exist. Sculptures among the many he destroyed that were supposed to survive only in recollection. 'Old Rope'. Not the teasing rope-pricks I had imagined at all, snaking their way into art history like Dali's moustache. These bunched clotted torsos of hemp were unmistakeably hanged figures, as you would see them after weeks rotting on a gallows. Here the flung transfixion of arms in agony. There a plunging neck and head. Abstracted only just enough to make the violence general. My mouth went dry.

I missed dinner. It got dark. I was still greedily opening image after image. Photos of Lou Bourden in a boat: a slight figure with a Jean Shrimpton fringe, screwing her eyes against the sun's dazzle. In another photo she was in a 1970s sweater and slacks with a cigarette in one hand and a paintbrush in the other, partially obscuring one of her own paintings, which was an odd premonition of Dacre's 'Interior Design' (1991) – a room wallpapered with images of cancer cells. She was really quite good, I thought. Another polaroid showed her leaning in to Dacre's rancorously intelligent scowl: on the ground their shadows merged into a single form, a chimera. The next photograph was of her apparently working on an inverted hunt modelled in plastic, the riders and hounds flayed and tied to the saddles of horses as stags are after a kill. This was, I decided, Dacre's 'Strange Game' (1989), in a much earlier phase of its imaginative life. In the third image, she was bending over a glass case that contained a single feather, kept aloft by a hairdryer. It was Dacre's 'F-aether' (1991), except that it wasn't. The sign on the case read **'Home Bird: L J. Bourden'**.

The truth dropped into my head like a bomb through a letterbox: a package that was both wholly unexpected and whose contents I somehow already knew. She wasn't his muse. She was the mainframe, the medulla . . . Something made me jump up from the chair where I had been hunched for several hours. It was raining hard, spattering on the glass as if someone periodically was throwing buckets of water against the windows. I switched on the light. I couldn't see the cat, but I sensed that he was in the studio.

'Sir?'

My brain had speeded up so much it was almost painful. I was excited and brilliant and outraged and mortified and cheated and finally just unbearably sad. My thesis had fallen to pieces. Works I had previously loved now struck me as toxic. Dacre's habit of destroying his work and eschewing its sale also appeared in a new light. He wasn't rejecting commerce, he was eliminating evidence. I would have to start over. It would take time. The thought of all my wasted months of writing that would have to be deleted, crushed the air out of my lungs. But maybe I could profit from being the first to know. I would have to work quickly. I began typing in a scathing tone, the tone of a wronged lover:

'Dacre's neediness is everywhere in his work. His own presence is that of a voyeur, a parasite.'

The next day I woke, felt for my glasses, and missed them on the nightstand. The cat must have knocked them off during the night. I stood up, took a couple of steps and felt something cold and wet under my right foot. Gross. GROSS. I took another step, more wetness. Stickiness. Something really disgusting that I couldn't quite make out. I started shivering uncontrollably. I had to crawl on my hands and knees and sweep-search the filthy floor. When my hand eventually found the arm of my glasses and I got them on, I saw what I had stepped in: a smear of entrails, and the tiny terrified mouse's head still goggling in disbelief. With blood on my glasses I hobbled down the open stairs and into the bathroom where I cowered under a hot shower for as long as the water stayed hot.

'Out,' I screamed when I saw the cat on the kitchen counter. 'Fuck off. FUCK OFF.' He slunk along the side of the studio, towards the outhouse. I locked the door; smoked a roll-up, defiantly, in the kitchen. It wasn't as if *Dacre* had smoked outside.

I returned to his computer, partly to reassure myself that the discoveries of the day before were still there. I wanted to tell my supervisor what I'd found, but my cellphone got no reception here. Besides, it was good to be the only one to know just for a day or two. I needed to think about it quietly, about what it meant. I started typing.

Rain drummed hypnotically on the wooden studio roof. I wrote on, and I could feel myself becoming fluent and speedy, though I was less certain about whether I was writing well or not. It was like driving drunk. The hours flew by. Usually, I put food out for the cat morning and afternoon, but that day I didn't, nor the next. I locked him out; I starved him out. I couldn't endure his wet fur on the bed, the little nooses of thread that his claws pulled out of my tights, my skirts. It was only when I forced him out of my mind that I realised how much space he had come to occupy, how his weight had been pushing me against an invisible wall. On the third day, I reluctantly opened the door, but no cat appeared. The next morning he was still not there.

The wind got up, blowing icy draughts through the kitchen and the bathroom, with its cratered lino and bath the colour of old teeth. I was nursing a mug of coffee, wearing both jumpers I owned and a double layer of socks and I was still cold. A tapeworm of guilt crawled in my stomach. At four-thirty it was already dusk. I stepped out of the studio and immediately was pushed sideways by a fierce gust, like the slipstream of a lorry speeding across the island. The noise I thought I had heard was louder now. A sort of mewling cry, over and over again. With the swoop and rush of storm in my ears it was hard to be sure, but it seemed to be coming from the outhouse. I allowed the wind to buffet me along the path toward it. Definitely the sound was stronger here. I imagined that the cat had found a way in. I should check, at least, to see if he was sick, or stuck.

To my surprise, the door was unlocked. The wind slammed it shut behind me. I felt in vain for a light switch on the right-hand wall. The noise was quite strong now.

'Sir?' I said.

Suddenly a light came on and I found myself in a kind of home cinema with a screen at one end and a projector hanging from the roof. No visible cat. When I stepped forward, however, the projector switched itself on and a single word came up on the screen in fat pink psychedelic letters: TRIP.

Another step. Complete darkness. Then there was a picture of a mouth open in terror.

My heart was thumping wildly; my own face seemed to belong to a puppet over whose expression I had no control. I took another step toward the screen.

Complete darkness again. Then, with a horrible sudden slap, a bird striking a pane of glass. Blood smeared as if on the camera lens itself.

'It's like "Shock and Augury", I thought. When you move, it trips a motion sensor, so you get the next image.'

Shaking, I took a step backwards. The screen changed again.

It was a huge clock. The tock, tock echoed through my own blood. It whirred and chimed and the door swung open to show a woman's naked body hanging by a coil of wire, a human pendulum, swinging from side to side with a creak that was also like the tread of someone coming up stairs.

I took one more step back. My hand was on the door. I knew what the last frame was before I saw it. 'No!' the woman's voice came through the loudspeakers. 'Help me. Oh god. NO . . . '

I stumbled back to the studio and stood trembling in the kitchen, looking for a phone. Of course there wasn't one. My knees buckled. It took me five goes to light a cigarette.

Eventually, I got up enough courage to pack my books, my files, my computer. I was as shaky as an old lady, cigarette dripping ash, looking two or three times for my toothbrush before realising it was in my hand. All I needed were my clothes. I sat on the bed, talking to myself for comfort, stuffing things at random into the rucksack, feeling how the dead smell of this place had become my smell, how I needed to scrub it out of my hair, my pyjamas, even my shoes. I stood, braced my back, hoisted the rucksack, and was three steps down the open stair when I trod on a body, a squirm of fur that broke my step with a yowl, my foot seeking the next tread in vain I swayed and grabbed at the non-existent handrail and fell in mind before I in body tripped and flailing plunged to the hard wooden floor striking my head on a whetstone of pain.

I woke choking in smoke so thick and acrid it was like a wire fist pressed down your throat. I tried to crawl. One arm didn't work at all, was floppy. That thing still on my back. I wriggled free of the rucksack as laboriously as an overturned beetle trying to right itself. No use trying to stand. Using my good arm, I shielded my face against the heat; coughing, choking, bum-shuffled toward what I prayed was the kitchen. I would not be his last work. I would not be his last work. I would not be his last work.

When they found me, I was face down on the stone path, with burns to my back and legs so bad that much of my skin is no longer my own or has changed its geography. I am a foreigner in my own land. The studio burned at such high heat that only mangled shapes later told of a saucepan, bath, a keyboard welded to a metal desk. Some wag, visiting, scratched 'You are Not a Winner' on a charred beam. You can still see the tarry square on the ground, as if a picture has been moved and the shadow of its frame remains. Dacre's work, given the oxygen of renewed controversy, is once more fashionable; others have mined an Estate I am now forbidden to touch, even should I want to comment, as an 'independent scholar' (currently seeking a position) on a topic where my opinions are notorious for their idiosyncracy. They call me a fantasist: a groupie who turned loopy; a squatter and an arsonist (though I was acquitted of that, the evidence being lacking and my own pain evident). I have told my tale many times without being believed. For nothing now remains of Dacre's final installation except my story. And as for the cat: nobody saw him but me.

NORMAN MacCAIG

Celtic Cross

The implicated generations made
This symbol of their lives, a stone made light
By what is carved on it.
                    The plaiting masks,
But not with involutions of a shade,
What a stone says and what a stone cross asks.

Something that is not mirrored by nor trapped
In webs of water or bag-nets of cloud;
The tangled mesh of weed
                    lets it go by.
Only men's minds could ever have unmapped
Into abstraction such a territory.

No green bay going yellow over sand
Is written on by winds to tell a tale
Of death-dishevelled gull
                    or heron, stiff
As a cruel clerk with gaunt writs in his hand
– Or even of light, that makes its depths a cliff.

Singing responses order otherwise.
The tangled generations ravelled out
In links of song whose sweet
                    strong choruses
Are these stone involutions to the eyes
Given to the ear in abstract vocables.

The stone remains, and the cross, to let us know
Their unjust, hard demands, as symbols do.
But on them twine and grow

beneath the dove

Serpents of wisdom whose cool statements show
Such understanding that it seems like love.

ADOMNÁN

Columba's Deeds

Like body armour
His monk's cowl guarded us.

He killed a wild boar
With his word.

One pinch of his fingers
Stopped chronic nosebleeds.

He knew where
To catch the best salmon.

He blessed small cows
So the herd would increase.

He prayed in the sea up to his knees
Till robber and blasphemer were drowned.

ADOMNÁN

Cronan the Poet

In County Roscommon, Connacht,
Where the River Boyle enters Lough Key
An Irish poet showed up for some *craic*.
After he'd gone, someone asked, 'Columba,
All the while Cronan the Poet was here
Why didn't you tap him for a song?'
'Ach, man, who could request a song
From a bard with just minutes to live?'
Next, from the farther bank of the Boyle
A shout comes: 'You know that poet, Cronan,
Who left half an hour ago, fit as a fiddle?
Right now he's been battered to death.'

ADOMNÁN

Neman

Scolded by Columba, Neman the thief
Laughed, and went on a spree.
'Neman, in the name of God, I tell you
Your enemies will catch you in a whore's bed
And send you to the devils in hell.'
Years later, near the mountain, Neman was nabbed
In flagrante delicto – beheaded.

ADOMNÁN

Day

When night
Had gone
The wind dropped
So we set out
From Saine
At first light
And soon
A breeze whipped
Our sails
As we sped
Home
To that longed-for
Iona harbour,
Dropping anchor
At the hour
Of Terce,
Then washing feet
And hands,
Going to pray
To meet
Our brethren
For mass
At the hour
Of Sext.
It was the feast
Of St Columba
And St Baithéne
And that first light
And that voyaging
And that landing
And that washing
And that praying
And the writing of this text
Were just one day.

ADOMNÁN

Raiders

Columba said, 'Where do you live?'

'I live near the shore at Cruach Rannoch.'

'Cruach Rannoch now is under attack.'

'Attack!' That word made the man weep,
Frightened for his wife and children.

'Your wife and children
Have managed to escape,
Though raiders have taken all your herd
And every stick of furniture.'

Every stick of furniture was gone.
So was the herd.
All this he found out from his wife and children
Just as Columba said.

JAMES BOSWELL

Tuesday 19 October 1773

The day was charming for a voyage to Icolmkill. When I went out, I met Miss Maclean, who said, 'I have been employed for you this morning. I have been scrambling among the rocks to get petrifications for you.'

She gave me a few, but none of them were curious. I once more paid my devotions to GOD in the old chapel.

After breakfast we took leave of the young ladies, and of our excellent companion Coll, to whom we had been so much obliged. He had now put us under the care of his chief, and was to hasten back to Skye. There was a kindly regret at parting from him which was both proper and pleasing. He had been a kind of banker to me, in supplying me with silver. There remained six-and-sixpence due by me to him on settling our accounts today. He desired that I should purchase with it a cap to Joseph's young son. A small circumstance shows benevolence. He and Joseph had been often companions.

Sir Allan had a good boat with four stout rowers. One of them, Lauchlan Dow ______, was a remarkably strong and clever fellow, either at sea or at land. All of them, and he in particular, took a great liking for me before we parted, as Sir Allan told me by interpretation. We coasted along Mull till we reached Gribon, where is what is called Mackinnon's Cave, an *antrum immane* indeed, to which the one at Ullinish is nothing. It is in a rock of a great highth just upon the sea. Upon the left of its entrance there is a cascade, almost perpendicular from top to bottom of the rock, of no great size, but very pretty. There is a tradition that it was conducted thither artificially, to supply the inhabitants of the cave with water. Mr Johnson gave no credit to this tradition. As his faith in the Christian religion is firm upon good grounds, he is incredulous when there is no sufficient reason for belief, being in this just the reverse of modern infidels, who, however nice and scrupulous in weighing the evidences of religion, are yet often so ready to believe the most absurd and improbable tales of another nature, that Lord Hailes said that somebody should write an '*Essai sur la crédulité des incrédules.*'

The highth of this cave I cannot tell with any tolerable exactness, but it seemed to be very lofty, and to be a pretty regular arch. After advancing a little, we found it to be forty-five feet broad. Afterwards we found a passage or gallery about four or five feet broad – for we did not measure it. Then we came to a place fifteen feet broad. There we found a large stone table lying on the floor. Sir Allan said it had stood on supporters or pillars, and we saw some broken stones near it, but Mr Johnson was of opinion that machinery sufficient to raise it could not be erected in the cave; so that there was a mistake as to the pillars. Sir Allan said there were stone benches, too, around the table. I think I saw some stones which may be called such. Where the table is, the floor of the cave is a good deal elevated above the floor of the entrance, by gradual progression. The floor is sometimes of loose pebbles; sometimes of a fine dry sand; sometimes embarrassed with large stones, I suppose fragments of the rock. As we advanced, the arch of the roof became less regular, the rock filling up a considerable part of the space on the left, but so as a man could clamber up it. A yard or two beyond the table, we found another heap of fragments, beyond which I could perceive that I might go; but as we had but one candle with us, to be a proof when the air should grow bad, and to give us light, we did not choose to risk its going out. Tradition says that a piper and twelve men advanced into the cave, nobody knows how far, but never returned. At the heap to which we went, which was 485 feet from the entrance of the cave, the air was quite good, for the candle burnt freely without the least appearance of the flame's growing globular; and there was as much light from the large mouth, though distant, as that a man would not find himself quite in a dismal state, and would find his way out tolerably well. Mr Johnson said this was the greatest natural curiosity he had ever seen.

We saw the island of Staffa, at no very great distance, but could not land upon it, the surge was so high on its rocky coast. We sailed close to a point called Ardtun, on the Mull coast, where we saw a miniature specimen of the Giant's Causeway, and some of the same kind of natural pilasters on rock as are described to be at Staffa. Sir Allan said people who had seen both were of opinion that the appearances at Ardtun were better than those at Staffa; prettier or finer, he said. If so, there must have been wondrous puffing about Staffa. He said if we had seen it, we should have had a controversy.

Sir Allan, anxious for the honour of Mull, was always talking of *woods* that he said were upon the hills of that island, which appeared at a distance as we sailed along. Said Mr Johnson, 'I saw at Tobermory what they called a wood, which I unluckily took for *heath*. If you show me what I shall take for *furze*, it will be something.'

Our rowers sung Erse songs, or rather howls. Sir Allan said the Indians in America sung in the same manner when rowing. We passed by the mouth of a large basin, arm of the sea, or loch, called Loch Scridain, upon the shore of which Mr Neil MacLeod, minister of Kilfinichen, lives. I had a letter to him from Kenneth Macaulay; and he was the best man we could get to show us Icolmkill with knowledge. But we were not sure of finding him at home, and thought it at any rate imprudent to go out of our way much, as we might lose a good day, which was very valuable. I however insisted that we should land upon the shore of Loch ________, which we came to a little after, but which, not being very far back into the country, cost us but a little deviation. My reason for insisting to land was to get some whisky or rum for our boatmen. The fellows were rather for pushing straight for Iona. But I could not be easy unless they had a *scalck*. Besides, the nearest public house was kept by Lauchlan Maclean, lately servant to Sir Allan; and we proposed to take him with us both as an additional rower and as quartermaster at Icolmkill, for which he was well fitted, having been with Sir Allan not only in the best parts of Scotland, but in many parts of England.

Sir Allan, like all other officers, who, though by their profession obliged to endure fatigues and inconveniences, are peculiarly luxurious, expatiated in prospect on the expertness with which Lauchlan would get on a good fire in a snug barn, and get us clean straw for beds, and dress us, along with Joseph, an Austrian campaigner, a tolerable supper. I take it the suffering, or at least the contemplating of hardships, to which officers are accustomed (for from Sir Allan's account even of the American expeditions, it appeared that though the poor common soldiers are often wretchedly off, the officers suffer little, having their commodious camp equipage, and their chocolate, and other comforts carried along in little room, and prepared by their men, who are most subservient beings), makes them fonder of all indulgences.

We went ashore upon a little rising ground, which is an island at high water. We sat down upon a seat of rock, and took a repast of cold mutton, bread and cheese and apples, and punch. Lauchlan Dow in the mean time ran to Lauchlan Maclean's house. When he returned with

Lauchlan Maclean, we had the disappointment of finding that no spirits of any kind were to be found. A burial some days before had exhausted them.

Mr Campbell __________, a tacksman of the Duke of Argyll's, lived not far off. Sir Allan sent the two Lauchlans thither, begging the loan of two bottles of rum. We got them, with a message that Mr Campbell had expected us to dinner, having heard that we were to pass; that he was sorry he had not then seen us, and hoped we would be with him next day. We refreshed our crew.

The weather grew coldish. I proposed an expedient to keep our feet warm, which was to strew the boat plentifully with heath, the chief production of the island where we dined. Accordingly I fell to work and pulled, as did some of our men, and Mr Johnson pulled very assiduously. Sir Allan, who had been used to command men, and had no doubt superintended soldiers making roads or throwing up ramparts or doing some other kind of work, never stopped, but stood by *grieving* us (the Scottish expressive term for overseeing as a taskmaster, an overseer being called a *grieve*; as my lord Loudoun tells, a countryman said to him, Mr Dun our minister was *grieving* my father, who was busy gathering stones to mend a road).

We made ourselves very comfortable with the heath. The wind was now against us, but we had very little of it. We coasted along Mull, which was on our left. On our right was the Atlantic, with Staffa and other islands in it for some part of the way. Then we came to a large black rock in the sea; then to Nun's Island, which it is said belonged to the nuns of Icolmkill, and that from it the stone for the buildings of Icolmkill was taken; as the rocks still there are of the same kind of stone, and there is none such in Icolmkill.

It became very dusky, or rather dark, about seven; for our voyage, by going along the turnings of the coast, would be, Sir Allan said, forty miles from Inchkenneth to Iona; so that we were benighted. Mr Johnson said, as we were going up the narrow Sound between Mull and Nun's Island, with solemn-like rocks on each side of us, and the waves rising and falling, and our boat proceeding with a dancing motion, 'This is roving among the Hebrides, or nothing is.'

A man has a pleasure in applying things to words, and comparing the reality with the picture of fancy. We had long talked of 'roving among the Hebrides'. It was curious to repeat the words previously used, and which had impressed our imaginations by frequent use; and then to feel how the immediate impression from actually roving differed from the one in fancy, or agreed with it. It will be curious too, to perceive how the impression made by reading this my Journal some years after our roving will affect the mind, when compared with the recollection of what was felt at the time. Mr Johnson said I should read my Journal about every three years. Joseph made a very good observation. 'Your journey,' said he, 'will always be more agreeable to you.'

I often do not observe chronology, for fear of losing a thing by waiting till I can put it in its exact place. Joseph said this one night as I was going to bed, and was resuming to him with much complacency some of our past scenes on this expedition. He meant what I have often experienced: that scenes through which a man has gone improve by lying in the memory. They grow mellow. It is said, '*Acti labores sunt jucundi.*' This may be owing to comparing them with present ease. But I also think that even harsh scenes acquire a softness by length of time; and many scenes are like very loud sounds, which do not please till you are at a distance from them, or at least do not please so much; or like strong coarse pictures, which must be viewed at a distance. And I don't know how it is, but even pleasing scenes improve by time, and seem more exquisite in recollection than when they were present, if they have not faded to dimness in the memory. Perhaps there is so much evil in every human enjoyment when present, so much dross mixed with it, that it requires to be refined by time; and yet I do not see why time should not melt away the good and the evil in equal proportions, why the shade should decay and the light remain in preservation. I must hear Mr Johnson upon this subject.

The boat had so much motion tonight that I had a renewal of the uneasiness of fear at sea; and I wondered how I could so soon totally forget what I had endured when driven to Coll. People accustomed to sail give every little direction with so loud a tone that a fresh-water man is alarmed. Sir William Temple's observation on the boisterous manners of seamen, from their being used to contend with a boisterous element, will apply in some degree to all 'who go down into the sea' – at least while they are upon it. Coll talks loud at sea, and Sir Allan talks loud at sea. I asked if we should not be quieter when we were in the Sound between Mull and Icolmkill. Sir Allan said no. We should have a rougher sea, as we should then have a stronger current against us, and have the Atlantic quite open from each end of the Sound. I yielded so much to fear as to ask if it would not be better that we should go ashore for that night on Mull, and cross the Sound in the morning with daylight. Sir Allan was for going on. Mr Johnson said, 'I suppose Sir Allan, who knows, thinks there is no danger.'

'No, sir,' said Sir Allan.

Mr Johnson was satisfied. I therefore had nothing to say, but kept myself calm. I am so much a disciple of Dr Ogden's that I venture to pray even upon small occasions if I feel myself much concerned. Perhaps when a man is much concerned, the occasions ought not to be called small. I put up a petition to GOD to make the waves more still. I know not if I ought to draw a conclusion from what happened; but so it was, that after we had turned the point of Nun's Island and got into the Sound of Icolmkill, the tide was for us, and we went along with perfect smoothness, which made me feel a most pleasing tranquillity.

In a little, I saw a light shining in the village at Icolmkill. All the inhabitants of the island, except perhaps a few shepherds or rather cowherds, live close to where the ancient buildings stood. I then saw the tower of the cathedral just discernible in the air. As we were landing, I said to Mr Johnson, 'Well, I am glad we are now at last at this venerable place, which I have so long thought that you and I should visit. I could have gone and seen it by myself. But you would not have been with me; and the great thing is to bring objects together.'

'It is so,' said he, with a more than ordinary kind complacency. Indeed, the seeing of Mr Samuel Johnson at Icolmkill was what I had often imagined as a very venerable scene. A landscape or view of any kind is defective, in my opinion, without some human figures to give it animation. What an addition it was to Icolmkill to have the Rambler upon the spot! After we landed, I shook hands with him cordially.

Upon hearing that Sir Allan Maclean was arrived, which was announced by his late servant Lauchlan whom we dispatched into the village, which is very near to the shore, the inhabitants – who still consider themselves as the people of Maclean, though the Duke of Argyll has at present possession of the ancient estate – ran eagerly to him. We went first to the house of ________ Macdonald, the most substantial man among them. Sir Allan called him the Provost. He had a tolerable hut with higher walls than common, and pretty well built with dry stone. The fire was in the middle of the room. A number of people assembled. What remained of our snuff was distributed among them. Sir Allan had a little tobacco, of which he gave several of them a little bit each. We regretted that there was not a drop of spirits upon the island, for we wished to have given them a hearty cup on occasion of a visit from Sir Allan, who had not been there for fourteen years, and in the interval had served four years in America. The people seemed to be more decently dressed than one usually finds those of their station in the isles.

Icolmkill pays £150 of rent. They sell about forty cattle and more than 150 bolls of barley; and what is remarkable, they brew a good deal of beer, which I could not find was done in any of the other isles. I was told that they imported nothing but salt and iron. Salt they might soon make. It is a very fertile island, and the people are industrious. They make their own woollen and linen webs, and indeed I suppose everything else, except any hardware for which they may have occasion. They have no shoes for their horses.

After warming ourselves in Mr Macdonald's, we were informed that our barn was ready, and we repaired to it. There was a fire in the middle of the floor, but the smoke was ceased before we went into the barn. We had cuddies and some oysters boiled in butter, that we might say we had fish and oyster sauce. Mr Johnson eat none of that dish. We had roasted potatoes, of which I think he eat one; and he drank a mug of sweet milk. The fire was then carefully removed, and good hay was strewed at one end of the barn. Mr Johnson lay down with all his clothes and his greatcoat on. Sir Allan and I took off our coats and had them laid upon our feet. But we had also a pair of clean sheets which Miss Maclean had put up, and some very good blankets from the village; so that we had a tolerably comfortable bed. Each had a portmanteau for a pillow. Mr Johnson lay next the one wall, I next the other, Sir Allan in the middle. I could not help thinking in the night how curious it was to see the chief of the Macleans, Mr Samuel Johnson, and James Boswell, Esq. lying thus. Our boatmen were lodged somewhere in the village. Joseph, Lauchlan Maclean, and Donald MacDougal, a fine smart little boy-servant to Sir Allan, lay across the barn, at a little distance from our feet. It was just an encampment. There was a good deal of wind blew through the barn, so that it was rather too cool.

WEDNESDAY 20 OCTOBER. Between seven and eight we rose and went to see the ruins. We had for our cicerone ________, who calls himself the descendant of St Columbus's cousin. It is said their family has from time immemorial had ten acres of land in Icolmkill rent-free, till it was lately taken from them by the Duke of Argyll. Sir Allan said if he recovered the island, they should be restored to their old possession. We had also a number of men following us. Our cicerone was a stupid fellow.

We first viewed the monastery of the nuns. The church has been a pretty building. Mr Johnson took a very accurate inspection of all the ruins, and will give a very enlarged account of them in the *Tour*, or whatever he shall call it, which the world will gain by this expedition, to which I have had the merit of persuading him. I shall therefore only mention such circumstances as struck me on a cursory view.

It shocked one to observe that the nuns' chapel was made a fold for cattle, and was covered a foot deep with cow-dung. They cleared it off for us at one place and showed us the gravestone of a lady abbess. It was of that bluish stone or slate which is frequent in Highland churchyards. At one end was carved the abbess with her crosier at her side, and hands folded on her breast. At another, with the heads in an opposite direction, a Virgin and babe. I think the figures at each end were entire, whole lengths. Round the stone was an inscription telling who the lady was. But I am, I find, growing minute when I write, though for the reason which I have mentioned it is unnecessary; and besides, I did not give exact attention to the nuns, as I considered that so many people had examined them: Dr Pococke, Dr Walker, Mr Banks, Mr Pennant; and when I saw Mr Johnson setting himself heartily to examine them, my mind was quiescent, and I resolved to stroll among them at my ease, take no trouble to investigate, and only receive the general impression of solemn antiquity and the particular ideas of such objects as should of themselves strike my attention.

We walked from the monastery of nuns to the great church or cathedral, as they call it, along an old pavement or causeway. They say that this was a street, and that there were good houses built on each side. Mr Johnson doubted if it was anything more than a paved road for the nuns. Some small houses now stand at various distances on each side of it. Mr Johnson said if there were houses there formerly, he did not imagine they were better. Indeed, when we saw how small a house the bishop had, it was not probable that inferior houses were better than what we now think poor cottages. Indeed, the houses here are all built of stone, as the inhabitants have without scruple made quarries of the walls of the religious buildings. The convent of monks, the great church, Oran's Chapel, and four more, are still to be discerned. Of some, more remains; of some, less. I restrain myself from saying anything in particular of them.

I was struck with a noble long cross called St Martin's Cross. But I must own that Icolmkill did not come up to my expectations, as they were high, from what I had read of it, and still more from what I had heard of it and thought of it, from my earliest years. Mr Johnson said it came up to his, because he had taken his impression from an account of it subjoined to Sacheverell's *History of the Isle of Man*, where it is said there is not much to be seen. Both he and I were disappointed when we were shown what are called the monuments of the kings of Scotland, Ireland, and Denmark, and of a king of France. There are only some gravestones flat on the earth; and we could see no inscriptions. How far short was this of marble monuments, like those in Westminster Abbey, and which I had imagined here! The gravestones of Sir Allan Maclean's family, and of that of MacGuarie, had as good an appearance as the royal ones; if they were royal, which Mr Johnson doubted.

We were shown St Columbus's well. I drank out of it. Mr Johnson had his drink from it last night. We were told that here, as at Inchkenneth, the water was conveyed in leaden pipes. All that I could observe was that at the well the water came out of a flat freestone with a springing motion, as if conducted to the orifice by a pipe. But whether there was a lead pipe or not is a moot point. We also looked at the __________ house, which has been inconsiderable.

We walked down again to our barn, where breakfast was prepared – milk, cheese, eggs, bread and butter. I slipped away and returned to the cathedral and its environs to perform some pleasing serious exercises of piety. I knelt before St Martin's Cross and said a short prayer. I went to the black stone on which the islanders of old used to swear. I had been shown a greyish piece of freestone, which they said was it; and I adopted their inaccurate information. I put my knees to this greyish freestone and said, 'I here swear with all the solemnity that any honest, honourable, and brave man ever swore upon this stone, that I will stand by Sir Allan Maclean and his family.' I had told Sir Allan that I would swear a covenant with him upon the black stone. I could not easily get him with me privately; so I went alone, and told him what I had done, which pleased him mightily; and I hope I shall have it in my power to convince him of my sincerity and steadiness.

My easiness to receive information in the isles was too great. Had not Mr Johnson been with me, I might have brought home loads of fiction or of gross mistakes. No wonder that he is in a passion at the people, as they tell him with such readiness and confidence what he finds, upon questioning them a little more, is not true. Sir Allan told me plainly that the greyish freestone which stood like a stone at the end of a grave, near the wall of the monastery, was the famous black stone. I, either not attending to the striking objection that it was not black, or thinking that the epithet 'black' might have been given to it from its solemn purposes and not from its colour (for I do not clearly remember how I believed implicitly), very gravely thought myself kneeling on that stone where so many chiefs and warriors had knelt. Sir Allan told me afterwards, of his own accord, that the black stone was quite sunk into the earth. However, I found (if Sir Allan could be credited as an antiquary a second time) that the black stone was sunk quite close to where the greyish stands; so that I really was upon the black stone while I swore to stand by Maclean.

I then went into the cathedral, which is really grand enough when one thinks of its antiquity and of the remoteness of the place; and at the end, I offered up my adorations to GOD. I again addressed a few words to Saint Columbus; and I warmed my soul with religious resolutions. I felt a kind of exultation in thinking that the solemn scenes of piety ever remain the same, though the cares and follies of life may prevent us from visiting them, or may even make us fancy that their effects were only 'as yesterday when it is past', and never again to be perceived. I hoped that ever after having been in this holy place, I should maintain an exemplary conduct. One has a strange propensity to fix upon some point from whence a better course of life may be said to begin. I read with an audible voice the fifth chapter of St James, and Dr Ogden's tenth sermon. I suppose there has not been a sermon preached in this church since the Reformation. I had a serious joy in hearing my voice, while it was filled with Ogden's admirable eloquence, resounding in the ancient cathedral of Icolmkill.

I had promised to write to my worthy old friend Grange from

Icolmkill. I therefore wrote a short solemn letter to him here. While I was writing it, Mr Johnson entered, that he might attentively view and even measure the ruins. I left him there, as I was to take a ride to the shore where Columbus landed, as it is said, and where the green pebbles called Icolmkill stones are found.

I eat some eggs for breakfast, while Sir Allan sat by me. ________ MacGinnis, whose horse I was to ride, came in. Sir Allan had been told that he had refused to send him some rum which he had; at which Sir Allan was in great indignation. 'You rascal,' said he, 'don't you know that I can hang you if I please?'

I, not adverting to the chieftain's veneration from his clan, was supposing that Sir Allan had known of some capital crime that the fellow had committed, which he could discover and so get him condemned; and I said, 'How so?'

'Why,' said Sir Allan, 'are they not all my people?'

Sensible of my inadvertency, and most willing to contribute what I could towards the continuation of feudal authority, 'Very true,' said I.

Sir Allan went on: 'Refuse to send rum to me, you rascal! Don't you know that if I ordered you to go and cut a man's throat, you are to do it?'

'Yes, an't please your honour,' said MacGinnis; 'and my own too, and hang myself too.'

The poor fellow denied that he had refused to send the rum. His making these professions was not merely a pretence in presence of Sir Allan. After he and I were out of Sir Allan's reach, he told me, 'Had he sent his dog for the rum, I would have given it. I would cut my bones for him.'

It was something very remarkable to find such an attachment to a chief, though he had then no connexion with the island, and had not been there for fourteen years. I was highly pleased with it, and so was Mr Johnson when I told him of it. Sir Allan, by way of upbraiding the fellow, said, 'I believe you are a *Campbell*.' MacGinnis is the name of a tribe of the Macleans.

I had a pleasant ride over some fertile land, while MacGinnis run before me. I saw on the right three rocks on the shore, which looked like haystacks, as the mountain at Talisker does; till upon getting to the ________ of them, they were seen not to be of a round form on all quarters. The shore is about two miles from the village. They call it *Portawherry*, from the wherry in which Columbus came, as I suppose;

though when you are shown the length of a vessel as marked on the beach by a heap of stones at each end of the space, they say, 'Here is the length of the *curach*,' using the Erse word.

I had from my earliest years been shown by my father an Icolmkill stone, and then been told of the venerable antiquities of that place. So I was curious to gather some of the stones myself. I did so, and was in a fine placid humour. I knelt on the beach and offered up a short prayer, supposing it to be actually the place where the holy man landed.

It was far in the forenoon when I got back to the village. But Sir Allan and Mr Johnson did not scold much. I put up a stone of the wall of the cathedral, to be preserved as a memento for devotion, and a stone of the convent of monks, as a talisman for chastity. The former was red; the latter, black.

It seems there is no peculiar words in English to signify the distinction between a sacred society of females and one of males. I thought a convent had been appropriated to monks, a monastery to nuns. Mr Johnson said no; for a monastery signified a segregation from the world of a society of either sex.

We had a goodly number of the people to launch our boat; and when we sailed, or rather rowed, off, they took off their bonnets and huzza'd. I should have observed a striking circumstance: that in this island which once enlightened us all there is not now one man that can read, and but two that can speak English. There is not a school in it.

There is, near the village, a hill upon which St Columbus took his seat and meditated and surveyed the sea. Icolmkill struck me as not so remote as I had imagined, there being so small a sound between it and the large island of Mull. But on the quarter where Columbus landed, it seems far enough in the western ocean; and besides, being near Mull in old times was being near a very rude country, and is so to a certain degree to this day.

ROBERT CRAWFORD

Iona

Doctor Johnson feels seasick. The small man who
As the years twitch past will slowly overtake him
Has gone off to scrabble for green stones.

Those bearded boatmen who rowed him here
Mutter in Gaelic. Johnson noticed their powder-red eyes
When they offered him oatmeal. He likes them,

Knowing all along their abbey is full of cowshit;
This place of beginnings is cold, bare, muddy.
He is starting to get tired of London.

ascribed to SAINT COLUMBA

An I Mo Chridhe

An I mo chridhe, I mo ghràidh
    An àite guth manaich bidh geum bà;
Ach mun tig an saoghal gu crìch
    Bithidh I mar a bha.

In Iona of my heart, Iona of my love,
Instead of monks' voices shall be lowing of cattle,
But ere the World come to an end
Iona shall be as it was.

Traditional translation

Isle of my heart, Isle that it loveth so,
Where chaunts the monk, only the kine shall low;
Yet before Heaven shall wax and Earth shall wane,
Iona, as she was, shall be again!

Translation from Mosse Macdonald, Iona
(Newdigate Prize Poem, Oxford, 1879)

BECCÁN MAC LUIGDECH

Tiugraind Beccáin do Cholum Cille

To-fed andes i ndáil fíadat findáil caingel;
Columb Cille – cétaib landa lethan caindel.

Caíni rissi: ríge la Día i ndeüd retho,
ríge n-úasal ó ro-cinni céim mo betho.

Brississ tóla, to-bert co crú cruü glinne
gabaiss foraib findaib coraib Columb Cille.

Caindel Connacht, caindel Alban, amrae fíadat
fichtib curach cechaing tríchait troich-chét cíabat.

Cechaing tonnaig, tresaig magain, mongaig, rónaig,
roluind, mbedcaig, mbruichrich, mbarrfind, faílid, mbrónaig.

Birt búaid n-eccnai hi cúairt Éirenn combo hardu,
amrae n-anmae, ailtir Lethae, líntair Albu.

Amrae tuire, teöir lemnacht, lethnaib coraib,
Columb Cille, comland gnátho gnóü foraib.

For muir gáirech, gairt in ruirich follnar mílib,
follnar mag ós mruigib réidib, rígaib, tírib.

Trínóit hi seilb siächt cobluth – caín con-úalath –
úasal la Día, díambo forderc fesccur mbúarach.

Búachail manach, medam cléirech, caissiu rétaib
rígdaib sondaib, sonaib tedmann, tríchtaib cétaib.

Columb Cille, caindel toídes teöir rechtae,
rith hi ráith tuir to-réd midnocht migne Ercae.

BECCÁN MAC LUIGDECH

The Last Verses of Beccán to Colum Cille

He brings northwards nearing the Godhead gathered bright chancels,
Colum Cille, cells for hundreds, haloed candle.

Cherished tidings: truth's kingdom completing my lifetime,
a lofty kingdom, for He laid out my life's pathway.

Passions he conquered, cast asunder sealed prisons;
over-powered them with pure habits, he, Colum Cille.

Connacht's candle, candle of Britain, blazing ruler,
rowed in currachs with a company of pilgrims past the sea's tresses.

Through the billowing bellicose margins, mane-like, seal-rich,
savage, skittish, seething, white-crested, welcoming, weeping.

Wisdom's upholder all over Ireland, exalted he was;
wondrous his title, tended is Brittany, Britain is sated.

Supporting column, contemplation's milk, mettlesome customs,
Colum Cille, consummate practice, brighter than baubles.

On the boisterous ocean he implored the Ruler who rules thousands,
who rules heaven above smooth moorlands, monarchs and countries.

In the Trinity's safe-keeping he sought a currach – courageous his leaving –
aloft with the Father, ever watched by him, night and morning.

Monks' shepherd, mediator of clerics, keener than any object,
than entries of monarchs, than moans of sickness, than serried champions.

Colum Cille, candle illuminating legal texts;
the hero's racecourse ran through the midnight of Erc's region.

Aiéir tinach, tingair níulu nime dogair,
dín mo anmae, dún mo uäd, hauë Conail.

Cloth co mbúadaib, ba cáin bethu. Ba bárc moine,
ba muir n-eccnai, hauë Conail, cotsid doíne.

Ba dair nduillech, ba dín anmae, ba hall nglinne,
ba grían manach, ba már coimdiu, Columb Cille.

Ba cóem la Día, díambo hadbae ail fri roluind,
ropo dorair, dú forriä imdae Coluimb.

Colainn crochsus, scuirsius for foill finda tóeba,
to-gó dánu, dénis lecca, lécciss cróeba.

Lécciss coilcthi, lécciss cotlud – caíniu bertaib –
brississ bairnea, ba forfaílid feisib tercaib.

Techtaiss liubru, léicciss la slán selba aithri,
ar seirc léigind, lécciss coicthiu, lécciss caithri.

Lécciss cairptiu, carais noä námae guë,
gríandae loingsech, lécciss la séol seimann cluë.

Columb Cille, Columb boíë, Columb biäss,
Columb bithbéo – ní hé sin in snádud ciäss.

Columb canmae, co dáil n-ecco, íarum, riäm,
ríaraib imbaiss, ima-comairc cách fo-n-gniäm.

Guidiu márguidi macc do Eithne – is ferr moínib –
m'anam día deis dochum ríchid re ndomuin doínib.

Día fo-ruigni, rígdae écndairc, hiland lessaib,
la toil n-aingel, hauë treibe Conail cressaib.

The air's make-peace, he mollifies the storm-clouds of surly heaven;
haven of my soul, safeguard of my creativity, Conal's descendant.

Declaimed for virtues, his ways gentle; galley of treasure,
tide of knowledge, Conal's offspring, everyone's counsel.

Crested oak-tree, soul's fortress, fast summit,
sun of clerics, consummate chieftain, Colum Cille.

Cherished by the deity, his dwelling was against an unforgiving cliff-face;
a challenge it was to uncover the position of the pallet of Colum.

He crucified his body, abandoned forever fair bodies;
bent on learning, he lay on flagstones, forsook padding.

He forsook bedding, forsook sleeping – sublime doings –
defeated angers, was ecstatic, had sparse mealtimes.

Manuscripts he owned, disowned completely claims of kinship:
in concern for learning he left off battles, abandoned castles.

He discarded chariots, chose currachs, challenger of error;
his exile was sun-like, by sail he released reputation's cables.

Colum Cille, Colum who was ever, Colum who will be,
eternal Colum, not he the safe conduct to cause keening.

Colum we keep singing, stand behind, before us, until death's meeting,
him we are serving through poetry's injunction which invokes him.

Him I implore, Eithne's offspring – opulence beyond riches –
on his right to bring my soul into heaven's kingdom before any other's.

He wrought for the Ruler a royal requiem within church ramparts,
at the request of angels, Conal's household's heir in vestments.

Cernach dúbart Día do adrad, aidchib, laithib,
lámaib fáenaib, findaib gartaib, gnímaib maithib.

Maith boí hi corp, Columb Cille – cléirech nemdae –
imbed fedbach, firían mbélmach, búadach tengae.

Victorious prayer: to praise the Deity, daily and nightly,
with hands in supplication, splendid alms-giving, and good actions.

Good his body, Colum Cille – cleric of heaven –
a husbandless multitude – melodious true one, tongue triumphant.

translated from the Gaelic by Meg Bateman

ADOMNÁN

The Excommunicant

St Brendan of Birr
Made sure
To kiss Columba
When Columba
Was excommunicated;
Then Brendan told
Those who recoiled
And said he should shun
Columba,
'In the skies
I have seen
A column of light
Rise
And go ahead of this man
Whom you despise
As soiled
And I have seen
God's unspoiled
Angels
Share his course
Across the moors.'

ADOMNÁN

The Loch Ness Monster

Set down this
Amongst Columba's acts
Among the Picts:
On the bank of the Ness
Where he came to bless
He saw a corpse
And heard how
A monster had mauled
The man as he swam
Across,
And how those
Who had tried to save him
Arrived too late.
'Swim,'
He called
To another man
Who then swam
Across,
And the hungry
Thing
Rose
From the muddy bed
Angry
At the swimmer.
The monster
Roared,
Churning
The water
As the watchers
Froze.
'Halt!'
Called
Columba,

'Go back!'
And though the monster
Was only a spear's length
From its prey,
Its strength
Vanished,
And it backtracked
As if hauled
Away
By ropes –
Recoiling
Through the roiling water,
Vanquished.

ADOMNÁN

The Whale Blessing

When Baithéne embarked for Tiree, Columba
Told him how last night a whale
Big as a hill had surfaced, flailing
Out of the deep, and soon again
Would rise between Iona and Tiree,
To which Baithéne countered simply,
'The whale and I belong to God.'
'Go in peace,' said the saint, 'your faith will guard you.'
So Baithéne's boat set sail for Tiree
And mid-way out across the Sound
The monster surfaced, yawning its jaws,
But Baithéne raised his steady hands,
Blessing the waves, blessing the whale,
Until the beast submerged, and was gone.

ADOMNÁN

The Trudge

On Iona, after a hot day's
Work on the harvest, the monks trudged back
Along the track that leads from the machair
On the west to the low east-coast
Field where the monastery stands.
Then each monk felt an odd excitement
Surge through his hands. Baithéne asked,
'Did you sense a sudden elation
Midway between the machair and the monastery?'
An old monk said, 'Yes. Every day
Just there I breathe a kind of fragrance
So heady it seems made up of all
The world's flowers pressed into one.
I feel a fire – not hellfire,
But quick, invigorating heat.
The pack on my back grows weightless.'
Shyly, every other harvest worker,
Though at first too tired to talk,
Confessed this too. They fell to their knees,
Unsure what to think, till, smiling, Baithéne
Explained, 'What you feel is the saint's warmth.
Columba knows how each of us labours
Long hours, trudging back late, and though
He can't come now to meet us in body,
In spirit he's with us as we walk.'

JENNIE ERDAL

Listening in the Loose Grass

It started with woodworm.

Ruth is perched on the loft ladder, fourth rung from the top, head poking through the hatch, awaiting the verdict. The man from Rentokil crouches at the far end of the attic, legs straddling the joists. *Anobium punctatum*, he says, elongating both words, as if to a simpleton, each syllable a tiny vocalised missile, launched across the roof space. That's what the experts say, those of us in the trade. He pauses, long enough for expertise to be noted. – People who're not in the trade, they call it woodworm. They're wrong of course. It's not even a *worm*. With a knowing smile he pulls himself up off his haunches. It's actually a *beetle*, he says, jubilant now, body arched under the coom, crawling towards her, a creature out of Kafka. – That's the *anobium* part. He reaches the hatch, his head level now with hers. – In *Latin*, that is.

Ruth is treated to a treatise on the life cycle of the beast. There are evidently four stages. He delineates each one. She has that confined feeling, the kind she used to get in the front row of the theatre, too near the action, too immediate. There is pupating, there is hatching, there are chambers and tunnels, eggs and exit holes. He says the beetles breed like nobody's business, and he purses his lips, pushing a thumb into a honeycombed joist. – It's a vicious cycle, you see. *Circle*, she wants to say, vicious *circle*. But she stops herself. This is a man who loves his job. He wipes his large hand over the dust and presents an outstretched palm to her face. And these are the faeces, he says, millions of faeces. He pronounces it *fishes*, which throws her for a moment. She wants this to be over. She is weary, short on sleep. – Can you fix it?

There is a long pause, as if her question might be the wrong one. She wonders for a moment if she has shown the wrong man into her attic. Fix it? he says at last, kneading the faeces into his trousers. Just you say the word, my dear, and I'll be back like a shot. We can't have the house falling about your ears, can we?

On account of the infestation Ruth took a lodger. The expense of drafting in professionals from the mainland – structural checks, replacement of timbers, the treatment itself – called for extreme measures. Most crofters did bed and breakfast to eke out their living. Diversification they called it. She had done it too at one time, but only to please her father. With him gone these past two years and her taking sole charge there was no longer the time or the inclination. In any case expectations were different now – *ong sweet* being the latest. Was the room *ong sweet*, people always asked. As if it were normal to have a bathroom in the bedroom, to pee in the place that was for sleeping.

The idea of taking a lodger arrived in Ruth's head at a meeting organised by the bird charity. Ruth had a weakness for charities. This one was trying to raise awareness for endangered birds, to get crofters onside, to generate funds for their work. We also need to find summer lodgings for a researcher in the field, announced the speaker, who wore a lapel badge that said *Julie: Liaison Officer*. Above her head was a huge slogan in garish green: *THREATENED SPECIES ACTION PLAN STEERING GROUP*. As a catchphrase Ruth decided it had nothing going for it: too many nouns, in confusing coalition, and no possibility of abbreviation or acronym.

Acronyms were on Ruth's mind because of their profusion the day before at a gathering in the same hall, where the man from Sustainable Tourism had spoken a strange new language. There were WEBS and TEES and even STAGS – revealed only later in the handout as Wider Economic Benefits, Transport Economic Efficiencies, and Scottish Transport Appraisal Guidance – all mixed together with market segments (MASSES) and vehicle operating costs (VOCS), and baked in a hot oven of interventions and location impacts (INLIMS). The island's future was balanced on the end of the speaker's acronymic tongue. He wore old man's trousers, tight at the top of the leg before expanding to embrace everything above. A mobile phone with a green blinking light was clipped to his belt. We need to bring the consumer to the product, he said, tapping the lectern with the blunt end of a pencil whenever emphasis was required. You are the *product*, tap tap. The consumer is interested in *you*, tap tap. This island is on *everyone's* tap tap itinerary. A causeway would liberate assets, he said. A causeway would encourage visitor motivations. There would be no acculturation, no loss of traditional employment systems. A kind of dead language, Ruth thought, nothing to do with their small island, the island-ness of the island. This tapping man had no words for what he had never felt and would never know.

At the causeway meeting it had been standing room only, and everyone with an opinion, but the speaker at the bird charity event was addressing a near empty hall – apart from Ruth just a few tourists who had wandered in to take shelter from the rain. Ruth knew of two possible reasons for the poor attendance. First, the charity's flyers had advertised membership at reduced cost for the *unwashed* – not the intended *unwaged* – an unfortunate error that deterred the islanders, ever on the alert for effrontery and none too familiar with the vagaries of autocorrect. And second, the charity had a habit of preaching to crofters, telling them they had an obligation towards threatened birds, that they should adopt practices to ensure their survival. As the locals were quick to point out, the birds came to the island year after year precisely because the crofters were doing something *right*. Over on the moral high ground of the mainland the birds had died out.

At the end of the talk Ruth enquired: How long? It would be three months, said the bird woman, herself as plump as a partridge – but very low maintenance, working at nights, sleeping by day. – And what sort of research? Oh, counting birds, she said, keeping records, no dirty work, nothing *to be frightened of*. Ruth had been merely curious, not frightened. She took the offered pen and signed the agreement. And so, between the yellow flag iris coming into bloom and the bracken turning golden, Ruth's life was set on a new course.

As she made her way home through the quiet of the island, emptied now of day-trippers, she thought of her attic with its millions of faeces, now magically dematerialising with each purposeful step. The sky had melded with the sea, and the wind had picked up from the west, bending the tall grasses at the edge of the machair. Duncan from the croft at the North End was approaching. – So you're taking a lodger, Ruthie? By osmosis, or some extra-sensory power, people in these parts knew about things before they had properly happened. Certain other things, also known about, were never mentioned. The two were in some contiguous relation, but the art was in keeping them separate. That's right, Duncan, she said, fixing her face in a way that would meet the demands of this sort of exchange. But Duncan had more urgent business. I need help with one of my ewes, he said – the lamb is breech.

Delivering a lamb legs first – as Ruth had once done years ago when her father was no longer up to it – was enough to get you a reputation for being an expert in breech births. This is what it was like here – you did something once, like mending a leaky tap, and before you had time to pack up your tools you were a master plumber.

By the time Ruth and Duncan reached the North End the rain was coming down again, a steady flow in the freshening wind. It was after nine, but the light was still good. The ewe lay on her side, pushing, but as Ruth came close she tried to stagger up to get away. The poor animal was at the end of its strength. Ruth rolled up her sleeves and wrapped one arm round the ewe, coaxing her down before delving the other arm into her body. She turned her arm slowly, feeling for a head, for a nose, but what she felt instead was the back end, stuck in the warm and wet of its mother. Duncan stood silent in the rain, watching, close enough to be part of the scene, far enough away to leave his options open. His weathered face, furrowed by days without human proximities, told of past catastrophes. Ruth's father had always said that hard work kept the bad stuff at bay, and she wondered briefly if Duncan had found it so.

Maybe you should let nature take its course, he said after a while, his voice raised above the wind, not critically or from a place of superior knowledge, rather in the way of someone who had nothing better to say and got by on old wives' tales. Sometimes nature takes the wrong course, Ruth said, and all you get are dead animals. Gently she took hold of one tiny leg and pulled it straight till it was out of the ewe. Then she went back in for the other leg. When the two soft wet stubs of the feet were out, she pulled with both hands until, in a splurge of red and gold and white, the lamb was free. She cleared the yellow slime from its nose and mouth and placed the newborn by its mother's head to be nuzzled. As it coughed and shuddered into life there was a quickening in her own breast, the sort of rush she got long ago, before everything was changed. Will it *live*? Duncan had moved closer. He was bending over the ewe, making soothing noises, telling her she'd done a good job. Ruth eyed him for a moment or two, before looking away over the rain-soaked field, remembering something she preferred to keep to herself. It will live, she said.

From the kitchen window she watches him make his way slowly through the bottom gate and up the track. Bert the collie dog stands on his hind legs beside her, looking through the same window, expectant. Bent like a question mark, weighed down by a large rucksack, and head tucked low into the drizzle blown in from the west, Ruth's lodger pushes a bicycle, an old style sit-up-and-beg with wicker basket up front. Over the rough ground he has to stop more than once to pick up things spilled from the basket. As he comes closer she sees that his clothes hang loosely on his frame. He could be a refugee fleeing the revolution, she thinks, a man betwixt and between, *déraciné*. Yet when she opens the door, what she sees is not a displaced person but a rather exotic specimen – smooth dark complexion, thicket of wild black hair, brown garnets for eyes, rinsed out golden at the edges.

Don, he says, showing two stacks of gleaming white teeth, Don McGeechan. He extends a hand so soft as to seem quite new and unused. The voice is in the middle range, songful and unexpectedly homegrown, a Scottish scratch in it. It's pretty wet out there, he says, shaking water out of his sleeves. Always plenty of weather, though none of it lasts for long, she tells him, feeling the familiar undertow that separates her from other people. – Thanks for having me to stay. I don't want to be any trouble.

Up close he is as thin as a wand. His skin is velvet, epicanthic folds on his upper eyelids, and hair so shiny it could have been painted on. No, no, Ruth says, don't go worrying about that. The words come out shriller than intended. I suppose not everyone will welcome what I'm here to do, he says. Never mind them, she says, already showing him to his room upstairs, we have plenty of lunatics here. The implication is that he too is a lunatic, not what she meant at all. She starts to row back. – I was thinking of George Eliot. In *Middlemarch* sane people do what their neighbours do, so that if there are any lunatics about they can be spotted straightaway and avoided. Her speech is rushed, fragmented. Why did she ever agree to a lodger? – But here on the island – she is rolling her eyes – I sometimes think this principle is reversed: only the sane stand out. Everyone else is in some sense deranged. There, she's said it now, there's no going back. But Don McGeechan laughs with all his white teeth, and because he laughs she does too.

The room was once her parents' bedroom. She can sense them here still, something to do with the complex smells collected in old fabrics.

She worries now that the lodger will sense them too. I hope you'll be comfortable here, she says, glancing at the bed where her father had spent his last days, his eyes clouded milky like those of a long-dead fish. She can hear his voice now too, telling her to come home, that everyone has a past, that here on the island it would stay in the past.

– Come down when you're ready, and I'll put the kettle on.

When the lodger appears in the kitchen, she finds herself hanging back, as if she might have better things to do, or perhaps to indicate that she has a separate life. Hold him at arm's length, she tells herself – this is a business arrangement after all. Her mother's instincts, which she has done much to combat, sometimes catch her unawares. Meanwhile the lodger has a zen-like air of containment, yet there is something unsettling about him, or maybe simply beguiling, a mystery waiting to unravel. She has become unused to the ways of men. In the time before crofting she knew about other people, other lives, but since returning to the island there has been a steady shrinkage and slippage.

With a mug of tea in hand they do what people do when they first meet, exchanging pleasantries, speaking the script of the non-acquainted. Who lives on the island? A mixture of natives and white settlers, she says. It's a sort of hierarchy – those that have been here for as long as anyone can remember, and those who have recently arrived. Like me, he says. She tells him that *recently* can mean anything from six weeks to six generations. He smiles, looking round the kitchen and into the hallway beyond. She looks too, through his eyes: faded wallpaper, the old table with the formica top, piled high with assorted clutter, the ant-heapishness of her life. She discovers he was born in Vietnam, but he has lived in Scotland for thirty years – practically a native! And his Scottish name – how did he come by that? His clear and patient answer betokens long practice. – *Nguyen Van Dung* was actually my given name. *Nguyen* is a surname and *Van* is sort of the equivalent of Mac, so *Nguyen Van* was changed to McGeechan when I first came to Scotland. He traces a thin finger round the rim of his cup, as if this information might be held there. *Dung* would naturally have been ridiculed at school, he says. Then sudden laughter, a burst of gunfire. – And so I became Don.

Afterwards the practical matters are sorted out. She will leave him to his own devices, she is an early riser, she is busy with the lambing, she sometimes rests in the afternoons and would appreciate quiet. He can have use of the kitchen – they should agree times – and there is a loo downstairs. The upstairs bathroom will be shared. It all sounds perfect, he says. He will keep himself to himself, try not to get in the way. He will be out every night between the hours of 11 p.m. and 3 a.m. – the best time for counting the birds – and for much of the day he will be asleep.

The bird that Don McGeechan has come to count is the corncrake, officially an endangered species in Britain, now confined to the Hebridean islands. Ruth feels something of a connection with corncrakes: sharing the same habitat, they are an embattled minority with an uncertain future. Their rasping call adds to her sleeplessness, yet it is a comfort. The male is the caller, the female silent. Which resonates too. The corncrake is also a reminder that just because something can't be seen doesn't mean it isn't there. Ruth's life is populated by absent presences.

When the bird people first came to the island to conduct tests, she recalls how they sashayed about in their high-vis vests, took soil samples, typed into their electronic notebooks. Using a machine called a penetrometer, which gave rise to much lewd hilarity amongst the islanders, they measured the height of the grass as well as its density. This led to a momentous discovery – something called *the sward penetrability quotient*. All that money and time and energy, scoffed the locals, to establish what was already known to anyone with eyes and ears: that corncrakes prefer loose grass, not the densely matted variety. When it came to 'conservation resources', however, local knowledge was often discounted. Wildlife was a noble cause, and it was for people in offices to decree the way the land worked.

Soon after arriving the lodger left his rent on the table in the hall, and there it had remained for a good few days, for Ruth did not want him to think that money was the nub of things. At first she found it hard to get used to a new presence in the house, and to the different sounds, both of which the dog took in his stride. But the lodger was as good as his word – quiet and considerate, keeping himself to himself, creeping out in dead of night and returning just as quietly in the small hours.

A routine established itself. Ruth was up and out before he stirred. She cooked in the early evening, while he made something to eat later, before going out to work. Only once had they stumbled into one another in the hallway, stalling as if they'd collided in the foyer of a theatre, waiting for the right greeting to come. After two weeks Ruth knew him scarcely any better than the island-baggers who walked past her gate. Then one night as she went upstairs to bed, Ruth caught a strange sound coming from his room. On the landing she stood perfectly still, straining her ears, bending into the sound, which she heard as a sort of keening, a soft ululation. She imagined Don McGeechan alone behind the closed door, tuned to some ancient lamentation, shoulders heaving, face crumpled, eyes salt-wet, trying to contain a secret sorrow. Tomorrow she would be kinder to him.

Ruth was a poor sleeper. For years, as a way of getting through the cool whispering hours of the night, she would listen to the World Service. Lying in the dark, a dot on her small island, she would marvel at the idea of being connected through a tiny transistor radio to people and places all over the globe. In the last year or two, she had tended towards the iplayer and podcasts, having defected from the World Service on account of the irritating jingles now played randomly between programmes. Since the arrival of her lodger, however, she more often lay awake listening to the *crex crex* of the corncrake, her head zinging with rhyming words – *mandrake, muckrake, headache, jailbreak, heartache, undertake, wide awake.* And now and then, on the skin of her closed eyelids, there would be a faint silhouette, out there somewhere on the island, listening also to the *crex crex*. And counting.

Next time she saw him Ruth asked how he had become involved with the Godfathers. The *Godfathers*? Oh, she said, bending down to hold Bert by the collar, – that was the local name for the bird charity people. But *why*? Addressing her answer to the dog, she said she supposed it was because the Godfathers rewarded good behaviour and punished bad behaviour. I see, he said, in a way that suggested he did not see. What I mean is, said Ruth, they have a kind of integrity, but the kind that can eliminate you if need be. Closing his double eyelids, the lodger narrowed his shoulders and crossed both arms over his chest, as if to make himself less of a target. He might have been facing a firing squad. – Not *literally* eliminate, of course. And with a swerve she asked him how his work was going.

His work mainly involved listening, he said, digging both hands deep into his pockets and starting to rock back and forth on his heels. You had to move quietly, learn to judge distances, be attentive. But above all you had to listen. Early in the mating season the male bird could call up to twenty thousand times over just a few hours. Listening was like looking, only more intense. You had to centre your whole body on your ears. She should come with him one night – he could show her. These words fell between one moment and the next, just managing to squeeze into the tiny space available. The corncrake was a very special bird, he said, outwitting capture, hard to pin down – a beautiful enigmatic shy creature. He hated the idea of its being hounded, flushed out, picked up, weighed and tagged – just so men in white coats could get an idea of numbers. He stopped, as if he'd heard himself say too much.

Ruth took up the thread. When the Godfathers visited with their tracking devices, she said, we all suspected them of moving the poor creatures around the island, to make the numbers look good. – Exactly! He had sensed an ally, as she had hoped. There was a touch of high definition about him now, eyes brighter, hair stiff as a broom. – And it's not as if tagging devices do any good. For a start only the calling male can be trapped, because only he can be located. The female is mostly silent and hidden. And the corncrake turns as he sings, so his song pulses like the beam of a lighthouse – which can make one bird seem like several. He was animated now, eyes darting about like flies trapped in a bottle. – I feel strongly about this, so strongly that I wrote to your Godfathers and offered to conduct the census aurally – using just my ears.

If only he hadn't bothered to add the bit about his ears, Ruth thought, as if she was someone who couldn't understand *aurally*. She must have a blank look about her. This sort of thing happened distressingly often.

He told her that all the previous census methods had been deeply flawed, resulting in corncrakes being either overcounted or under-counted. But my method actually works, he said. My method is accurate. – And what *is* your method?

It was based on his ability to hear individual corncrakes, he said – quite without vanity or affectation. He could differentiate their calls. Other methods lumped the birds together, effacing their individuality. He could hear each bird – not just the male *crex crex*, but the more sporadic high-pitched *cheep* of the female and even her tender *ooh-ooh-ooh peep* to her chicks. He explained that it was a gift, not something you could buy or ask for or otherwise be sure ever of getting. It was in his blood, imbibed with his mother's milk, nothing consciously learned. He thought it had something to do with the six tones in his native language, each tone subtly distinct from the other. They helped you listen, and listening made you hear better. The tones were also used in a vocal technique that had no equivalent in English – an amazing thing, a form of heightened speech, a kind of a tonal prayer. It was called *Đoc Kinh* – something like cantillation, but not the same. Even now he practised it every night, in memory of his parents.

The following evening as Ruth was shutting up the hens, he appeared at the door of the hen hut. – Sorry to interrupt. He peeped into the hut as if it might contain something he needed to be aware of and avoid. – Can I cook for you tomorrow? It's my birthday. The smile opened up around his stacks of white teeth. Good, he would prepare a Vietnamese feast.

In the kitchen he turned out to be masterful. I never travel anywhere without these five ingredients, he said – lemon grass, soy sauce, ginger, chili, lime. He held up each in turn for examination, a conjurer about to perform a magic trick. Five was the vital number, he explained, with the five elements in nature corresponding to the five tastes. Spicy was metal, bitter was fire, salty was water, and so on.

– And what about earth and wood? Ruth was eager to show she could measure up. Ah, that's sweet and sour, he said, crushing crystals of sea salt now with the back of a spoon. And salt – he let a few flakes fall through his fingers – salt was the connection between the living and the dead.

Over dinner, as splendid and colourful a meal as Ruth had ever set eyes on, she asked him about cantillation. Was it part of his religion? No, for him it was cultural, a way of paying homage to his roots. – In fact, I have no time for religion.

With his breath he made a swishing noise, skates stopping on ice. – Sorry, perhaps you . . . ? No, no, please don't worry, said Ruth. Religion is important in these parts of course, but I've never been able to get a handle on it. I always think it must be like the queen in *Alice* – believing six impossible things before breakfast. His smile was now the smile of friendship. It seemed to say something had shifted between them. My parents were devout, he said. When we left Vietnam on the boat they prayed all the time. It made no difference. We were adrift for weeks in the South China Sea, without food and little water. Eventually we were picked up by a British freighter, but by then I had lost my whole family – parents, grandparents, brothers, sisters. Even now, thirty years on, there is a space around me where they used to be. He paused, his eyes, black as coal, scanning the present space around him. – And I sometimes think that those lost were also *me*.

Outside the sun was setting. Shafts of light lay on the water like beaten gold. Ruth opened the kitchen door and moved into the cool of the evening. The lodger followed, and they leaned side by side against the garden wall. The day had stalled, and couldn't get going again. After a while she asked: How on earth did you *cope*? The question hung in the air, waiting for an answer. He examined his hands, as if expecting them to tell him something. In Vietnam, he said at last, people believe that when you are in need of a teacher, a teacher will appear. And when I came to Scotland this happened to me. There was a lovely old lady, older by far than my grandmother, who volunteered to teach me English. One day, when she found me weeping, she told me: Memories make life beautiful, but only forgetting makes it bearable.

But did you never think *why me?* Almost everything sounded wrong the moment she said it. Yet she was intently listened to. Even the space between words was intense. He had a way of listening to silence too, tilting his head as he did so. – I think the small boy that this happened to must have thought *why me*, at least to begin with. But the grown man came to understand that every day, somewhere in the world, people are tortured, babies starve. My family lost their lives at sea, yes, but even here on this island there have been drownings. Every day there is pain and grief. Why should *anyone* be exempt?

Why indeed, thought Ruth, who had a sense of being unwound, cotton spinning off a reel. The feeling settled in her mouth, where it turned bitter, competing with the after-tang of beautiful food. It had to do, she thought, with always being outside someone else's story, with no one inside hers. It's so hard to get beyond your own story, he said, as if reading her thoughts. If you are a survivor you are always pitied. And pity is hard. It relies on a version of events that starts with tragedy. As the survivor you have to slot in as best you can.

The sun had gone down, the horizon now a single shimmering silver line. Beyond the sprinkle of houses and lines of washing, the gentle waves lifted the creel boats by the jetty. Of course, he said, parents don't put their children in a leaky boat if the land is safe. Even so, it's important not to invite pity. To be pitied – nothing could be worse.

She had an urge to repay his candour, match it with a thick slice of her own. Instead she played with the hem of her jersey, scrunching it up and straightening it again and again, during which she did not tell him about the long-ago accident on the way back from Brighton: about the black ice, the skid down the embankment, the crack of an ancient oak, the deafening blare of the horn, the smell of petrol. She said nothing about the contents of the car spread all around, the shreds of ordinary living, the toys, an infant cup that still contained milk. Nor the hideous bright of the hospital, the tubes coming out of her husband and son, the monitors and beeps, the buzz of urgency, before the hush of *I'm sorry.*

Instead she pushed different words around her mouth till they slotted into the small gaps between what was said and what was meant. The life I have now, she whispered, well, it isn't the life I thought I would have. There was another life, but it was cut short.

And in a voice so gentle she would remember it always, he said: *do you want to tell me about it?*

That night she wept in her sleep. She could hear herself sobbing, but it was deep in a dream and in any case she needed to stay in the dream because Jack was alive and her little boy had grown into a fine young man, and for a brief time she too was younger, and every dream might still come true. When she woke it was with the familiar promise of old, and only when she was halfway out of bed and reaching for her dressing gown did she remember, with hammering heart and pressure in the skull, that the dream life was gone.

May gave way to June. The summer ferries disgorged their regular loads: sightseers, pilgrims, heritage poppers, mystics, peace lovers. The weather was poor for the time of year, sudden squalls coming in like dark fingers lain across the land. Ruth felt sorry for the bedraggled tourists, but she had her own worries too. Whenever the wind got up and the temperature fell, one or two pregnant ewes would run off in search of nonexistent shelter. A few new mothers even abandoned their lambs. The lodger, sounding apologetic, said the weather made no difference to corncrakes, whose calling went on regardless. And even in the driving rain he could single out the birds, dozens and dozens of them, each of their songs lyrically distinct.

But soon the weather settled and the days warmed. The island was suddenly lit yellow with wild iris. For Ruth everything seemed now to be happening very slowly and very quickly. There had been a gentle movement towards a new way of living, like a quarrel being put straight, for good and forever. From the kitchen window Ruth watched the lodger scatter scraps and the hens come running. He had asked to help with the chores, and she had accepted. At some level they were amazed by one another. Cooking for two had become an elevated act, shared between them and performed with care and kindness. In the evenings after supper he played the old piano, which had sat silent for years. He had spent a week doing repair work before tuning it to something he called *equal temperament*, a phrase Ruth thought sounded sweet on the tongue.

When the chosen night arrives, the sky is lemon wild with purple streaks. They venture into the twilight, walking down the track and along the road past the jetty. There are few signs of life, but even at this hour Ruth knows there is no chance of going unnoticed. Beyond the road the ancient headstones in the graveyard look like rotting teeth, all gaps and blacknesses. Halfway across the island a dog barks, a lone living creature. As always there is the sound of the sea, but tonight it is just a rumour. As they walk he speaks in hushed tones, as if in preparation for a solemn act, about his feeling for the corncrakes. After a while a kind of intensification takes place, he says. Gradually you let the *crex crex* in, and you begin to pick up the different calls. It feels like oneness, without separation. Listening is the thing. Listening can make you well again, heal the broken bits.

When they reach the place for tonight's count he unrolls a travel rug and spreads it on the ground. At the edge of the long grass they settle down into the quiet of the space, lying back under the huge sky. They might be survivors of some natural disaster, the last two people alive. Try first to listen to the stillness, he says, and then let go, into it. Soon you will forget where you begin and where you end.

CHRISTABEL SCOTT

from *Iona: A Romance of the West*

I begged Iona for her company
And gentle guardianship across the moor
That leads unto that rocky little bay
Where Saint Columba landed long ago,
Called Port-na-Curraich to this present day.
She would not come until her brother said
That I would never find the way alone,
And needed that I should be guided there;
So just to please us both Iona came,
And as we went along she told me names
Belonging to each little island near.
She showed me 'Macher' and the 'Spouting Cave,'
And told me how the little farm was called
'Back of the Ocean,' just because it looked
Unto the western boundary of sea.
And so at last we came unto the bay
Where Columb landed in his wicker boat
Full thirteen hundred years ago and more.
We wandered down the little strip of grass,
Which once was covered by the ocean foam,
Unto the pebbled shore, where lay such great
And infinite variety of stones,
It seemed as if it were a playing-ground
For all the wonders of the mighty deep;
Here lay great boulders of the bright red rock,
And here were whitened pebbles, smooth and round,
Worn by the tumult of a thousand storms.
All colours of the rainbow seemed within
This great kaleidoscope of shingled shore,
From brightest granite to the pale sea-green
Of that reputed talisman from death,
Iona's famous pebble of the sea.
I searched in vain for one of these bright stones;

All shades seemed there except the liquid green.
At last Iona gave a little cry,
'Here is a beauty I have found for you;
And if you wear it as a sacred charm,
No danger can approach you from the sea.'
She made me take it, and I'll have it set
With burnished gold to hang upon my chain.
I thought she looked a vision of delight
As, seated on the rough and shelving bank,
Amid the brightness of the shore and sky,
She was the only living thing in sight.

ADOMNÁN

Bed

‘Woman, why
Try
To deny
Your husband sex?
Let us fast,
You, I,
And your husband. You
Are subject to his law.
Let us pray.’

Her reply:
‘Columba, I know
What is impossible
Will be possible
Through you.’

And next day
She said, ‘Now
This man I loathed,
Somehow –
It makes no sense why –
Is the man I love.’

And as the sun moved
Lower in the sky
They took off their clothes
And went to bed.

ADOMNÁN

The Cry

On Iona's good earth
One day, reading,
He heard a cry
From Ireland
And ran to pray,
Pleading
To try
To take away
A woman's pain
Where she lay
In agony,
Giving birth.

ADOMNÁN

Mother

During pregnancy
She dreamed
An angel
Brought her
What seemed
A coat
Coloured
With the colours
Of every flower;
After an hour
The angel
Snatched it back,
Raising it up,
Then let it drop
And float,
Glowing,
Through the air.
'Why
Take it back?'
She asked.

'Because to lack
That garment
Is your gift.'

Then she saw
The robe shift,
Seem to lift,
And fly,
Glowing,
Billowing on and on
Outwards
Across the globe,

Still one,
But growing
Broader than moors,
Sturdier than mountains,
Wider than forests.

'This dream
Is of the greatness
Of your son.'

ADOMNÁN

The Foster-Mother

Her tall
Brother
Nailed
A block of salt
On one wall
Of the house
Of the foster-mother
Who could hardly see;
And when fire
Razed the village
Every other
Building
Was torched,
Every other wall
Fell
Except that lea
Wall;
Where
Her brother
Had hung the saint's salt,
It was still
Hanging there
On its small
Unscorched
Nails.

ADOMNÁN

Erc

'On you go. Row across the Sound to Mull
To catch Erc, the poacher, in the hills.
Last night, alone, he sneaked over from Coll,
Making his upturned boat a den,
Camouflaging it with grass,
Hiding, waiting to embark at night
For the seal colony – the one that's ours –
He wants to smuggle our pups.'
So the monks set out, arrested Erc,
Dragged him to Columba. 'Erc, Erc, Erc,
Why ignore *Thou shalt not steal*?
Just ask – we'll give you what you need.'
So Erc was handed butchered mutton
And later, as soon as Columba foresaw
Erc on his deathbed, he had him sent
A big beast and six sacks full of grain –
The saint's gifts, for the funeral feast.

JOHN MacGILVRAY

from *Elegy on Donald McLean, Esq. of Coll* (1787)

See how Iona's mouldering walls decay,
Where priests and heroes once were used to pray;
The heifer treads upon the learn'd and brave,
And squalid moss conceals Columba's grave.
The characters of ruin we can trace
Through all the precincts of the holy place.

WILLIAM WORDSWORTH

Iona
(Upon Landing)

How sad a welcome! To each voyager
Some ragged child holds up for sale a store
Of wave-worn pebbles, pleading on the shore
Where once came monk and nun with gentle stir,
Blessings to give, news ask, or suit prefer.
Yet is yon neat trim church a grateful speck
Of novelty amid the sacred wreck
Strewn far and wide. Think, proud Philosopher!
Fallen though she be, this Glory of the west,
Still on her sons, the beams of mercy shine;
And 'hopes, perhaps more heavenly bright than thine,
A grace by thee unsought and unpossest,
A faith more fixed, a rapture more divine
Shall gild their passage to eternal rest.'

RUTH THOMAS

All the Treasures We Can Have

There was something funny about going to an island. The only island she'd ever been to (unless you counted St Michael's Mount) was a place called Sifnos, off the Greek coast. She'd gone there with her parents the previous summer.

'Wasn't it lovely, that time in Sifnos?' her mother would sigh sometimes, and Catherine would try to recall what had been lovely about it. All she could remember was an algae-bright raised swimming pool, a lot of heat and hills and whitewashed buildings, and a man called Theophilus who'd kept bringing them pomegranates. He'd just kept turning up with them and leaving them in a basket outside their apartment door. This strange gift. They hadn't known what to do with them, and in the end her father had put them all in a bag weighed down with stones and thrown them into the sea.

'But we could have let them float away like little boats!' Catherine had protested, standing beside him on the gritty beach.

'Yes, but they weren't little boats, Catherine, they were fucking fruit!' her father had said, striding empty-handed back up to their apartment.

'But what about Theofferlus? Won't he be sad?'

'I don't give a monkey's about Theophilus.'

This summer they were going to an island again – a place called Iona. It sounded quite Greek but it wasn't, it was in Scotland. It was, her mother said, going to be nothing like Greece.

*

Catherine's best friend at school was called Fiona, coincidentally, and you pronounced her name to rhyme with Iona. That was quite funny too. Although Catherine had always known it was pronounced oddly – even before they'd met – because that was what Fiona's mother yelled as she walked her children up to school.

Paul!
Kevin!
Mary!
Steven!
Fie-oh-nah! Fie-oh-nah!

The Walshes always set off ages before they needed to, and you could hear them coming a mile off.

'Oh, it's Mrs Walsh: it must be twenty past eight,' Catherine's father would joke: he made that joke a lot. And then after a couple of minutes you would see them all progressing past the window: this little line of Walshes, pressed tight up against the verge to keep safe from the cars. Mrs Walsh, squat and overweight, walked at the back of the line, and every few seconds she would open her mouth and bellow her children's names into the air.

Paul!
Mary!
Steven!
Kevin!
Fie-oh-nah! Fie-oh-nah!

Catherine would stand at the kitchen window and watch them. There was something ceremonial about it: it was like looking at a little flotilla. Sometimes she would imagine the stretch of road the Walshes had already been along in that careful line before they'd got as far as their house. She pictured them plodding solemnly past the broken-down Working Men's Club, and the playing field that everyone called The Rec, and the Women's Institute and the electricity substation and the funny old house that was supposed to be haunted: she would think about all these places as Mrs Walsh's voice grew nearer and nearer. The Walshes were *from gypsy stock*, people had said when they'd arrived in the village that spring: and they said this in a way that seemed a strange mix of admiration and contempt. The Walshes knew how to ride horses bareback and how to fist-fight and how to jemmy open people's car doors. Fiona's father had been caught doing that the previous year, which was why he was in Maidstone Jail. Dirty tink, people said. Yes, they might have managed to get themselves into one of those swish new council houses – they might have swapped their caravan for a house but you couldn't remove the gypsy that easily. *You can take the gypsy out of the caravan, but can you take the caravan out of the gypsy?* a Rotary Club woman named Mrs Nelson had proclaimed, confusingly. It was even rumoured that the Walshes sometimes ate hedgehogs baked in clay. And Mrs Walsh was said to have a crystal ball, and to know how to use it. Also, Fiona had had her ears pierced when she was seven months old, and had worn gold hoops ever since: Fiona herself had told Catherine this, in class.

Sometimes, standing at the kitchen window in the mornings, Catherine would wave to Fiona as she walked past. Fiona never waved back. Waving to people was not what the Walsh children did.

'Fie-oh-nah!' Mrs Walsh yelled.

'What a fishwife that woman is!' Catherine's father said. 'She should be selling jellied eels at Billingsgate!'

'What's a fishwife?' Catherine asked. She thought of the old women who'd hung around the harbour, that summer on Sifnos. All those serious looking women in headscarves, wearing black. They'd looked a bit gypsyish themselves, she thought; but maybe they were more like fishwives. And she wondered if the man called Theophilus – who was, himself, a fisherman – had had a wife.

'What do fishwives do?' she asked.

Her father didn't reply. He put a piece of toast in his mouth and just stared out through the window for a moment, at Mrs Walsh shouting her children up the road. *They all have exactly the same colour hair*, Catherine thought. Even Mrs Walsh. A pale, apricot-ish orange. On misty mornings in particular, there was something very pretty about it.

*

The things she and Fiona liked doing most at school were: colouring in, litter-pick in the park with a big, kind woman called Mrs Barry, and Music and Mime classes (*'Now pretend you're a rabbit, children, running faster and faster . . .'*)

Also, singing. Their own songs, though: the only *school* song they liked was one called 'Daisies are our silver' – it was pretty, that song, unlike the ones they usually had to sing. Unfortunately though, their headmistress had been phasing out *Daisies are our Silver* recently and had replaced it with clapping songs about Jesus.

She and Fiona hated all those songs. That was just the way it was, though. You couldn't pretend to like something you hated, just as you couldn't pretend to hate something you liked. It was the same with people: some people you just liked, and that was all there was to it.

'Who did you play with at lunchtime today, sweetheart?' Catherine's mother had asked her once or twice in the past term.

'Fiona Walsh,' Catherine had said.

And her mother had become rather quiet.

'Weren't Emily and Katie around to play with today?' she'd said. 'I thought you normally played with them.'

'Not always.'

And after a while she had stopped bothering to tell her mother that she'd spent play-time with Fiona Walsh again, and not with Emily and Katie; they had wandered off by then anyway, and had joined the people who didn't like Fiona Walsh.

'It don't bother me,' said Fiona one lunchtime, pulling a piece of chewing gum out of her mouth and then spiralling it back in again. 'Does it bother you?'

'No.'

It didn't. One day – quite soon, really – they were going to leave. They were just not going to be at that school any more.

And at playtime they went down to the little grassy area behind a strange, staircase-shaped wall that seemed to be there just because it *was* staircase-shaped, and they made daisy chains, and pulled up grasses. (*Here's a tree in summer, here's a tree in winter, here's a bunch of flowers, here's some April showers!*) And at lunchtime they sat alone at two sides of a hexagonal formica table, put their hands together when the headmistress told them to and mumbled *For what we are about to receive may the Lord make us truly thankful.*

(*Fiona Walsh has spitted in the water jug!*
Fiona Walsh has put salt in the sugar!
Fiona Walsh has wet her knickers and she's got boy's pants on!)

And in Assembly in the mornings they shared the same falling-apart song book and sang 'Build Up One Another', and 'The Ink is Black, the Page is White', and 'Daisies are our Silver'.

(Daisies are our silver,
Butttercups our gold.
These are all the treasures
We can have or hold.)

Which was the only one they liked.

*

'I'm going to a place called Iona this summer,' Catherine told Fiona on the last Friday of term.

'Where's that?'

'Scotland'

'I've never been to Scotland'

'Neither have I'

'But you *are* going there now'

'I know'.

The Walshes themselves weren't going anywhere, Fiona told her. Except maybe Camber Sands. Apart from that they were going to stay put in their new house, and their dad was going to be with them again in August.

'That sounds nice,' Catherine said cautiously, wondering if Mr Walsh was coming out of jail.

And she'd smiled at Fiona, and envied her pretty apricot-coloured hair.

'When you get back from holidays', Fiona added, 'you can come round my house. I've got a blue rug in my room, and when you get out of bed in the mornings and put your bare feet on it, it's all lovely, it's like putting your feet on a big blue sheep.'

'I'd like to,' Catherine said, a fearful kind of excitement lighting up her heart at this invitation. She tried to imagine what it might be like, setting foot in the Walshes' solid brick council house at the end of the village. It was somewhere you were not really supposed to go. Probably even more so if Mr Walsh was going to be in it.

'If you like', she said, 'you can come round to my house too, before we go away. Why don't you come round before we go to Scotland, and you can meet my mum?'

Fiona had not gone round, though, and met Catherine's mum.

That had not happened.

And then summer had begun, and Catherine's father had squashed all their luggage into the boot of their car and driven them all the way up to Oban – 'thank God we're finally getting away!' her mother had proclaimed melodramatically as they'd driven past the village's *end of speed restriction* sign. It had taken eleven hours to get there and Catherine had been sick twice, once in a field in Staffordshire, a herd of cows watching her, and once in the toilets of a Little Chef, her mother holding onto her forehead with her flattened palm as if that would somehow make things better – and then, onto Oban for a night, to stay in a hotel called, bafflingly, The Falls of Laura.

And then they had taken the ferry across to Mull. And then on again, to Iona.

'The thing about islands, Catherine,' her father had said, as the three of them stood on deck, peering down at the dark green water slopping against the hull, 'is you can go there, and think . . .' – and his voice altered suddenly – became almost quite choked – '. . . you can think: "*I could just stay here, and maybe I don't ever have to go back.*" '

'Yes, that's just what I was thinking,' Catherine's mother said, a little grimly.

Catherine was aware of them glaring at each other, above her head.

'The trouble with you, Helen,' her father hissed after a moment, 'is you don't seem to appreciate when someone's trying to do the right thing. You don't seem to be able to do that. I mean, I can't imagine anyone else looking so pissed off about going on holiday!'

'Oh!' said her mother. 'Is that what this is? A holiday?'

Catherine peered into the water. She recalled the holiday they'd been on, to Sifnos. And also the one the previous autumn, to Cornwall, when they'd walked across the causeway to St Michael's Mount and got the bottoms of their trouser-legs soaking wet. Her parents had also had a row then, she remembered. Something about not waiting for the tide to turn.

'Christ, I don't know why the fuck I bother, I really don't!' her father shouted now, as the ferry bore them onwards, towards Iona.

'No: I don't know why the fuck *I* bother!' her mother said.

Catherine looked down at the water. She could see a couple of jellyfish floating around down there, their bodies as weird and transparent as ghosts. She thought of those drowned pomegranates.

'Did you see the jellyfish?' she asked.

But it appeared that her parents had not seen the jellyfish.

*

Their guesthouse was painted white, like the houses on Sifnos. Except Iona was not hot and sunny. The house was run by a woman called Mrs Hale. It stood on a hill in the mist, and had its own set of postcards in a rack, with a sign on it saying GUESTHOUSE CARDS 50p.

While her parents were carrying their luggage up the stairs, Catherine pulled a card out of the rack and looked at it. The weather in the background was identical to the weather that day. Standing in the house and holding one of the postcards was, she thought, like being in a never-ending picture-within-a-picture. Maybe, if God existed, he was standing in the sky holding a massive postcard depicting the guesthouse with Catherine standing in it, holding a postcard.

On the back of the cards, there was a line of print that said *A Judge's Picture Postcard. Looking east to Mull and west to the Atlantic*. She couldn't imagine what that meant. It just did not say anything to her at all, apart from the fact that they were a long way from home.

'Have you got 50p, Dad?' she asked her father as he headed up the stairs.

'No', he said, 'I'm carrying the luggage in.'

There were pens, too, sitting in a mug on a small side-table: they all had tiny ferry boats in the barrel, and when you tipped one of them up, the boat slid along its own viscous little sea, then reversed back when you tipped it the other way. *Caledonian MacBrayne*, it said on the side.

Guesthouse Souvenir Pens: £1, said a sign beside the pen mug.

Beneath the postcard rack there was also a puffy, leather-bound Visitors Book. It reminded her of the big ceremonial bible at school, or one of those pub menus. It was the sort of thing that might advertise chicken burger and chips. Looking at the page it was opened at, she saw that the week before, some people called The Sadler Family from Liverpool had stayed there: Gemma Sadler aged eleven had written:

We made friends with a seal pup!

and Greg Sadler (age unspecified) had written:

Very memorable trip to the abbey this week. Had an enjoyable meal in the Heritage Garden Café.

There was also someone called Ellen McCroy from West Virginia. Ellen McCroy had written, in large round writing:

Some day I hope to return to this beautiful spot! What a special place!

It made Catherine think of another song she and Fiona Walsh used to sing sometimes at school – 'Some-daay my prinnnce will co-mmme, some-daay he'll ma-rry meee!' they would bellow, running around the playground. For some reason, they'd always felt slightly hysterical, singing that song.

'If I'd known we had to leave the car on Mull I'd have booked a place there!' her father said, putting the last two suitcases down on the lobby floor.

Catherine's mother folded her arms.

*

Upstairs, the guesthouse smelt of pine wardrobes and Airwick air freshener and old casserole. There was a creaky floorboard beneath the carpet at the top of the stairs and a high round window she wasn't quite tall enough to see through.

'Do you know what that little beach is called over there?' her father asked after he'd stowed away the suitcases in the bedrooms; and he lifted Catherine up so she could peer through. 'It's called The Bay at the Back of the Ocean. Isn't that an amazing name?'

Catherine did not know what to say. Something about the word 'ocean' made her insides curl with sadness, like that sentence that Ellen McCroy had written in the Visitors Book. And those jellyfish bobbing about in the water. And those pomegranates drowned in a sack.

'I didn't think oceans could *have* backs,' she said.

Her father didn't reply. Then he put her down again. 'You are very literal-minded,' he said.

'What do you mean?' she asked.

He laughed. 'That's exactly what I mean,' he said. And then he headed down the carpeted stairs to look for her mother.

After he'd left, Catherine stood on tiptoe and squinted out through the window for a while. It was like looking through a porthole. Her armpits hurt a little bit, from where her father had been holding her. The ocean looked very huge and grey and she could not even imagine what was on the other side of it. 'Hello,' she wrote with her finger in the condensation of the window-pane. And then she drew a face: a circle, two dots and a curve. Then she walked back across the landing into her little room, and unpacked her suitcase. She put her collection of knitted animals across the top of the bed, and placed her clothes in the little chest of drawers. She put her underwear at one end of the drawer and her trousers and skirts at the other end and everything else in the middle. She had been brought up to be neat. She picked up a seashell that someone had left on top of the chest of drawers, put it to her ear, listened to the sea, and put it down. Then she went out onto the landing again to look for her parents. They were downstairs somewhere: she could hear their voices before she could work out quite where they were – it was a bit like hearing Mrs Walsh before seeing her rounding the bend in the road.

'. . . and you've got the fucking nerve to drag us all the way up here just because you think . . .' her mother was saying.

And her father was saying 'Don't tell me what *I've* got the nerve to be fucking doing!'

It was strange how often that word appeared in their arguments, Catherine thought. She didn't know what *fucking* meant but she knew it was not a good word.

*

On her way back past the little reception table, she stopped for a moment and picked up the biro with the little boat in it, that lay on top of the Visitors Book. She wrote *Catherine Louise Jones* beneath the Sadlers from Liverpool and Ellen McCroy, then slipped the biro into her pocket. Then she hitched up her jumper, picked up one of the guesthouse postcards, tucked it into the waistband of her skirt, opened the front door and went outside. '... and if you honestly think for one moment I'm going to let you just ...' her father was shouting; and she shut the door behind her.

It was rather cool outside considering it was August and not even evening yet: it was not even the end of their first day there. She thought: we are going to be here for twelve more days and twelve more nights. There was a fine rain but it was more like a hovering cloud than something falling. It just crept up to your face and hair and got them wet without you thinking it would.

'Iona,' Catherine said out loud, and she put her hands in her cardigan pockets and walked a little way down the path. She felt a huge kind of emptiness in her chest, as if she'd swallowed some of the cloud and just had to keep it in there now, indefinitely. 'Iona,' she said again, heading straight into a field full of thick wet grasses that stuck to her legs and covered her tights with burrs and seed-heads. The sky seemed to be a much bigger thing, somehow, in Scotland. It seemed to really mean something. She stooped, picked a stalk of grass and pulled the seed-head off it. From where she stood now she could see the sea, and if she turned ninety degrees she could see the sea and if she turned 180 degrees, she could see the sea. Only the presence of the guesthouse behind her prevented an absolute view of water and of sky. A little further down the hillside, before the grass gave way to sand, she could also make out something that looked like a chapel. It was small and had a cross on its roof. What was it about islands, she wondered, that made people want to build little chapels on them? What was it that made people think about God? And she thought of a little chapel she and her mother had visited one afternoon on Sifnos – and of the man called Theophilus, whom they had bumped into while they were there.

She breathed in a scent of pure sweetness: of air and grass and earth and water. Then she headed across the field, towards a stile she could see at its far end. It was one of those crooked stiles like the one in the rhyme about the crooked man walking a crooked mile. From a distance the pathway that led across the field had looked as if it was painted white, but when she got close to it she realised the whiteness was actually daisies: it was covered with daisies, she realised, as she began to walk along it; and on either side of the path there were buttercups. A line of gold and then white and then gold, as if it had been planned.

*

When she got down to the beach she took out the postcard she'd stolen off the little table in the hall, and the biro, and found a large, flattish rock to sit on. The sand beneath her shoes made her think of pale brown sugar.

She clicked the point up on the biro.

Dear Fiona, she wrote, *I am on Iona.*

And then she stopped writing and started to giggle. It was ridiculous, that rhyme. *Dear Fiona, I am on Iona.* She couldn't think what to add to it now, having written that. She didn't know what she wanted to say anyway, about Iona – about the hugeness of the sea, or the guesthouse that smelt of Airwick air freshener, or about the Visitors Book, or Oban, or the little porthole that her father had lifted her up to look through. She thought about the notes she and Fiona wrote to each other sometimes in class, and about the wild singing they did, and the handstands and the playing tag. Also about the milk-bottle crate they had to lug around the corridors sometimes, and the litter-picks they had to do on the village green with Mrs Barry. *You are my best friend*, Fiona had said to her once, while they were plodding around the grass with their litter-pick sticks. And then she had come across and put her mouth right up close to Catherine's ear so all her words came out hot and close and complicated, and whispered 'I wish you were my sister.'

She looked at the printed writing again at the bottom of the card.

A Judge's Cards picture postcard. Looking east to Mull, and west to the Atlantic.

It didn't tell her anything.

I miss you, she wanted to write. But instead she wrote

There are lots of buttercups and daisies here.

And then she just sat with the card and the biro in her lap and watched a little white seabird for a while: it had very long pale orange legs, and was walking slowly along the edge of the water, dipping its bendy beak into the wet sand. She didn't think she'd ever seen a bird like that before – there weren't birds like that in Kent, not even at

Dungeness, and she certainly couldn't remember seeing any birds like that on Sifnos. If there had been any birds like that on the seashore, her dad would have scared them all away, lobbing pomegranates like that into the water. 'What a terrible waste,' her mother had said when they'd returned to the apartment empty-handed. And then she'd begun to cry.

After a moment Catherine picked up her biro again and wrote

There are seals here but I haven't met one yet. What are you doing at the moment? Have you been to Camber Sands? Love from –

but before she could write her name, she heard it. She heard someone calling her name – *Cath-rin! Cath-rin!*. This strange, desolate wail.

She turned to look back up at the guesthouse. There was the figure of her mother, tiny in the distance, running back and forth across the top of the field.

*

Catherine got up from the rock, her damp skirt sticking to her behind.

'I'm over here!' she shouted, waving the postcard in the air. And she watched, as, soundlessly – like someone in a silent film – her mother heard her, stopped running and turned towards her. She stood absolutely still for a moment. And then she began to head across the field.

'What on earth did you go off like that for?' she asked when she'd reached the start of the little beach and began scrunching across the sand towards her. 'Why didn't you tell us you were going out? We've been going nuts!'

'I just thought I'd go for a walk,' Catherine said, peering at her mother: she was out of breath and pink-cheeked from running, and there were tears in her eyes: her face was all wet with the mist and her own crying. 'I couldn't have gone very far, could I?' she added. 'We're on an island.'

'Yes, but that's not the point!' her mother said. 'What would have happened if you'd fallen in the sea!'

'Why would I fall in the sea? What would I want to go in the sea for? It's freezing! It's not like Greece!'

Her mother did not reply. She just went very quiet for a moment. Then she said, 'No. It's not like Greece.'

And she looked out at the sea, its great grey expanse, as if she was trying to work something out. As if she was calculating how long it might take to get to the other side of it. She seemed very tired suddenly, it seemed to Catherine.

'What was the sea called, where we were that summer?' Catherine asked her.

'It was called the Aegean,' her mother replied, gazing out.

'And does the Aegean join up with this sea?'

'I suppose', she said. 'Eventually.' And she turned, smiled, put her hand out and stroked Catherine's cheek – *little peach cheeks*, she used to say, when Catherine was very small.

'Did you see that lovely path of daisies', she said, 'in the middle of the field?'

'Yes, I did,' Catherine said. 'It made me think of that song we sing at school. That one that Fiona and I sing.'

'Do you?'

'Yes – the one about daisies being silver, and buttercups being gold.'

Her mother looked at her.

'You do know the Walshes are moving on this summer, don't you, sweetheart?' she said. 'You know they were only in that house temporarily? While Mr Walsh was . . . not with them.'

'Oh,' Catherine said. She felt a peculiar sensation inside her chest suddenly: a strange, wild kind of plummeting.

'You did know, didn't you?' her mother said.

Catherine felt her mouth go a strange shape. She looked down at the sand.

'Yes,' she whispered. 'I think so.'

Because somehow she had known. She had. It was what some people just *did*: they moved on. They set up home somewhere for a while, and then they headed off again. And that was what made them interesting. Only she still had a longing to go to Fiona's house, as she'd promised she would – to be transported there across time and space and to put her bare feet on the fluffy carpet that was like a big blue sheep.

'The funny thing about being away,' she said, her voice coming out rather high and bright, 'is sometimes, people seem to be in your head even more. Don't they? Even when you're not with them. Even when you're not even in the same place at all'

'I know,' her mother said. 'It *is* funny.'

And she frowned out at the sea.

'Mum,' Catherine said. And she took a step towards her across the pale-sugar sand, and put her arms around her waist. *East to Mull*, she thought, *west to the Atlantic.* She imagined they were probably facing west at that moment. But if you turned 180 degrees, you would be facing east – and all the seas did link up eventually, she thought, whichever direction you set off in; and after a long, long time and a great big sea crossing, you would get all the way to the Aegean. And she thought of the pen and postcard she'd taken without paying for them; and of Mrs Walsh, wanting to keep her children close; and the man called Theophilus, who had given her mother all those pomegranates.

MICK IMLAH

I

Elderly, veiny, eccentric: our guide, running
a leak from his nose, with not enough coat

to keep out the flat rain or hail of Iona,
is 'taking the story on from Columba'.

For here, as our Lord's first millennium bumped
on its dark philological bottom or *nadir*,

they carried the freezing body of Fergus Mor,
crawled through the winter to give him grace;

Fergus, whose ancestral line or graveway
appears as a series of pock marks in the grass.

Is nothing sacred? Not the burial ground
of the ur-kings, the first Scots known by name?

'. . . And Fergus's son was Domangart Macfergus;
and he "begat" Comgall MacDomangart;

who in his turn begat – *aheugh!* – MacComgall,
begat Ferchar . . . begat Ainbcellach Mac

cheugh! Mac Ferchar, begat *aheugh!* Muiredach
Mac – heigh, ho – Eochaid the Venomous –

and thirty more I *could* name, but for this
caaatchoo! – down to your own John Smith. *Ahem.*'

ROBERT CRAWFORD

MC

'Going to hell in a hurry. Send *The Wykehamist.*'
1916, awarded Military Cross.

MA, BD. At Nakusp, BC,
Preaches to thumbless lumberjacks. Takes tea at Harvard.

New charge – galvanic Pope of Govan –
Unemployed and Iona Abbey

Rebuild one another as ordered.
World War Two: 'I am a man

With a jammed Bren gun, but not so jammed.
I hit with one bullet in five.'

Old age, psoriasis: put feet in poly bags.
Tell Duke of Edinburgh: BAN THE BOMB.
Immersion

In mud, weeds, leaves, preaching
Christ of Ecology at Morven, car converted

To diesel in the 70s. Public weeping when wife dies,
Wrinkles in the age of the image.

We Shall Rebuild. Iona rebuilt.
We Shall Rebuild. Yells: 'I have maintained

This single-minded passion for so many years
By being deaf.' Military. Cross.

HERMAN MELVILLE

Clarel

XXXV

In spot revered by myriad men,
Whence, as alleged, Immanuel rose
Into the heaven – receptive then –
A little plastered tower is set,
Pale in the light that Syria knows,
Upon the peak of Olivet.
'Tis modern – a replacement, note,
For ample pile of years remote,
Nor yet ill suits in dwindled bound,
Man's faith retrenched. 'Twas Hakeem's deed,
Mad Caliph (founder still of creed
Long held by tribes not unreknowned)
Who erst the pastoral hight discrowned
Of Helena's church. Woe for the dome,
And many a goodly temple more,
Which hither lured from Christendom
The child-like pilgrim throngs of yore.
'Twas of that church, so brave erewhile –
Blest land-mark on the Olive Hight –
Which Arculf told of in the isle
Iona. Shipwrecked there in sight,
The palmer dragged them from the foam,
The Culdees of the abbey fair –
Him shelter yielding and a home.
In guerdon for which love and care
Received in Saint Columba's pile,
With travel-talk he did beguile
Their eve of Yule.
The tempest beat;
It shook the abbey's founded seat,
Rattling the crucifix on wall;

And thrice was heard the clattering fall
Of gable tiles. But host and guest,
Abbot and palmer, took their rest
Inside monastic ingle tall.
What unto them were those lashed seas?
Of Patmos or the Hebrides,
The isles were God's.
                                        It was the time
The church in Jewry dwelt at ease
Tho' under Arabs – Omar's prime –
Penultimate of pristine zeal,
While yet throughout faith's commonweal
The tidings had not died away –
Not yet had died into dismay
Of dead, dead echoes that recede:
Glad tidings of great joy indeed,
Thrilled to the shepherds on the sward –
'Behold, to you is born this day
A Saviour, which is Christ the Lord;'
While yet in chapel, altar, shrine,
The mica in the marble new
Glistened like spangles of the dew.
One minster then was Palestine,
All monumental.
                                Arculf first
The wonders of the tomb rehearsed,
And Golgotha; then told of trees,
Olives, which in the twilight breeze
Sighed plaintive by the convent's lee –
The convent in Gethsemane –
Perished long since. Then: 'On the hill –
In site revealed thro' Jesu's grace' –
(Hereat both cross themselves apace)
'A great round church with goodly skill
Is nobly built; and fragrant blows
Morning thro' triple porticoes.
But over that blest place where meet
The last prints of the Wounded Feet,

The roof is open to the sky;
'Tis there the sparrows love to fly.
Upon Ascension Day – at end
Of mass – winds, vocal winds descend
Among the worshipers.' Amain
The abbot signs the cross again;
And Arculf on: 'And all that night
The mountain temple's western flank –
The same which fronts Moriah's hight –
In memory of the Apostles' light
Shows twelve dyed fires in oriels twelve.
Thither, from towers on Kedron's bank
And where the slope and terrace shelve,
The gathered townsfolk gaze afar;
And those twelve flowers of flame suffuse
Their faces with reflected hues
Of violet, gold, and cinnabar.
Much so from Naples (in our sail
We touched there, shipping jar and bale)
I saw Vesuvius' plume of fire
Redden the bay, tinge mast and spire.
But on Ascension Eve, 'tis then
A light shows – kindled not by men.
Look,' pointing to the hearth; 'dost see
How these dun embers here by me,
Lambent are licked by flaky flame?
Olivet gleams then much the same –
Caressed, curled over, yea, encurled
By fleecy fires which typic be:
O lamb of God, O light o' the world!'

In fear, and yet a fear divine,
Once more the Culdee made the sign;
Then fervid snatched the palmer's hand –
Clung to it like a very child
Thrilled by some wondrous story wild
Of elf or fay, nor could command
His eyes to quit their gaze at him –

Him who had seen it. But how grim
The Pictish storm-king sang refrain,
Scoffing about those gables high
Over Arculf and good Adamnan.

The abbot and the palmer rest:
The legends follow them and die –
Those legends which, be it confessed,
Did nearer bring to them the sky –
Did nearer woo it to their hope
Of all that seers and saints avow –
Than Galileo's telescope
Can bid it unto prosing Science now.

attributed to ST COLUMBA

Noli Pater

Noli Pater indulgere tonitrua cum fulgore
ne frangamur formidine huius atque uridine.

Te timemus terribilem nullum credentes similem
te cuncta canunt carmina angelorum per agmina.

Teque exaltent culmina caeli vaga per fulmina
O Iesu amantissime, O rex regum rectissime.

Benedictus in saecula recta regens regimina
Iohannes coram Domino adhuc matris in utero
repletus Dei gratia pro vino atque sicera.

Elizabeth Zachariae virum magnum genuit
Iohannem baptistam precursorem Domini.

Manet in meo corde Dei amoris flamma
ut in argenti vase auri ponitur gemma.

after a medieval Latin hymn attributed to Columba in the Irish Liber Hymnorum

Father, curb frightening thunder and lightning,
So we are not smashed by its bolts and blasts.

All-Powerful One, we fear you, we know none comes near you.
All hymns aspire toward your massed angel choir.

Lightning-strike riven, let the hilltops of heaven
Praise Jesus, gentle lover, true ruler of rulers.

John, blessed forever, God's just law-giver,
Goes before the Lord, who in woman till now was enwombed,
Flushed with Grace Divine in place of wine.

Zachariah's Elizabeth was a great man's mother,
Her son John the Baptist the Lord's precursor.

My heart still holds God's loving flame
As a silver vase enfolds a gold gem.

ADOMNÁN

Calm

'Stop bailing now!'
He commanded
In a storm.
'Be still and pray.'
The holy man
Stood in the prow,
Raising his hands,
And as they began
To understand,
So, slowly,
The storm
Passed away.

ADOMNÁN

Fifty Yards

He kissed his old uncle, sending him off
As Prior to Hinba: 'Friend, set out
On your journey: I don't hope to see you
Ever again in this life.' Days later,
His uncle fell ill, and, suddenly homesick
For Iona, was brought back by boat.
Columba strode to meet him at the harbour;
Yet the old man tottered, sagged, and slumped
As the saint approached. Fifty yards
Separated them, but before each saw
The other, the Prior dropped down dead
Outside the door of the corn-kiln.
A cross was raised there; another set
Fifty yards back. The saint's word held.
Those two crosses still stand today.

LIONEL JOHNSON

Saint Columba

to Dr Sigerson

Dead is Columba: the world's arch
Gleams with a lighting of strange fires.
They flash and run, they leap and march,
Signs of a Saint's fulfilled desires.

Live is Columba: golden crowned,
Sceptred with Mary lilies, shod
With angel flames, and girded round
With white of snow, he goes to God.

No more the gray eyes long to see
The oakwoods of their Inisfail;
Where the white angels hovering be:
And ah, the birds in every vale!

No more for him thy fierce winds blow,
Iona of the angry sea!
Gone, the white glories of thy snow,
And white spray flying over thee!

Now, far from the gray sea, and far
From sea-worn rocks and sea-birds' cries,
Columba hails the morning star,
That shines in never nighted skies.

High in the perfect Land of Morn,
He listens to the chaunting air:
The Land, where music is not born,
For music is eternal there.

There, bent before the burning Throne,
He lauds the lover of the Gael:
Sweet Christ! Whom Patrick's children own:
Glory be Thine from Inisfail!

ADOMNÁN

Lightning

In mid-sentence
While copying a book,
Columba's look
Changed
And he yelled,
'Help!
Help!'
Then, when
Some of his men
Ran in,
He felt compelled
To explain,
'I saw
A man start
To fall
From high on part
Of the main
Gable wall
At Durrow,
So I sent
The angel who stood
Here with me:
He sped
Across the sea
At lightning speed,
So before
Yon man hit the ground
That angel was there
To catch him
And the monks found him,
Not even scared
But held fast,

Blessed,
Seconds ago
At Durrow
Beneath the north gable wall.

ADOMNÁN

Old

Worn out,
He was taken
To the machair
In a cart
To visit workers
Working outdoors
Towards the west.
'I have started
To long for rest
More
Than anything;
But, so that Easter
May be no sadder,
I've prayed
And delayed
My going.'
Then he gave his blessing,
Looking eastward
Across that island
Where no adder
Can live,
And soon he smiled
And started to give
An account of an angel
(Sent to recover
A long loan)
Flying through the roof;
And he blessed
A white horse,
Laying its head
To his chest;
And he blessed
The grain

In the grain shed
Where a millstone
Now
Holds the base
Of a cross
Set up in due course
To stand forever
From age to age
Showing how
His pilgrimage
Was over.

ADOMNÁN

Retreat

He made a decision
To go away
Alone
On retreat
To pray
In a wild place
Where
He had this vision:
All day
There
An array
Of devils
Fought him,
Beat him down,
Attacked
His soul.
Yet, though alone,
He found faith
To defeat
Those devils
And drive them away,
And so, in fact,
The whole
Community
On Iona
Was saved
Only
Because
On that lonely,
Stony

Tract
Of heather,
He beat
Those devils
On his wilderness
Retreat.

WALTER SCOTT

from *The Lord of the Isles, Canto IV*

Merrily, merrily goes the bark
    On a breeze from the northward free,
So shoots through the morning sky the lark,
    Or the swan through the summer sea.
The shores of Mull on the eastward lay,
And Ulva dark and Colonsay,
And all the group of islets gay
    That guard famed Staffa round.
Then all unknown its columns rose,
Where dark and undisturb'd repose
    The cormorant had found,
And the shy seal had quiet home,
And welter'd in that wondrous dome,
Where, as to shame the temples deck'd
By skill of earthly architect,
Nature herself, it seemed would raise
A Minster to her Maker's praise!
Not for a meaner use ascend
Her columns, or her arches bend;
Nor of a theme less solemn tells
That mighty surge that ebbs and swells,
And still, beneath each awful pause,
From the high vault an answer draws,
In varied tone prolong'd and high,
That mocks the organ's melody.
Nor doth its entrance front in vain
To old Iona's holy fane,
That Nature's voice might seem to say,
'Well hast thou done, frail Child of clay!
Thy humble powers that stately shrine
Task'd high and hard – but witness mine!'

JOHN KEATS

Letter to his Brother, while travelling with Charles Brown, 23 and 26 July 1818

My dear Tom,

Just after my last had gone to the Post in came one of the Men with whom we endeavoured to agree about going to Staffa – he said what a pitty it was we should turn aside and not see the Curiosities. So we had a little talk and finally agreed that he should be our guide across the Isle of Mull – We set out, crossed two ferries, one to the isle of Kerrara of little distance, the other from Kerrara to Mull 9 Miles across – we did it in forty minutes with a fine Breeze – The road through the Island, or rather the track is the most dreary you can think of – betwen dreary Mountains – over bog and rock and river with our Breeches tucked up and our Stockings in hand – About eight o Clock we arrived at a shepherd's Hut into which we could scarcely get for the Smoke through a door lower than my shoulders – We found our way into a little compartment with the rafters and turf thatch blackened with smoke – the earth floor full of Hills and Dales – We had some white Bread with us, made a good Supper and slept in our Clothes in some Blankets, our Guide snored on another little bed about an Arm's length off – This morning we came about six Miles to Breakfast by rather a better path and we are now in by comparison a Mansion – Our Guide is I think a very obliging fellow – in the way this morning he sang us two Gaelic songs – one made by a Mrs Brown on her husband's being drowned the other a jacobin one on Charles Stuart. For some days Brown has been enquiring out his Genealogy here – he thinks his Grandfather came from long Island – he got a parcel of people about him at a Cottage door last Evening – chatted with ane who had been a Miss Brown and who I think from a likeness must have been a Relation – he jawed with the old Woman – flatterd a young one – kissed a child who was affraid of his Spectacles and finally drank a pint of Milk – They handle his Spectacles as we do a sensitive leaf –.

July 26th Well – we had a most wretched walk of 37 Miles across the Island of Mull and then we crossed to Iona or Icolmkill – from Icolmkill we took a boat at a bargain to take us to Staffa and land us at the head of Loch Nakgal whence we should only have to walk half the distance to Oban again and on a better road – All this is well pass'd and done with this singular piece of Luck that there was an intermission in the bad Weather just as we saw Staffa at which it is impossible to land but in a tolerable Calm Sea – But I will first mention Icolmkill – I know not whether you have heard much about this Island, I never did before I came nigh it. It is rich in the most interesting Antiquties. Who would expect to find the ruins of a fine Cathedral Church, of Cloisters, Colleges, Monataries and Nunneries in so remote an Island? The Beginning of these things was in the sixth Century under the superstition of a would-be Bishop-saint who landed from Ireland and chose the spot from its Beauty – for at that time the now treeless place was covered with magnificent Woods. Columba in the Gaelic is Colm signifying Dove – Kill signifies church and I is as good as Island – so I-colm-kill means the Island of Saint Columba's Church – Now this Saint Columba became the Dominic of the barbarian Christians of the north and was famed also far south – but more especially was reverenced by the Scots the Picts the Norwegians the Irish. In a course of years perhaps the Iland was considered the most holy ground of the north, and the old kings of the afore mentioned nations chose it for their burial place – We were shown a spot in the Churchyard where they say 61 kings are buried 48 Scotch from Fergus 2nd to Mackbeth 8 Irish 4 Norwegian and 1 french – they lie in rows compact – Then we were shown other matters of later date but still very ancient – many tombs of Highland Chieftains – their effigies in complete armour face upwards – black and moss covered – Abbots and Bishops of the island always of one of the chief Clans – There were plenty Macleans and Macdonnels, among these latter the famous Macdonnel Lord of the Isles – There have been 300 Crosses in the Island but the Presbyterains destroyed all but two, one of which is a very fine one and completely covered with a shaggy coarse Moss – The old Schoolmaster an ignorant little man but reckoned very clever, showed us these things – He is a Macklean and as much above 4 foot as he is under 4 foot 3 inches – he stops at one glass of wiskey unless you press another and at the second unless you press a third.

I am puzzled how to give you an Idea of Staffa. It can only be represented by a first rate drawing – One may compare the surface of the Island to a roof – this roof is supported by grand pillars of basalt standing together as thick as honey combs. The finest thing is Fingal's Cave – it is entirely a hollowing out of Basalt Pillars. Suppose now the Giants who rebelled against Jove had taken a whole Mass of black Columns and bound them together like bunches of matches – and then with immense Axes had made a cavern in the body of these columns – of course the roof and floor must be composed of the broken ends of the Columns – such is Fingal's Cave except that the Sea has done the work of excavations and is continually dashing there – so that we walk along the sides of the cave on the pillars which are left as if for convenient Stairs – the roof is arched somewhat gothic wise and the length of some of the entire side pillars is 50 feet – About the island you might seat an army of Men each on a pillar – The length of the Cave is 120 feet and from its extremity the view into the sea through the large Arch at the entrance – the colour of the colums is a sort of black with a lurking gloom of purple therin – For solemnity and grandeur it far surpasses the finest Cathedrall – At the extremity of the Cave there is a small perforation into another cave, at which the waters meeting and buffetting each other there is sometimes produced a report as of a cannon heard as far as Iona which must be 12 Miles – As we approached in the boat there was such a fine swell of the sea that the pillars appeared rising immediately out of the crystal – But it is impossible to describe it –

Not Aladin magian
Ever such a work began,
Not the wizard of the dee
Ever such dream could see
Not St John in Patmos isle
In the passion of his toil
When he saw the churches seven
Golden aisled built up in heaven
Gazed at such a rugged wonder.
As I stood its roofing under
Lo! I saw one sleeping there
On the marble cold and bare
While the surges washed his feet
And his garments white did beat

Drench'd about the sombre rocks,
On his neck his well grown locks
Lifted dry above the Main
Were upon the curl again –
What is this and what art thou?
Whisper'd I and touch'd his brow.
What art thou and what is this?
Whisper'd I and strove to kiss
The Spirits hand to wake his eyes.
Up he started in a thrice.
I am Lycidas said he
Fam'd in funeral Minstrelsey –
This was architected thus
By the great Oceanus
Here his mighty waters play
Hollow Organs all the day
Here by turns his dolphins all
Finny palmer's great and small
Come to pay devotion due –
Each a mouth of pea[r]ls must strew
Many a Mortal of these days
Dares to pass our sacred ways
Dares to touch audaciously
This Cathedral of the Sea –
I have been the Pontiff priest
Where the waters never rest
Where a fledgy sea bird choir
Soars for ever – holy fire
I have hid from Mortal Man.
Proteus is my Sacristan.
But the stupid eye of Mortal
Hath pass'd beyond the Rocky portal
So for ever will I leave
Such a taint and soon unweave
All the magic of the place –
'T is now free to stupid face
To cutters and to fashion boats
To cravats and to Petticoats.

The great Sea shall war it down,
For its fame shall not be blown
At every farthing quadrille dance.
So saying with a Spirits glance
He dived –

I am sorry I am so indolent as to write such stuff as this – it cant be help'd – The western coast of Scotland is a most strange place – it is compos'd of rocks Mountains, mountainous and rocky Islands intersected by Lochs – you can go but a small distance any where from salt water in the highlands I have a slight sore throat and think it best to stay a day or two at Oban[. . .]

Your most affectionate Brother
John –

MEAGHAN DELAHUNT

To Pick Up a Stone

A solitary gull surveyed her from the ferry handrail. It fixed an eye on her as if it knew her intimately, knew everything: *What is the point of makin amends, takin stock, callin yerself to account?* She reached for her sunglasses and the seagull flew off; the question trailed in its wake and she shut her eyes for a moment. It was a question that wouldn't let her be. That night in the long ago, for example, one night among many. She remembered the drive across the border, herself ten weeks pregnant and how she'd delivered Callum, her childhood friend, to the dark. She'd left him there and kept driving. But what would it even mean, *to call herself to account*? Brigid opened her eyes and put her sunglasses on although the day was not bright. She could see the island coming closer. She glanced around the deck, looked at people looking. No one paid her any attention. There was a young boy sitting apart from his family, head down, swiping at a small screen. A teenage boy. Could be the age of her grandson. Might even *be* her own grandson, how would she know? She looked around but couldn't see the boy's father. Sometimes, she was caught out like this and her thoughts strayed to a different life. Against all expectation, after that night, after she'd driven over the border, she'd had the child, and afterwards, she'd given the child up. By then she was in London with a new name and a new address and had started work in the English Department. It was a big job. The exact co-ordinates of the park; the bandstand; where the soldiers would be; how to minimise civilian casualties.

The rest, as they say, is history.

But gettin back to that night: she'd said to Callum, I'll meet ye at the church, I'll pick ye up after the cards. There was nothin unusual in that. They'd all been friends since they could walk. And every Wednesday night, Callum and her brother Brendan the priest, and the card game at the Priest's House. For years it'd been a fixture. There was a meetin down south, she'd said. We'll go together, drive back the next day. And Brendan hugged Callum before he got into the car, she remembers that clearly, the light above the door, the long shadows cast: it lacked only crow of the cockerel, the palm of silver. Callum folded his big frame into the car, an overnight bag at his feet, its leather strap wound tight around his wrist, not lookin at her, lookin straight ahead even when she took the unfamiliar route from Derry, he didn't protest, and he could've done somethin, what with her brother the priest and that rough embrace – but Callum knew the score, knew what was what and when she drove over the border and slowed the car and the men stepped out from the trees, he looked at her, direct, 'Brigid', he said. 'I know.' He was twice her size; he could've taken the wheel, taken her by the throat. And she'd delivered Callum to the sure red-dark and the men with the guns. *Was he a tout now, or was he not?* The words like a noose round his neck and there was no way that state of affairs could continue – *an informer?* – that kind of uncertainty. Not with the Brits on the streets. Not with a war goin on.

*

She's disappointed when they get to the island. She thought they'd land exactly where Columba landed. She thought she'd walk up onto a pebbled beach, then climb the hill, turn her back to the old country and so on, just like the saint. Her own private steps in his steps. Instead they landed at the main port in cold rain and hard wind and were funnelled into a squat grey building – a cafe restaurant. She took off her sunglasses, wiped the wet off them. By now, it was too cold to stay outside, to explore, to go anywhere. It was late June, summer, and it was freezin. She queued up at the self-service counter, along with everyone else. Some great holy place, she rolled her eyes – all them holy places the same – straight in with the food and the merchandise – pots of tea and scones – then across the road to find a hat in the gift shop, perhaps a fleece, some gloves. She'd left most of her clothes behind; she'd left in a hurry. In the change room she tried on the hat and almost didn't recognise herself. Her long, greying fair hair – now it was dark and short. The colour made her look gaunt and pale. It made her look older. She took out her passport and held it up to her face. The new passport from Glasgow. She had to admit, them Glasgow Irish had done good. They'd understood exactly what was needed. She couldn't fault them; they were as good as if she'd trained them herself. She bought a fridge magnet for that time in the far off when she might have a place with a fridge. She bought a Columba key ring on a whim.

Despite herself, she could still be whimsical. And wasn't that what she'd always been told, by her mam and her da and the nuns at school? Told that she was too dreamy and vague. Not a skerrick of commonsense. She could've been a poet, her mam once said, a writer. It was all there, so it was, in her name. And, unbidden, the many meanings of her name come to her in the shop: St Brigid – patron saint of poets and blacksmiths, of dairymaids and newborns, of healers and midwives, of cattle, of nuns, of boatmen. She paused. Then the word rose up, out-of -the-blue, she'd learnt it in the long ago, at school, and then forgotten, before her life took the turns it had – St Brigid, patron saint of *fugitives*. For godssake. Her own name playin tricks on her like that. She hadn't become a poet, not at all. But a life on the run, well, she could write the handbook on the subject. But. To get back to the common sense. And wasn't that what the men had said in the training? When it was all about the firearms and gelignite and precision long-range timers? That she didn't know her erse from her elbow, did everything the hard way. Where was her common sense?

Common sense is overrated, she'd said.

Her own way was slow, odd; it was not methodical, that she could admit. She didn't have what ye'd call a logical mind. She needed to feel her way into a situation. She needed to imagine her way in. She had good visual and spatial memory, for sure. She never forgot a face, which had been her salvation, and not only *her* salvation, many a time. She had a steady hand and a keen eye. Good focus. She was the best sniper in Derry. But the thing they never took into consideration, not her parents, not the nuns, not her comrades even, was this: lessons learnt the hard way are the lessons that stick. Nothin about this life came easy, but when it came for her – and it came for her young – life on the move, jail, the hunger, solitary – what she could draw on was more than common sense. She could draw on the imagination. She could draw on reserves of the soul. She could draw on the birds flyin past the prison yard; see in them all sorts of future and past. Read their arcs through the sky. And then, over time, after she'd proven herself, handled the weapons, dismantled the guns, covered her tracks, *survived*, they'd all been forced to change their tune.

Ye don't untie a knot by cuttin through it, she'd said to them.

*

And now, here she was, herself, on St Columba's island. The place he'd ended up. A place that yoked her to the place she'd left. That first day, after she'd prised herself from the gift shop and the gee-gaws and made her way to the hotel, the rain still teemin, she'd felt strange and alone. It did not feel like a holy site to her although the Abbey reared up to her right and the ruined Nunnery lay to her left; its pink granite slick in the wet, its boundary wall made of wooden crosses, it seemed to her. She felt that here was a place where she had to keep her wits about her. It felt chill and inhospitable. In the hotel, she'd unpacked her suitcase, turned on the television, watched the news. She hadn't expected to see herself on the news, not yet, but she had been warned. The only item from Ireland flashed up: an open pit, diggers, a forensics team. Some godforsaken beach in County Louth. The presenter said something about the *disappeared*. She sat back, absorbing it all. So, she thought. It's all on. And they know what they're lookin for. And soon, it will be time to move.

*

When she got walking on the second day, when the rain eventually stopped, she noticed that there were no oak trees on the island; there were birds aplenty but no oak trees. *My Derry, my little oak grove*, Columba once wrote. But here on Iona there was nothing to remind him of home. From the jetty she turned left following the tarmac road, past the fire station and the war memorial and then struck out across the island. The long, rough grass here caught the wind and the light; colours of purple and silver and green. Small irises shone yellow as she walked to the Bay at the Back of the Ocean and climbed the nearby hill. It was the Hill of the Back to Ireland. She stood there, wind-riven, like the old saint before her, looking out over the Bay, just to check for herself. So, it *was* right, just as it was written in the life of the saint. Ye could not see Ireland from here. There were no oak trees and ye could turn yer back on Ireland. Perhaps from the first, in her own life it was written. As a schoolgirl, walkin past the checkpoints, or at home, with her aunt with the one arm – a livin martyr in their own house she was, and never a word of complaint – all her aunt's stories: how the grenades had blown when she moved the box. And later, the guns packed in the car: Armalites under the dog blanket, timers concealed in the back, perhaps it was always goin to lead this way, if she survived, away from

Ireland, to some other place. And as a child weren't they always sayin goodbye to people? That's what she was used to. Always sayin goodbye. Back then they'd assemble at Leac na Cumhadh near Derry, the place where Columba was born. And the next morning, they'd gather near the stone of the saint and walk some of the way to the port with those destined to far places – Canada, America, Australia.

Why are they always goin? Brigid had asked this of her mother, when her favourite Aunt Aoife got ready to leave.

Because, said her mother, bending low and taking the child's face in her hands. Because Ireland makes it difficult to stay. But see this stone, now? Brigid knelt down and put out her hand to the surface of the stone. It was all rusty, blood-coloured. There were copper coins pressed into it. Like touching a red moon, she thought, if ye could touch the moon. The stone of sorrows, her mother said. And the story ran that St Columba had at one time come here and seen a man so weighted with sadness, so full of loss, that the poor man could not go on. And St Columba blessed the man, blessed a cup of water from the nearby well and the man drank the holy water and the sorrows were lifted. St Columba himself had left from here to his own exile in Scotland. And so, her mother said, if we leave a coin at this stone, say our goodbyes from here then no harm can befall us. St Columba is all for the exile and the emigrant, she said, if he's for anyone. She clasped the child Brigid to her side, waving to her sister Aoife until she was out of sight and then wiped her eyes defiantly and they both walked back the way they had come.

*

Brigid stood on the Iona pier, watching the next ferry come in. Out in Martyrs Bay there was a large French cruise ship and a private helicopter circling the island. She tracked the helicopter. She watched it dip and swoop. In her old life, a helicopter always meant trouble. Her mind snares on the blades and she's back there, decades before, in Belfast: a British military helicopter. The shadow of it overhead. A great dark thing sharking the Lower Falls. The loudspeaker: talk of curfew, talk of being shot if ye broke curfew, she thinks of her mother and all the other mothers and the children and people floodin the streets after thirty-six hours, the curfew finally over, and no food because the Brits had emptied the shops. And she picks up a stone to hurl at the soldiers. How good that felt. That's what ye did. That's what people do. They use bin lids to signal an enemy approach; they leave the door open so ye can slip through; they change street signs to disorient patrols. They march for better housing; equal rights, against harassment. *Let me be clear, yer Honour. I never went to war, the war came to me.* The man in the uniform, ye got at him to get a message through to Whitehall. That was all there was to it. That was what war meant. That's what us volunteers understood.

*

Here, on this beach, looking over St Columba's Bay, Brigid picked up two stones. According to local legend, if you wanted to leave something behind, you threw one stone back into the sea. The other stone was to keep: a commitment to the future, some hope or new direction. She smiled to herself, a sad half-smile. She was no longer sure what she could commit to; the great commitments of her life whirled as dust behind her. She stood looking out over the Bay, the fifty cairns at her back, but could not find the strength to throw one pebble into the sea or to keep one pebble in her pocket. What need had she of a stone to take back? Certainly not to the old flat and her old life. Not with people lookin for her. Not any more. And after all, it wasn't so easy, despite the pilgrim lore, to throw one thing away and to keep another. One thing here, another there. Black-and-white, like that. Certainty, commitment. These words from the past. When she first joined up she'd been a teenager and they told her, quite calm, no holdin back, that there was only two places she was headed, if she committed herself, if she stayed the course, two places only: to the jail or to the cemetery.

*

That first week, she returned each day to the south of the island, to the Port of the Coracle and to the Port of the False Man. She wondered at the cairns – had the monks built them as a penance, way back, or was it the medieval pilgrims? She got into the habit of picking up two stones from the shore. Weighing them in her palm. Most days, she'd stand looking out over the Bay; clenching and unclenching her fists; but she still couldn't throw one back into the sea and still couldn't keep one.

She was neither here nor there. She was, for the first time since her sixteenth birthday, quite literally, at sea. So much sacrificed for so little, it seemed to her now. What if ye fought a war and after the peace, no one came to comfort ye? What if the peace ye fought for is nothing like what ye'd imagined? The dream of yer life turned sour. Where is the comfort in that?

*

She told the woman behind the counter in the General Store, when asked, that she was writing a book. It was the first thing that came into her head; godonlyknows – the island was awash with notebooks and easels in the summer. All manner of artists and writers.

And should I have heard of you? the woman behind the counter asked.

I don't think so, Brigid said.

And have you published?

Not really.

And is this your first book?

Yes, said Brigid. My first.

Well, now. The woman was kindly and talkative. A novel, is it?

Yes, a novel.

Write about what you know, the woman is breezy and assured as she opened the till. That's what they say.

Is it now? said Brigid, feeling guarded.

You're Irish? the woman asked.

I am.

Well, plenty to write about there, she laughed and shrugged at the same time.

Brigid attempted a smile.

I'm of Irish descent myself, the woman said in her very English accent. So many stories!

That there are, said Brigid, feeling morose. Plenty of books on the Irish.

Ah, but they're all miserable!

I see. Brigid couldn't help herself: And it's the happy Irish ye're wantin?

Yes, exactly! the woman beamed.

Do they exist?

The woman's smile dropped and she drew herself up a little. Of course. My family was very happy.

Good luck to them, Brigid said, trying to lighten her tone. Of course they was happy. Brigid wanted to get the hell out of there. She waved to the woman. Goodbye to ye now. Good luck. She turned her back and as soon as she was out of the shop opened her bottle of water and sighed a long sigh. *For Christsake.* In her mind, as she walked back to the hotel, just to amuse herself, she started to make a list of all the things she knew. What this life had taught her: how to get past a checkpoint; how to tie a tourniquet; how to work with Semtex – the beauty of it – brick red, malleable. How to mix fertiliser and diesel oil, pack it in a tin, make a handle for the tin. *Ignite.* For sure, I know how to lie and dissemble. How to run a tight team. But – hell on earth ye could never put all that in a story, she thought. Then there were the other forms of knowing. The body memories. How the body feeds on its very own self when starved. First it draws on the fat, then the muscle and finally the brain. Make a story from that! Some godawful happy Irish story. I could tell ye a thing or two, she said to the woman in her mind. Brigid was all fired up in this imaginary conversation. Things ye would never believe. In another place and time – oh, the tales I could tell – and not one of them tales would be happy. How could ye put such things in a story? In such a story they'd make the girl a monster, she thought. A girl like that would always be a monster in a story. Whereas, in her own way, she, herself, and everyone she knew were good people. She'd trained to be a nurse but her training got interrupted. In her defence, ye could say the British Army came and interrupted it. If somethin was worth believin it was worth fightin for. St Columba knew that. Back in the day, they were all warriors, them monks.

There'd been mistakes, course there had been. She had good days and bad days with the past. All those lives and so on. Overall, though, she had no regrets. Well, maybe one. How the peace had turned out. It threw everything into question.

Write about what ye know, she shook her head. *Not the sort of things I know, missus. Not that sort of knowledge.*

*

She tried to avoid breakfast in the hotel, even though she knew it was the most important meal and so on, but food was still difficult. Decades on, still difficult. And breakfast was the worst, what with the eggs and the juice and the milk. It was the same with the loud noises, when she first got out of jail: she couldn't handle the choke of buses, of cars in the street. Couldn't walk into a pub or a restaurant. The people, the clink of glasses, the clatter of forks and knives and spoons on a table. Everything strained through her. Prison sound was what she got used to. The turn of a key. The voices over the loudpeaker. The scrape of a chair in the meal room. The approach of certain steps on the concrete. When she was inside, all her senses got tuned to a certain pitch. She felt sounds through her feet, through her limbs; she had eyes at the back of her head. In solitary, though, she learnt there was no such thing as total silence. And with the blows: her hearing, anyway, the damage done. Though the guards denied the blows. Of course they did. And sometimes, in the mornings, was it the shrill of the alarm or the shrill in her head that woke her? Even this, she had become used to. A human being adapts. She was a livin testament to that proposition. But with the food. She looked down at her hotel breakfast. She pushed aside the orange juice, the jug of milk, the plate of eggs. Her jaw ached just looking. She felt the wooden clamp at her mouth, the rubber hose down the throat. It seemed to her, since that time, as if she could no longer see food as nourishment. She looks at food and feels her jaw prised open and the tube forced down and the milk-soaked glucose and the iron and the juice poured straight in. Worried that she'd choke and that would be the end of her. The kindness of the doctor: *My girls*, he used to call them, the political prisoners, the ones like her: *My girls*, he'd say, after the guards had left with the clamps and the hoses: *Why do this to yerselves*?

*

Her teeth, her hair, her bones. That time bore down, left its trace on her, no doubt about it. She'd aged badly, ye could say. Aged a decade by the time she got free. At night, in bed, her jaw hurt, her ears flushed with sounds not heard in the world outside. If she lived to be an old woman, her bones would be brittle.

If she lived to be an old woman.

On this island, in this hotel, she was still tryin to sort the sounds. The particular creak of a floorboard or door or window. The groan of the pipes. These were things she needed to know. Here, she checked the windows and floorboards. Was she worried about gettin arrested? she asked herself in the quiet of her room. Of course, yes. She was no longer young. No longer so resilient. But she was more worried about gettin shot. And not only by her erstwhile enemies. At this, she permitted herself a tight smile.

*

In recent years, it was the peace she'd found difficult, more difficult than the war, and she had no time for Good Friday, none whatsoever, and would never truly accept it. She'd broken with them – her former friends and section commanders – some now high up in Stormont. And she wanted to say: We fought a war for so many years. Someone had to make a war for ye to be a peacemaker. And now ye keep a distance. Now ye disown us. For the Union Jack to fly steady? For things to stay the same? Tell me – hand on heart – we fought a war for that?

*

The weather turned fine. She watched another procession of people arrive. All quiet. No cars. She watched the golf buggy take the luggage up to the Abbey. She could feel the longing in the pilgrims. It surrounded them like a coloured light, an aura, ye could say. They lit up, ready for transformation in a holy place. She felt this like a wound inside. Each day, she forced herself out. One afternoon she saw four white swans glide across Columba's Bay. The swans were very white against the dark of the water and she wondered whose souls they were – for birds are soul-carriers, she was sure of that – and what were they doin here, in this place, and had they followed her and to what purpose? The thought gave her pause. The hardest thing she ever done was drive those people over the border. And now these swans. What were they tryin to say? What was it they wanted her to know?

*

In her room, she watched the twenty-four hour news. Everything on a loop. Waiting. The news from Ireland: a man had been found, dug deep in that beach in County Louth. Traces of the man – one shoe, a leather bag strap, pieces of bone. DNA. She knew who it was, even before they said; the police were piecing the evidence. Again the digger in the sand, the forensics team. There may be more than one body. She turned off the sound and sat on her bed, she hugged a pillow to her chest; her free hand clawed the bedspread. And then there she was. Herself on the screen, in black-and-white, with her long fair hair and round face and mini-skirt. An earlier incarnation of herself. She stared hard at the photo from forty years before, surprised to find herself once again, A Most Wanted Person.

*

She went down to the port and scanned the faces of all the pilgrims and of all the day-tourists. And she decided then and there that she would walk a route for luck, one last time before she left. She went to the Abbey to pick up a stick. It was a long carved stick, strong and heavy, and a man at the Abbey said, It's yours for as long as you're here. He was a walker himself, he told her, leaving today. Take it as a gift. He smiled at her.

Thank you, she said. She moved off away from the man, holding the stick, waving at him. The kindness of strangers, enough to make ye weep. She made for the Bay at the Back of the Ocean but didn't walk in a straight line or obey any maps. She was done with any of that. She set off on her own pilgrim route with two stones in her pocket and the Columba keyring. She still couldn't throw one stone away, still couldn't make that decision. She set off walking. The machair was green and firm underfoot. And for sure, she would keep the stick. She tested its weight and heft, measured its use. She would keep this with her. And it wouldn't look strange – just a woman, carrying a stick. For wasn't she a pilgrim now, she thought. Surely – after all this time, to make amends, one final walk – surely, some manner of pilgrim now?

ADOMNÁN

Machair

As they were building
Drystane dykes
On the west coast
Round the machair,
He started to speak:
'My children, today
Is the last day
You will see my face
Here at the machair.'
And when he saw
They looked alarmed,
He began to pray,
Then prophesy,
And to lay
Down the law:
'From now on
No venom
From adders will harm
Beasts or men
On Iona
As long
As all who plough
Or build
Or talk
Or live
Or walk
Stay strong
And keep Christ's commandments.'

ADOMNÁN

Script

At the very end
He climbed a small hill
And stood
A short time
On its summit
Blessing the island,
Forecasting its story,
Then walked back
Past a bend
In the track
To the monastery
To copy
The Psalms,
And at verses
Ten to eleven
Of the thirty-fourth
Psalm –
'They that seek
The Lord
Shall lack
Nothing that is good' –
He gave up
His pen.
'Tonight
I must stop.
Now, friend,
It is your turn
To write.'

ADOMNÁN

Diarmait

One day
Royal
Columba's
Loyal
Servant
Diarmait
Was about to die,
And Columba
Prayed,
'Now,
O Lord,
Hear my word:
Let Diarmait
Live on
After I
Am gone.'
And when
All was said
And done,
Diarmait
Grew well
Again,
And did
Live to tell
How
Columba
Died
In his stead.

ADOMNÁN

Columba's Death

At the midnight bell
Columba hurried
Alone
Into the church,
Kneeling in prayer
At the altar,
Till the whole
Abbey was full
Of pure light.
Then as Diarmait
Neared the church door
The light was failing,
So Diarmait,
Feeling his way
Through the dark,
Called, 'Father,
Where are you?'
And when men
Came with lamps
It was evident
The saint
Was dying,
Though there was joy
In his eyes.
Diarmait held
Columba's head
And raised
Columba's weak
Hand
And kept
It raised

So he blessed
The choir of monks,
Though he could neither stand
Nor speak;
And then
Columba was dead.

Praising God,
The monks wept.

ADOMNÁN

Drought

During a drought
After Columba was dead,
The sky molten iron,
Earth dry
As brass,
We walked
Out,
Proud,
Across parched grass,
And ploughed,
Sown, scorched fields,
Then took
The books
He had copied,
The white coat
He had worn
When he died
And shook
The coat
Three times
Then read
Aloud
From those books
At Sithean,
The Hill
Of the Angels,
Where, some nights,
Bright
Spirits in a dance
Had once
Had their fill

Of chatting with the saint,
And then,
In the still
Afternoon,
Once again,
As if by chance,
Came the rain.

ADOMNÁN

The Work

I, Adomnán,
Have tried not to shirk
Setting this down
As best I can
In a plain
Style, though worn out
By the day-in,
Day-out
Demands
Of almost non-stop work.

CONTRIBUTORS

ADOMNÁN was born in Ireland and became ninth abbot of Iona in the year 679. Active in arguments about the date of Easter, he was involved in establishing Adomnán's Law, which offered protection to the clergy, women and children in time of war. As well as *De Locis Sanctis*, an account of the sacred sites of Jerusalem and the Holy Land, based on the narratives of the traveller Arculf who was said to have been shipwrecked on Iona, Adomnán wrote in Latin prose a *Vita Sancti Columbae* (Life of Saint Columba), on which the verse paraphrases in the present anthology are closely based. He died on Iona in 704.

MEG BATEMAN is a poet and scholar who is Professor of Gaelic at Sabhal Mòr Ostaig on Skye, part of the University of the Highlands and Islands. Her collections of poetry include *Orain Ghaoil / Amhráin Ghrá* (Coiscéim, 1990), *Aotromachd agus Dàin Eile / Lightness and other Poems* (Polygon, 1997), *Soirbheas / Fair Wind* (Polygon, 2007), and *Transparencies* (Polygon, 2013). With Robert Crawford and James McGonigal she edited *Scottish Religious Poetry* (Saint Andrew Press, 2000); her translations appear in *Duanaire na Sracaire / Songbook of the Pillagers: Anthology of Scotland's Gaelic Verse to 1600* (Birlinn, 2007) which she co-edited with Wilson McLeod; with Anne Loughran she co-edited *Bàird Ghleann Dail / The Glendale Bards* (Birlinn, 2014).

JAMES BOSWELL toured his native Scotland in 1773 with Samuel Johnson, about whose life he went on to write. Regarded by many as the greatest English-language biographer, Boswell (1740–95) had studied Rhetoric and Belles Lettres at the University of Glasgow with Adam Smith. His first book, *An Account of Corsica* (1768), dealt with an island, and his *Journal of a Tour to the Hebrides* (1785) deals with an archipelago. Son of an Ayrshire judge, Lord Auchinleck, Boswell was a professional lawyer and a vivid memoirist as well as author of his celebrated *Life of Samuel Johnson* (1791).

GEORGE BUCHANAN was one of the greatest Renaissance Latinists. Poet, dramatist, historian, and political theorist, he was probably a native Gaelic speaker. Born in 1506, he was educated and later taught at the University of St Andrews, spent much of his career on continental

Europe and was arrested by the Inquisition in Portugal. Buchanan went on to become a tutor to King James VI and I as well as author of a substantial Latin history of Scotland which was still a school text in Enlightenment Scotland.

AMY CLAMPITT was born in 1920 and grew up in an Iowa Quaker family. Later she moved to New York and worked as an editor and freelancer. She published her first full-length collection of poems, *The Kingfisher*, at the age of sixty-three, and went on to publish four other collections before her death in 1994. In 1997 her *Collected Poems* was published in America by Knopf and in Britain by Faber, with a foreword and memoir by Mary Jo Salter.

SAINT COLUMBA arrived in Iona in the year 563 when he was in his early thirties. Born in Donegal, and educated in Irish monastic foundations, he seems to have quarrelled seriously with some of his mentors and came to Scotland as an exile. Tradition has it that he landed on Iona at what is now known as St Columba's Bay. He founded the monastery which later became Iona Abbey and was remembered for his love of writing as well as for his piety. To him are attributed several impressive Latin hymns. He died on Iona in 597 after making arduous journeys among the Picts in eastern Scotland. Many miracles were attributed to him; he and his followers were regarded as the founders of many monasteries and churches.

ROBERT CRAWFORD was born in Lanarkshire in 1959 and grew up there. He has published a *Selected Poems* (Cape, 2005) and seven collections of poems in English, most recent of which is *Testament* (Cape, 2014), as well as poetry in Scots including the versions of classic Chinese poems in *Chinese Makars* (Easel Press, 2016). His biographies include *The Bard: Robert Burns* (Cape and Princeton, 2009) and *Young Eliot: From St Louis to 'The Waste Land'* (Cape, 2015). With Mick Imlah he edited *The Penguin Book of Scottish Verse* (2000). Professor of Modern Scottish Literature and Bishop Wardlaw Professor of Poetry at the University of St Andrews, he has won Scottish Arts Council Book Awards, the Saltire Book of the Year Award, and the Saltire Research Book of the Year Award.

ALAN DEARLE, Dean of the Faculty of Science at the University of St Andrews, is an experimental computer scientist whose primary research interests are in the confluence of programming languages, databases, middleware, distributed systems and operating systems. He created the Grasshopper Persistent Operating System with Professor John Rosenberg of Sydney University, and has worked on reflective middleware, global ubiquitous computing, computation in appropriate geographical locations, P2P systems and most recently languages for sensor nets. Throughout his career he has maintained close links with industry and has been a consultant to Iona Technology, Reuters Research and Standards Group, Enigmatec Corp. Currently he is on the technical advisory board of Cloudsoft Corp.

MEAGHAN DELAHUNT was born in Australia and grew up there, publishing her first novel, *In the Blue House*, with Bloomsbury in 2001. That novel was awarded a Commonwealth Fiction Prize, and was followed by *The Red Book* (Granta, 2008) and *To the Island* (Granta, 2011). Meaghan Delahunt now lives in Edinburgh and has been awarded a Saltire Prize as well as being longlisted for the Orange Prize for Fiction. Her collection, *Greta Garbo's Feet and Other Stories* was published in 2015. Her short stories have been broadcast on BBC Radio 4 and her work has been widely translated. She has taught creative writing at the University of Stirling and is a qualified Hatha/ Vinyasa Flow Yoga teacher.

JENNIE ERDAL studied philosophy and Russian at the University of St Andrews and has worked as a translator. The first book she wrote under her own name was *Ghosting* (published by Canongate in Britain and by Doubleday in the US), which became a BBC Radio 4 Book of the Week. It tells of her childhood in a Fife mining village and her long-term work as a ghost-writer for Naim Attallah, owner of Quartet Books. Her first novel, *The Missing Shade of Blue* (Little, Brown, 2012) is set in Edinburgh; she is now completing her second novel. She lives in Fife.

LOUISE IMOGEN GUINEY was born into an Irish-American family in Boston in 1861. Educated in Providence, Rhode Island, she lived most of her life in Massachusetts, publishing her first collection of poems, *Songs at the Start*, when she was twenty-three. She went on to write essays, fairytales, and biography as well as several further volumes of poetry, most celebrated of which was *A Roadside Harp* (1893). She crossed the Atlantic several times, and had a particular interest in the heritage of English Catholic writing. Her co-edited anthology of *Recusant Poets* was published posthumously in 1939.

SEAMUS HEANEY won the Nobel Prize for Literature in 1995. Born in County Derry in 1939, he grew up on a small farm there and studied English literature at Queen's University, Belfast, where he also taught. His collections of poetry include *Death of a Naturalist* (1966), *Field Work* (1979), and *Seeing Things* (1990). Among his many essays are pieces on the Scottish poets Robert Burns, Robert Henryson, and Sorley MacLean. He also published translations of poetry by MacLean and Henryson. In the early twenty-first century he visited Iona with the novelist Andrew O'Hagan.

MICK IMLAH (1956–2009) liked to assert that he was born in Aberdeen, though he spent his early childhood in Milngavie before the family moved south and he was educated at Dulwich College in London. After studying and teaching at Oxford, he edited the magazine *Poetry Review* before becoming poetry editor at Chatto & Windus, then at the *Times Literary Supplement*. He published *Birthmarks* (Chatto, 1988) and *The Lost Leader* (Faber, 2008) as well as co-editing *The Penguin Book of Scottish Verse* (2000). After his death his *Selected Poems* appeared in 2010 and his *Selected Prose* in 2015.

LIONEL JOHNSON (1867–1902) was an English poet and critic. Educated at Oxford University, he became a Catholic convert and published his *Poems* in 1895, following it with a further collection entitled *Ireland and Other Poems* two years later. He died young after struggling with alcoholism and feelings of guilt associated with his homosexuality. He introduced his cousin, Lord Alfred Douglas, to Oscar Wilde with notorious and tragic results.

SAMUEL JOHNSON, lexicographer, playwright, novelist, and poet in both English and Latin, spent most of his life in London but travelled north to Scotland with his friend James Boswell in 1773. By that time the publication of his 1755 *Dictionary*, his novel *Rasselas, Prince of*

Abyssinia (1759), and his editing of the *Rambler* had helped establish him as England's leading man of letters. His *Journey to the Western Islands of Scotland* (1775) was not welcomed by all Scottish readers, but has established itself as a classic eighteenth-century travel narrative – a sort of home-grown alternative to the European Grand Tour.

JOHN KEATS trained as a doctor at Guy's Hospital, London, and is remembered as one of the greatest of the Romantic poets. Born in London in 1795, he published *Endymion* in 1818; his second book of poetry, *Lamia, Isabella, The Eve of St Agnes and Other Poems*, appeared in 1820, by which time it was clear that he was suffering from tuberculosis. Though Keats is often regarded as sickly, his making an extensive tour of Scotland as a young man, often covering substantial distances on horseback and on foot, shows his physical resilience as well as his love of Romantic northern terrain.

DAVID KINLOCH's first full-length collection of poems, *Paris-Forfar*, was published by Polygon in 1994, and followed by *Un Tour d'Ecosse* (Carcanet, 2001), *In My Father's House* (Carcanet, 2005), and *Finger of a Frenchman* (Carcanet, 2011). His most recent publication is the pamphlet *Some Women* (Happen*Stance*, 2014). Born and raised in Glasgow, he studied at the universities of Glasgow and Oxford, and is now professor of creative writing at the University of Strathclyde. He has also written and edited several studies of French and Scottish literature.

SARA LODGE was born and educated in Edinburgh, then studied at Cambridge and Oxford. Author of two critical books, *Thomas Hood and Nineteenth-Century Poetry: Work, Play and Politics* (Manchester University Press, 2007) and *Jane Eyre: An Essential Guide to Criticism* (Palgrave, 2009), she is now working on her first collection of fairytales and on a study entitled *Inventing Edward Lear: Nonconformity and the Art of Nonsense*. She teaches in the School of English at the University of St Andrews.

NORMAN MacCAIG's *Poems*, edited by his son Ewen, was published by Polygon in 2005 with an introduction by Alan Taylor. Born in 1910 in Edinburgh and educated there, he began to publish poetry in the

1930s. His collections include *Far Cry* (1943), *Riding Lights* (1955), *Rings on a Tree* (1968), *A Man in My Position* (1969), and *Voice Over* (1988). He was awarded the Queen's Gold Medal for Poetry in 1985. MacCaig worked as a schoolteacher for many years, then taught at the University of Stirling. He lived most of the year in Edinburgh, but spent much time also in the West Highlands.

JOHN MacGILVRAY was Master of the Grammar School in Lestwithiel (now Lostwithiel) near Bodmin in Cornwall. A university graduate, he published his *Poems* in London in 1787. The book includes paeans to 'The Caledonian Spring' and 'The Grampian Mountains', but reviewers were not enthusiastic. The *Critical Review* thought that 'Some passages, particularly of a descriptive kind, bear marks of genius, but not of a very superior kind.'

MOSSE MACDONALD from Nottingham entered his poem 'Iona' for the University of Oxford's Newdigate Prize competition while he was studying as an undergraduate at Brasenose College, Oxford. When he won, it was recited in the university's Sheldonian Theatre on 18 June 1879, and published shortly afterwards. Later he became a curate in Fulham and in Nottinghamshire.

VICTORIA MacKENZIE wrote a doctoral thesis on modern poetry and science and is completing her first novel. She has won several awards for her short stories and recently completed a writing residency at Cove Park supported by Creative Scotland. In 2016 she was awarded a New Writers Award by the Scottish Book Trust. She teaches creative writing for the Open College of the Arts, and lives in Fife.

FIONA MACLEOD was the pen-name of William Sharp (1855–1905), an author whose work helped define the internationally acclaimed 'Celtic Twilight' movement. Born in industrial Paisley, he spent time in Glasgow, London, Paris, in the Highlands and elsewhere. Poet, essayist, anthologist, biographer, and author of several prose fictions, he published such volumes as *The Gypsy Christ* (1895), *The Mountain Lovers* (1895), and *From the Hills of Dream* (1896). 'The Sin-Eater' may be his finest piece of fiction.

BECCÁN MAC LUIGDECH, like Columba, seems to have been linked to the Uí Néill family in Ireland. In the 630s he was involved in the running of the monastery on Iona. Later he sailed northwards to the Hebridean island of Rhum where he lived as a hermit for years, dying there in the year 677. Several Gaelic poems are attributed to him.

CANDIA McWILLIAM was born in Edinburgh, where she now lives. Educated at Cambridge, she published her first novel, *A Case of Knives*, in 1988. Her second novel, *A Little Stranger*, appeared the following year. In 1994 her novel *Debatable Land* won the Guardian Fiction Prize, and was followed three years later by her short story collection, *Wait Till I Tell You*. In 2010 Cape published her memoir *What to Look for in Winter: A Memoir in Blindness*. She has been awarded the Betty Trask Prize, Scottish Arts Council Book Awards, the Premio Grinzane Cavour, the Sky Arts Award, and the Hawthornden Prize.

HERMAN MELVILLE (1818–1891) is most famous as the author of the novel *Moby-Dick* (1851), though he also published other novels as well as many short stories and poems. Born in New York, he worked briefly as a schoolteacher before going to sea. He sailed to Liverpool in 1839, and, though he spent much of his life in Massachusetts, he later sailed to the Middle East. His long poem *Clarel: A Poem and Pilgrimage in the Holy Land* was published in 1876 and demonstrates his familiarity with Admonán's account of conversing with Arculf about 'the holy places'.

EDWIN MORGAN published his breakthrough collection of poems, *The Second Life*, in 1968 at the age of forty-eight. He lived almost all his life in Glasgow where he became a professor of English literature at the University of Glasgow. Among his many collections of poetry are *From Glasgow to Saturn* (1973), *The New Divan* (1977), and *Sonnets from Scotland* (1984). He wrote an opera libretto, *Columba*, for the composer Kenneth Leighton. Towards the end of his life he was appointed Scotland's first Makar or National Poet. His many translations range from versions of medieval Latin to translations of modern Russian, Hungarian, Italian, Spanish, and Brazilian poets.

THOMAS PENNANT (1726–1798) was a Welsh traveller, antiquarian and naturalist who published *A Tour in Scotland and Voyage to the Hebrides* in 1774–6, following the success of his earlier 1771 account, *A Tour in Scotland*. Pennant's work was familiar to many later travellers, including James Boswell and Samuel Johnson. Later, in 1782, he published *The Journey from Chester to London*.

CHRISTABEL SCOTT published her verse novel *Iona: A Romance of the West* in London in 1896, having previously published *Sketches from Nature*. A reviewer in the *Glasgow Herald* thought that 'The story' of *Iona* was 'written in simple and even graceful language'. More harshly, a critic in the London *Times* wrote that, 'We cannot pretend to judge Miss Scott's Gaelic songs, but as to her English versification we may venture to remark that it is not good to terminate each of 35 consecutive lines with a monosyllable, as she does on pages 72 and 73.'

WALTER SCOTT (1771–1832) was born and grew up in Edinburgh and the Scottish Borders. A lawyer by profession, he soon became a best-selling poet, authoring book-length poems including *The Lay of the Last Minstrel* (1805) and *The Lady of the Lake* (1810). When he turned to writing fiction, *Waverley* (1814) and the many novels that followed were even more successful, making him arguably the single most influential novelist in the worldwide history of the novel.

WILLIAM SHAKESPEARE, the world's most famous dramatist, lived from 1564 until 1616, a period during which political relations between Scotland and England changed markedly. Several of Shakespeare's plays concern themselves with the political status of Britain and Britishness. Not least among such works is 'the Scottish play', *Macbeth*, which presents England's northern neighbour as strife-torn, bloody and in need of English intervention. *Macbeth* can be seen as articulating political propaganda. It also contains the playwright's only mention of Iona (which he terms 'Colmekill').

KENNETH STEVEN learned to walk on Iona and has returned there many times since. His novels include *Dan*, which was shortlisted for the Saltire First Book Award and is the first book in his Highland Trilogy. His collection of short stories, *The Ice*, was published by Argyll in 2010. His collection of poems, *Iona*, is published by the Saint Andrew Press, and *A Wee Book of Iona Poems* is published by Wild Goose Publications, the publishing arm of the Iona Community.

ROBERT LOUIS STEVENSON (1850–94) was born in Edinburgh, where he grew up and went to university. A great Francophile, he published *An Inland Voyage* in 1878 and *Travels with a Donkey in the Cevennes* in 1879, and became a highly accomplished poet, though he is best remembered as the author of such prose fictions as *Treasure Island* (1883), *Strange Case of Dr Jekyll and Mr Hyde* (1886), and *Kidnapped* (1886). The last of these includes the chapter entitled 'The Islet', which forms part of the present anthology. Stevenson is a wonderfully lively letter writer; it is worth noting that the cuisine of the Argyll Hotel has improved immeasurably since he stayed there.

RUTH THOMAS was born in Kent and studied at the University of Edinburgh. Her first two collections of short stories *Sea Monster Tattoo* and *The Dance Settee* were published by Polygon and her third collection, *Super Girl*, by Faber in 2009. Faber have also published her novels *Things to Make and Mend* (2009) and *The Home Corner* (2013). She has won or been shortlisted for various awards including the John Lewellyn Rhys Award, the Saltire First Book Award, and the V. S. Pritchett Prize. She lives in Edinburgh and has been a lecturer in creative writing at the University of St Andrews.

ALICE THOMPSON was born and brought up in Edinburgh, studied at Oxford, and was the keyboard player with post-punk 1980s band the Woodentops. Jointly with Graham Swift she won the James Tait Black Memorial Prize for Fiction for her first novel, *Justine* (Canongate, 1996). Her other novels include *Pandora's Box* (Little, Brown, 1998), *Pharos* (Virago, 2002), *The Falconer* (Two Ravens Press, 2008), *The Existential Detective* (Two Ravens Press, 2010), *Burnt Island* (Salt, 2013), and *The Book Collector* (Salt, 2015). She has received a Creative Scotland Award and her work has been translated into several languages. She teaches creative writing at University of Edinburgh.

QUEEN VICTORIA reigned from 1837 until 1901, making her Britain's second longest reigning monarch. During all this time she made many visits to Scotland, most frequently to Edinburgh and to her beloved Balmoral, but never quite made it onto the shores of Iona. She was a gifted artist, a dedicated diarist, and Empress of India.

WILLIAM WORDSWORTH was born in Cockermouth, Cumbria, in 1770. He read the poems of Burns in his teens and was a lifelong Scotophile. After studying at Cambridge, he shared with his friend Samuel Taylor Coleridge the volume *Lyrical Ballads* (1798). His other collections included *Poems in Two Volumes* (1807), *Miscellaneous Poems* (1815), and the long autobiographical poem *The Prelude*, published in 1850, the year of his death. He visited Iona while touring Scotland in 1835.

ACKNOWLEDGEMENTS

The editor wishes to acknowledge the Royal Society of Edinburgh and the Scottish Government for the award of an Arts and Humanities Network Grant which made possible the 'Loch Computer' project, part of which involved the commissioning of several of the poems and most of the stories in this book. More information, reflections, images and artwork can be found on the project's website (just google 'Loch Computer'), developed by Dr Alice Crawford and hosted by the University of St Andrews Library. Other works from the project have been published in 2016 by Easel Press of Edinburgh in the limited edition artists' box *Loch Computer.* A whoop of glee goes up to and from all the Loch Computer network's members: Meg Bateman, Alice Crawford, Robert Crawford, Al Dearle, Meaghan Delahunt, Jennie Erdal, Jen Hadfield, Sara Lodge, Norman McBeath, Peter Mackay, Candia McWilliam, Vicky MacKenzie, Leena Nammari, Michael Nott, Helen Pain, Dave Robertson, Don Sannella, Ruth Thomas, Alice Thompson, Colin Waters. Gratitude is owed also to several institutions who hosted Loch Computer meetings: the Poetry House, School of English, University of St Andrews; the Farr Institute and the School of Informatics, University of Edinburgh; the Scottish Poetry Library; and to the Edinburgh College of Art at the University of Edinburgh for hosting the Loch Computer exhibition during the 2016 Edinburgh International Science Festival.

The editor and publisher would like to thank the following publishers, authors, translators, and editors for permission to reproduce work: Birlinn for 'Delightful to Be on the Breast of an Island' translated by Meg Bateman from Anon., 'Meallach Liom Bheith i n-Ucht Oiléin', and for 'The Last Verses of Beccán to Colum Cille' translated by Meg Bateman from Beccán mac Luigdech, 'Tiugraind Beccáin do Cholum Cille', in Wilson McLeod and Meg Bateman, ed., *Duanaire na Sracaire / Songbook of the Pillagers: Anthology of Scotland's Gaelic Verse to 1600* (Birlinn, 2007), as well as for extracts from *To the Hebrides: Samuel Johnson's Journey to the Western Islands of Scotland and James Boswell's Journal of a Tour to the Hebrides*, edited by Ronald Black (Birlinn, 2007), and for Norman MacCaig, 'Celtic Cross', from *The Poems of Norman MacCaig*, ed. Ewen McCaig (Polygon, 2005); Jonathan Cape and Penguin Random House UK for 'Iona' from Robert

Crawford, *A Scottish Assembly* (Chatto & Windus, 1990), and for 'MC' from Robert Crawford, *Talkies* (Chatto & Windus, 1992), and for 'The Marble Quarry' from Robert Crawford, Testament (Cape, 2014); Carcanet Press for 'Between the Lines' from David Kinloch, *Finger of a Frenchman* (Carcanet, 2011), and for 'The Maker on High', translated by Edwin Morgan from the Latin of the 'Altus Prosator' in Edwin Morgan, *Collected Translations* (Carcanet, 1996), and for 'Columba's Song' from Edwin Morgan, *Collected Poems* (Carcanet, 1990); Faber and Faber for 'I' and 'The Prophecies' from Mick Imlah, *Selected Poems* (Faber and Faber, 2010); Faber and Faber and Farrar, Straus & Giroux for 'Gravities' from Seamus Heaney, *Death of a Naturalist* (Faber and Faber, 1966) (also published in the USA in Seamus Heaney, *Opened Ground: Selected Poems, 1966–1996* (Farrar, Straus & Giroux, 1999)); Alfred A. Knopf, and Random House Inc. for 'Westward' from Amy Clampitt, *Collected Poems* (Alfred A. Knopf, 1997) (also published in the UK by Faber and Faber in 1998); Wild Goose Publications for three untitled poems from Kenneth Steven, *A Wee Book of Iona Poems* (Wild Goose Publications, 2015).

Copyright remains with the individual authors and translators of the following works which appear here for the first time: Robert Crawford's verse versions of passages by Adomnán and of the 'Adiutor Laborantium', the 'Noli Pater' and 'Fil Súil nGlais'; 'The Iona Machine' by Alan Dearle; the poems 'Peploe and Cadell in Iona' by Meg Bateman and 'Icolmkill' by Robert Crawford; the stories 'To Pick up a Stone' by Meaghan Delahunt', 'Listening in the Loose Grass' by Jennie Erdal, 'The Grin Without the Cat' by Sara Lodge, 'The Loopholes of Retreat' by Candia McWilliam, 'Crex Crex' by Victoria MacKenzie, 'All the Treasures We Can Have' by Ruth Thomas, 'Hologram' by Alice Thompson. Norman McBeath retains the copyright of any specially taken photographs of Iona used in *The Book of Iona*. Finally, thanks to Hugh Andrew, Edward Crossan and colleagues at Polygon for helping to bring this volume into being; and to Melissa Wetton-Boyle for clearing the copyright permissions.